Byrd Nash

College Fae
Junior

BANE
OF HOUNDS

Copyright © 2020 Byrd Nash   www.ByrdNash.com
Cover Art by Original Book Cover Design
Publisher: Rook & Castle Press

ISBN 978-1-7348938-7-8
Library of Congress Control Number: 2020909179

Publisher's Cataloging-in-Publication Data
provided by Five Rainbows Cataloging Services

Names: Nash, Byrd, author.
Title: Bane of hounds : college fae junior / Byrd Nash.
Description: Tulsa, OK : Rook and Castle Press, 2020. | Series: College fae,
    bk. 3.
Identifiers: LCCN 2020909179 (print) | ISBN 978-1-7348938-4-7
    (paperback) | ISBN 978-1-7348938-7-8 (paperback) | ISBN
    978-1-7348938-3-0 (ebook : Kindle) | ISBN 978-1-7348938-6-1 (ebook :
    epub)
Subjects: LCSH: College students--Fiction. | Magic--Fiction. | Fairies--
    Fiction. | Animals, Mythical--Fiction. | Fantasy fiction. |
    Bildungsromans. | BISAC: FICTION / Fantasy / Contemporary. |
    FICTION / Fairy Tales, Folk Tales, Legends & Mythology. | FICTION
    / Coming of Age. | GSAFD: Fantasy fiction. | Bildungsromans.
Classification: LCC PS3614.A724 B36 (print) | LCC PS3614.A724 (ebook)
    | DDC 813/.6--dc23.

Other Books by Byrd Nash

College Fae Series

#1 Never Date a Siren
#2 A Study in Spirits
#3 Bane of Hounds
#4 Coming 2021

Fae Magic Adventure Series

#1 Knight of Cups

Fairytale Series

The Wicked Wolves of Windsor
and other Fairytales

Dance of Hearts ~ Cinderella retelling

Snarling people have snarling dogs,
dangerous people have dangerous ones.
Sir Arthur Conan Doyle

Dedications

I told my Love a Story
That had no end.

Table of Contents

Junior Year, Fall Semester
Leopold-Ottos-Universität
Geheimetür
Bewachterberg

In Europe there is a special place where
humans and fae attend college classes together.
Beware though, the university does not
guarantee your safety.

Chapter One
Keeping the Peace

Brigit Cullen was cold. She should be home studying for a test, not hunkered behind a hedge waiting for a wailing wraith to scream an omen of death.

"You'd think the banshee would adhere to some sort of schedule. It's a full moon. Why can't she show herself before we freeze to death?" Brigit grumbled to her companion, Logan Dannon.

As a dryad, the fall and winter seasons of the Human Lands made Brigit feel sluggish. Her home in the Perilous Realm had a more temperate climate than the city of Geheimetür.

Bewachterberg was south of Germany and Switzerland. Surrounded by mountains, it could get chilly even in the fall. Dealing with the cold was one of the many adjustments she had to make these last two years as a student at Leopold-Ottos-Universität Geheimetür.

She gave a sulky sideways glare at Logan. His human metabolism made him better at handling the frosty climate of mid-October. Or maybe it was the heavier coat?

When Logan didn't respond, she muttered again, her breath making fog clouds in front of her nose, "After all, it's not like we're being paid by the chancellor to solve his little problems."

"Chancellor Bandemer is good at delegating things that annoy him," agreed Logan, who was behind the bushes with her.

Chancellor Bandemer had appointed Logan and Brigit as Student Liaisons last year after the events in the library. They were tasked to mediate complaints between the fae and humans. After their initial elation, they both learned that dealing with difficulties between students from two vastly different cultures was a big headache.

Thinking upon their most recent adventure, Brigit's complaint turned into a rant.

"Last month, I cut my weekend plans short to trudge through the Geheimetür sewage system to bargain with a tommyknocker. Did we get any thanks for passing along the warning from that fae mining spirit to the chancellor? No! All I got was a stench that took a week to get out of my hair!"

"The knocker told us that bridge was going to collapse," Logan reminded her. "That saved lives, Brigit. We might not get much thanks from Bandemer, but never doubt it, we are doing good work."

Logan's calm reply stirred up her torpid blood.

"Frost on the pumpkin, Logan! Do you like being Bandemer's unpaid lackey?"

"We do get one credit hour of coursework for it," he reminded her.

Brigit exploded and uttered every colorful fae curse and swear word she could think of. She only stopped when she noticed the smile Logan was trying to hide behind the upturned collar of his coat.

"You did that on purpose!"

"You feel warmer now, don't you?" Before she could answer, Logan pulled off his gloves and handed them to her. "It would be easier to wait if you weren't so cold. Try these. They're thermal."

Brigit pulled them on with stiff fingers. She preferred wearing organic material, so she could talk to her clothes, but the relief they gave made her sigh.

Logan threw his arm over her shoulders, drawing her tight against his side. The maneuver was awkward because they were sitting on their heels behind the bushes, but his solid body blocked more of the wind. She put her head on his chest and burrowed deeper.

"Look, I also have a test tomorrow. I don't like this either. If the banshee doesn't appear in the next hour, we call it a night, okay?"

"Agreed," she mumbled against his coat.

After a moment's silence, Logan asked, "What do we know about the banshee?"

"The appearance of a banshee heralds the death of someone. She seems to be focusing on the third floor of the dormitory where a human, O'Conner, lives. His family history fits the profile of being a likely target. This banshee comes from a Gaelic fae court. Fae folk from that region seem especially attached to family bloodlines."

Huddled like a chick tucked under a hen's wing, Brigit gave him a sly smile as she added, "Something you would know about, Logan."

Logan didn't take the bait about his grandmother, the Celtic goddess, the Morrighan. Last year, their meeting with Bandemer exposed Brigit as a fae princess and Logan's family tree. Brigit hadn't allowed him to forget it.

He deflected, "Like the brownie?"

The brownie, who managed their housekeeping, had initially been attached to Brigit's ex-roommate, a troll from Scotland. Somehow, the dryad had convinced her to come live with them.

"Kinda. But the brownie was able to break her Bond of Servitude because Sam's behavior was bringing out her boggart side. If she had stayed, she would have transformed. A lawyer told her it was a repudiatory breach so she had the legal right to terminate the contract." Brigit shook her head, her tight black curls bouncing, as she said, "Banshees, however, tend to stick to blood ties. Silly old-fashioned creatures."

"If she won't leave, would the chancellor force O'Connor to withdraw from the university?"

"Maybe if she would show herself, we could find out!"

As if Brigit's words had summoned her, a strange cry started in the air above their heads. Brigit felt a cold shiver of fear up the back of her neck. It was a disconcerting noise even for someone like herself, used to the ugly natures of the fae.

Logan bent closer and whispered in her pointed ear, "My flight response is really kicking in."

"It's the banshee. Her purpose is to unnerve you."

"It's working," Logan's reply was terse.

Sometimes she forgot Logan wasn't fae. For humans targeted by a banshee's bloodcurdling screams, it was probably horrifying. Brigit reached over and gave Logan's hand a reassuring squeeze.

The shrieking was piercingly shrill. It started low, and built in intensity until the glass windows in the dormitory vibrated in their frames. The screaming woke students in the dorm. Faces, appearing as shadows, peeked out from behind drapes.

This was the reason they were there. Students were threatening to stop paying dorm fees if the banshee situation wasn't sorted out soon. No one felt safe. In typical fashion, Bandemer shoved the problem onto his Student Liaisons.

Logan and Brigit stood up, but she had to take a moment to stomp feeling back into her feet, which had fallen asleep. They could now both see the ghostly apparition of the banshee.

She was suspended in mid-air, hovering outside the third floor of the dormitory hall. Since the banshee's face was towards the building, they only saw the back of her form. In some ways, she was similar to the ghosts they had met in the library, for she was as insubstantial as a spectral vapor.

Brigit estimated the banshee to be at least seven feet. If her height didn't betray her as fae, her torso would have, for it was not of human proportions. Instead she was long and thin, like a sapling, and her arms were branch-like, almost as long as her torso.

The banshee wore a long white dress. The skirt and its train billowed away from her body like the tail of a wispy cloud. Her thick red hair fell past her ankles and their snake-strands whipped around as though torn by a strong wind. Only the chilly night air was still.

Recovered from their first fright, Logan and Brigit could now understand the words she was screaming.

"Tomorrow, you will have a pop quiz in biology!"

Brigit and Logan stared at each other in surprise.

"Your roommate ate the last cookie from the tin."

At this, Logan raised his eyebrows and Brigit rolled her eyes.

"Professor Steingard doesn't like you. Your face reminds him of his nephew, who he hates."

Brigit cupped her hands around her mouth. She shouted up at the banshee floating above them.

"By the authority vested in me by the chancellor of Leopold-Ottos-Universität Geheimetür, Bewachterberg, I command you float down here and explain yourself!"

The banshee didn't seem to hear them. Their voices couldn't compete with the noise she created.

Brigit took to throwing rocks at her. While they passed harmlessly through her body, it did get her attention. The banshee drifted down to hover a few feet above the ground.

Brigit, who had seen many scary things during her childhood in the Perilous Realm, did not flinch from meeting the bloodstained weeping woman's gaze.

"Look, banshee, there have been complaints."

The fae's mouth formed an O in agonized surprise.

"I must issue my prophecies," sobbed the banshee. "It's part of who I am—my mission."

Her chest swelled as she took a deep breath to start another scream. Brigit interjected hastily, "We heard what you said. That didn't sound very dire. Since you aren't here to issue a warning about an imminent death, why are you here?"

Logan avoided the banshee's gaze by looking down at the toes of his sneakers. His bard magic let him know the truth from the banshee's spoken words. "She's lonely."

"Lonely?" Brigit repeated Logan's word in surprise. "All of this," the young woman waved a hand in an emphatic circle over her head, "because you're lonely?"

The banshee's wail was mournful, but not as piercing. Brigit almost laughed at her attempt to scream a polite explanation. It made for a weird effect.

"The ó Conchobhair family will not suffer another loss

for me to announce until Sean turns 84. What am I supposed to do until then? I'm bored staying on the moors back home!"

She turned a weeping face back to the dormitory windows and gave a pitiful shriek at the anonymous glass, "On Wednesday, you will meet a girl who will break your heart!"

Logan said to Brigit, "I thought banshees only predicted death? I don't get it."

The banshee turned back to them. Bowing her head, the red hair obscured her face, as she explained.

"Traditionally, banshees favored death. But in these times, women don't die in childbirth, burying their bairns year after year. Science helps them live longer. I've had to get creative."

Her voice cracked with sorrow. "As a prognostic, a fae Cassandra, I can foretell all significant events. No matter how small or large, I know it before it happens."

"I'm sorry about that," said Brigit, "but you can't haunt the campus. Some of us have tests to take and studying to do. We need our sleep."

"She needs a job," Logan pointedly said to Brigit. "An occupation to keep her busy. Something like what we do."

Nodding her head in sudden agreement, the dryad asked the banshee, "You seem pretty good at predicting unpleasant things. Does that work only for the O'Connor bloodline? Or can you do it for anyone?"

The banshee mused over Brigit's question. Her red eyes went unfocused as she intoned solemnly, "Your mother arrives soon."

The prognosticator turned to Logan, but he held up a hand to stop her. "Hm, no thanks. I'm good. I'd rather my future come as a surprise."

Brigit fished in her jean pocket for a stiff piece of card stock. The last time she visited the chancellor's office, she had swiped a stack of his business cards.

"Here, take this," she raised the card high so the banshee's thin hand could take it. "Meet me tomorrow at Chancellor Bandemer's office. He can find something more interesting for you to do than wailing over the loss of someone's cookie stash."

After convincing the banshee to leave, Logan and Brigit walked back to the main bus stop on campus. Due to the restrictions on vehicles allowed in Geheimetür, the bus service still made stops every hour despite the late hour.

Brigit could open a portal, using the Perilous Realm as a stepping stone to easily travel the distance between the campus and their apartment. In the past she avoided doing so in order to prevent her parents discovering her. But now, she didn't because it made Logan uneasy.

Since getting ill after a visit to her parents, Logan was hesitant to experience traveling the portals of the Perilous again. Brigit was committed to changing this attitude of his. Her thoughts on how best to do this were interrupted by her companion.

"Now is the time for magic to happen."

Startled, Brigit exclaimed, "What?"

"Don't you feel it? The wind is kicking up. Something is in the air."

Brigit gazed up to the sky, noting the full moon. There was a breeze on her cheek, and a quiet to a landscape vacant of traffic and people. The world seemed to be holding its breath. Magic indeed.

"There's a ring around the full moon. That means it will snow in three days." Logan told her, but Brigit was distracted and didn't hear.

She took off, shouting, "Hey! What do you think you're doing?"

Being a runner, Logan was at Brigit's side in a moment. She pointed ahead of their path, "Some guy was shoving something down in the trash. There! Do you see him? He just took off!"

Chapter Two
Backward Pawn

B y the time Logan and Brigit reached the bus stop shelter, the shadowy person running from the scene was long gone. But instead of pursuing him, Brigit started to investigate the trash barrel.

"He acted sketchy. Secretive," she told Logan. "I'm sure he put something in here!"

She removed the trash lid and dumped it on the ground. It gave a deep ring when it struck the concrete sidewalk.

"See! I told you!" On top of the garbage was a crumpled paper sack. Brigit's sensitivity to the magical aura of other fae alerted her. "Whatever fae it is, it's weak, dying."

Logan picked up the bag with both hands and Brigit cautioned him, "Gently! Gently! Put it on the ground, not the concrete."

Logan peeled back the paper to reveal a body, covered in black fur. It was about the size of a shoebox.

"It's a puppy!" he told her. Brigit, her hand hovering above the body, said, "I think it's a True Beast, like Jib!"

Kneeling on the ground, Logan laid his hand on the puppy's rib cage. It took several moments before he felt the slight rise of its chest. He reassured Brigit, "Still alive, but just."

"Wood magic has some limited healing powers. It's not my usual talent but let me see—"

Brigit let out a worried sigh. Her mother had forced her to study healing energies, but Brigit lacked true skill. Fae magic was sorted into seven types: wood, metal, stone, water, wind, flame, and time/memory. Water magic, like her friend Celia had, was the better affiliation for such work.

Well, Brigit would see what she could do.

Settling herself cross-legged on the hard ground, she placed one of her hands on the dog's head and another flat on the grass.

As a dryad, her wood magic was connected to the earth and growing things. She quieted her breathing and used a visualization meditation taught to her by a fae tutor.

Closing her eyes, Brigit expanded her magical senses to touch the aura of the small dog Logan cradled in his lap.

In surprise, her eyes opened and her hand flew to cover the area of her left breast. Under her coat, the leaf printed into her skin was pulsing.

The leaf was a twice given gift: it came to Logan from the grove of her home in the Perilous Realm when he had played a truth game with her father. Later, Logan had given it to her as a heart-gift.

Two summers ago, Brigit had slept with it and overnight it had dissolved into the dryad's body. Only a silver outline of the leaf's pattern remained on her brown skin to show where it had become one with her.

From the leaf, Brigit was given the image in her mind of a plant she knew well.

"What's wrong?"

Hand shaking, Brigit told Logan, "The leaf says the Black Dog is poisoned. With wolf's-bane."

The three returned to the apartment quickly via the Perilous Realm. Realizing the necessity of getting home swiftly, Logan didn't squawk about the shortcut.

Rummaging under her bed, Brigit found the unicorn cup her father had gifted her last year. Its pearly surface was smooth to the touch, well-worn by generations of fae queens who had used it.

A unicorn horn was able to turn any liquid into a healing draft. Brigit was hopeful that it would help their patient. When the horn's water bubbled, signaling a change, they rubbed the water on the dog's gums. Next, they raised the puppy's head and gave him a few drops.

"Not too much!" Logan said, "We don't want the water getting into his lungs by mistake."

Logan's cousin, Evelyn, had interned summers at a veterinarian's office, and he had often helped her with sick patients. He massaged the dog's throat to get him to swallow.

They watched and waited. Slowly, the dog's labored breathing eased and the color of his gums turned from white to a healthier pink. With the crisis past, the three fell into an exhausted sleep an hour before sunrise.

Brigit woke up abruptly. Her breathing was shallow as if she had been running for some time. She was clammy and shivering.

Feeling a bit panicked, it took her a moment to shake off her dream and realize where she was. She was still in Logan's bed at the apartment, the rescued fae dog cuddled between them. She reached out a hand, and saw that it was trembling.

She calmed herself and rested her fingers on the puppy's fur, scanning the Black Dog's aura. His magical aura was a more healthy shade, though still not as deep a color as she would like.

Each fae had an aura, its vibrancy related to the being's health and type of magic. Most of the time, Brigit could use it to determine the being's magical affiliation. For instance, the puppy was clearly a Black Dog. Brigit's discerning power had failed her only once, when she met with a Doppelgänger.

He was breathing better; his rib cage rose and fell in a healthy rhythm. He was probably still recovering, but seemed to be on the path to wellness. Still, Brigit planned on getting him a proper checkup with a professional.

Looking over the dog's head, she saw Logan was still

deeply asleep. She took a moment to examine her roommate's face: those ridiculously long eyelashes, and that wild lock of hair that refused to be tamed.

On the surface, he seemed the same guy she met two years back, but something was different. Oh, he was still that quiet, self-deprecating human, still curious, although not (thanks to her) as naive about the fae.

She examined him with a critical eye as he slept. The physical changes were easier to see. Logan was leaving his youth behind. The tall, almost gangly form of a teenager was transforming into that of a man. His shoulders were broader and filled a t-shirt that was undoubtedly a bit tighter. His jawline had sharper angles. Was he taller?

But now there was a quiet to him she couldn't figure out. A contemplative silence he would lapse into when others were talking. A way his eyes would change as if they were holding back secrets.

Logan still hadn't told her all of what happened when they were separated by the griffins last fall. After she had recovered, Brigit discovered the monster vanquished, and the librarian Burkhalter in the hospital.

He had given her the briefest of explanations before changing the subject. In the months that followed there seemed to be no way to bring it back up again for he clearly did not want to speak of it.

She suspected it had something to do with his bard talent. He'd always been reluctant to discuss his powers, preferring that others would forget he could discern truth from lies. His reticence made her suspicious.

Brigit reached out to touch Logan's cheek but stopped when she noticed the time on the digital clock on the bedside table. She needed to get to her appointment with the banshee.

She slid off the bed, trying to ease off the mattress without shaking it. On bare feet, Brigit crossed the living room to her bedroom.

She was still in her clothes from last night, so Brigit hastily changed into a clean hoodie and a pair of jeans. After doing her hair and brushing her teeth, she headed to the kitchen wondering what the brownie had for breakfast.

What she found was Jib. The black cat was giving her a death-laser of a glare.

"What is that hound doing here?" it growled. Brigit shushed the púca, her finger covering her mouth in the age-old gesture for silence.

"Don't get territorial, Jib," she whispered. "Logan and I found him last night. He was in a bad way and needed our help."

The cat's black fur was spiky. Little electric charges sparked across its body. "This apartment isn't big enough for two beings, a brownie, a púca, and some smelly dog!"

"Nah, moggie, there you be wrong. Every place be needing a moggie by the hearth, and a dog at the door. T'will help with security," said the brownie.

The brownie was sipping tea from a tiny teacup. It was one of a set for dolls that Brigit had bought for her to use. She was only about three feet tall so had to stand on the chair to reach the table.

"Exactly!" Brigit agreed. "There's room for us all. Besides, you're out prowling all night anyway. During the day, you're either watching television or sleeping. When was the last time we had a good chat?"

"Chat?" hissed the cat. "By their majesties' request, I am here as your adviser. How can I advise when you don't listen to me? I'm telling you now that Black Dog is nothing but trouble."

While Jib continued to complain, Brigit grabbed a muffin from the plate. At least someone got their work done without having a hissy fit.

"It's just temporary. After he is checked by a vet and gets better, we'll re-home him."

"That's what all new dog owners say."

Brigit was long inured to Jib's sarcasm. She shrugged the púca's concern away.

"You should be more concerned with the fact a fellow fae was attacked right on campus and left for dead. That's a criminal act that requires Balance."

Jib turned its shoulder away and started taking a bath. Brigit gave the brownie a "what can I do?" shrug. Pulling out a pad from the junk drawer, she wrote a note to Logan and stuck it on the fridge door.

Before leaving, she shook her second muffin at Jib to emphasize her words, "Don't disturb either of them. Let them sleep. I'm warning you."

Chapter Three
Job Interview

rigit found the banshee waiting for her in the shadow of the administration building. "Glad you came."

The weeping lady appeared nervous. She bit her lip, and looked from side to side, as she told Brigit, "I don't like being out during the daytime hours. It's dangerous! A dragon just passed by me less than an hour ago!"

Brigit very much doubted a dragon was walking around the campus. This banshee seemed the over-emotional, hysterical type of fae that Brigit found draining to deal with. It would be a pleasure to shove the problem of what to do with her to the chancellor.

"No need to worry. You're with me now," Brigit reassured her. "Nothing bad will happen."

Brigit's words caused the banshee to sob harder. Fat blobs of bloody tears ran down her thin, wan cheeks as she wailed, "Everyone on campus knows that Princess Cullen attracts trouble! Last year, you got the librarian eaten by griffins!"

Outraged at the unfairness of the accusation, Brigit exploded, "That is not true! Go ask Frau Burkhalter at the library — it was some sort of bookworm thing that tried to eat her."

The banshee was still wailing when Brigit hustled her into the building. They drew a few stares from human students, but not from the staff. The university personnel continued working without acknowledging the floating apparition.

When they passed by the elevators, the banshee made a scene. The creature started citing the death statistics of elevator travel in a loud voice. Now everyone turned to stare.

"Last year, elevators and escalators killed 48 people in the Human Lands."

"Yeah, but you're a banshee. You could tell me if the elevator was going to cause an accident."

"I would be with you on the elevator, so I would not know what our fate would be riding inside such a dangerous box. No prognosticator can ever predict danger to themselves. That would operate against how our magic works."

Brigit wasn't going to argue. She opened the door to the

stairs and restrained herself from pushing the banshee across the threshold. She did step aside, and the banshee floated up the steps ahead of her in the stairwell. Brigit followed.

"I haven't been around many harbingers so didn't know your limitations. I'm sorry."

"I'm not a harbinger! I'm a Cassandra. Big difference. I can see the future and give warnings or advice on a wide variety of futures. A harbinger is a one-note wonder."

When they gained the fifth floor and exited the fire door into the hall, the banshee froze in place. From behind her, Brigit walked through her freezing vaporous form; it felt like being plunged into a mountain stream in March.

Brigit demanded impatiently, "What is it this time?"

"A wet floor caution sign!" the banshee wailed in a piercing shriek that made Brigit cover her sensitive ears. "We need to wait until it dries. I could slip and break my neck."

Stepping away from the cold spot that the banshee's presence generated, Brigit saw the shiny hall floor. She tapped the toe of her sneaker on the tile, leaving a wet footprint. It was damp but drying fast.

"I'm going ahead," she told the banshee. "Just float above it."

The banshee and all her dire warnings were getting on Brigit's nerves. She was careful where she placed her feet, walking around the edge of the hall. When Brigit made it safely to the chancellor's outer office door, she beckoned the banshee to follow.

The weeping lady drifted back and forth, her manner

indecisive. At Brigit's urgent hiss, she floated higher. Once she got four feet above the floor, she had to bend her tall form to clear the ceiling. In a mad dash, she swept over to where the dryad stood.

"Good girl," Brigit told her. "I knew you were brave. Now, let's go in and demand to see Bandemer."

"Do you think he will be happy to see us? I hear he is a very busy man."

Brigit changed her laugh into a cough. The banshee was a sorry bag of worry and it would serve the chancellor right if they interrupted his day. She opened the door to his outer office and found it empty.

"We're in luck! His secretary must have stepped away from her desk. Probably dispatched to get the old French fop some tea made from the tears of fish. Or something else equally time consuming and near impossible."

Brigit didn't wait to hear what the banshee thought. She went to another heavy oak door and tried to turn the knob. At first the handle didn't move.

Identify yourself, demanded the old door.

Being a dryad, Brigit was used to wooden doors opening at her request and was slightly irked by its refusal.

Brigit Cullen to see the Chancellor on urgent business.
Wait. I will see if he wishes to speak with you.

It took a moment before the lock released and the door said they could enter. Brigit strode confidently into Bandemer's office. But before she could say anything, the fae chancellor preempted her.

He stood up, coming from behind his desk, saying in

buoyant French, "Ah, my favorite dryad. By chance, is this the lovely banshee I've heard so much about?"

Since all languages were one in Bewachterberg due to fae magic, Brigit heard the greeting in her native tongue, with the French a light whisper underneath.

The chancellor was wearing his usual 18th-century garb, including a neon-green moire satin frock coat with a purple waistcoat. He wore pink ribbons on his wrists and matching green garters below his knees.

While the banshee was an ephemeral being, the chancellor was able to pick up her limp fingers with his own. Some magic trick, thought Brigit, who despite herself, was impressed.

"Enchanté. Far lovelier than the reports we've heard, isn't she?"

Off to the side stood the man Bandemer had addressed: a tall, elegant, and extremely handsome person in his middle years. Probably as arrogant and power hungry as the chancellor was Brigit's scathing, one-minute analysis of the newcomer.

"Indeed," was the man's non-committal reply.

"Mlle. Brigit Cullen, this is my assistant, M. Peter Darcy. He is in charge of my upcoming symposium. Why don't you formally introduce us to your lovely companion."

"Banshee, this," Brigit's flat hand gestured palm upward, "is Chancellor François Auguste Bandemer. He will find you an outlet for your talents. Keep you happily occupied until you can take delight in predicting O'Conner's death sixty or so odd earth years from now."

Bandemer clasped his hands together, causing the lace at his wrists to flutter. His gesture seemed to indicate he was vastly pleased by Brigit's statement, but the dryad saw the sardonic gleam in his eye.

Hm, she may have overstepped. Perhaps she should have sent Logan? He was far more diplomatic when dealing with Bandemer's ego. Besides, Brigit always felt the chancellor treated Logan a bit more carefully than he did her.

"A job?" asked Bandemer coyly, putting a finger to his chin. "A capital idea. I wonder what talents the banshee has that we could use in our operation here?"

Brigit gave a brief rundown of the weeping lady's ability for predicting disaster, as long as it didn't include her mortality. As the dryad talked, the remote expression on the chancellor's austere features froze to sub-zero temperatures. Seeing it, Brigit grew more stubborn about her plan for the chancellor to take over the problem the banshee presented.

Before the discussion could result in blows, M. Darcy said in a gravely voice as handsome as his face, "Risk-based asset management."

"M. Darcy, you have a mind like a trap. Bravo!" Bandemer gave a light, short clap-clap with the fingers of one hand upon the soft palm of the other. "Like all job applicants, we shall give our banshee a little test before we assign her a position that best fits her gifts."

The banshee was too star-struck by Bandemer to string together a sentence, so it was up to Brigit to ask, "What's this risk-based asset whatever? Why would she be good at it? How will she be paid?"

"It's an analysis of what consequences might happen given a certain scenario," explained Darcy. "From there, the type of risks would be evaluated."

"For example," the fiendish gleam in Bandemer's inhuman frigid-blue eyes intensified as he interrupted his companion and asked the banshee, "what if Mlle. Cullen," he gestured to Brigit, "was to form a Life Bond with Logan O'Dannon? Let us assess the risk of such a union between humans and fae."

"I wish your speculation about Logan and I would stop. Get your nose out of our business. We're just friends — co-workers — and roommates."

While Brigit protested, Bandemer and Darcy waited for the banshee to speak. The creature turned her red, weeping eyes to observe Brigit. The dryad felt a cold breeze sweep through her. It was a shadow of what she had felt bumping into the creature at the top of the landing.

"There are too many variables to evaluate such a contingency," the prophetic Cassandra said hesitantly. This earned her a warning glare from Brigit, who snarled at her, "Keep out of my business."

The chancellor, seeing how irritated Brigit was becoming, encouraged the banshee to continue speculating. "I would find your answer amusing."

The banshee simpered, which was a ghastly look considering her bleeding eyes. She explained, "The top three reasons unions fail is due to money, infidelity, and sexual incapability."

"Watch it!" snapped Brigit, shaking a clenched fist under

the banshee's nose. To evade the threat, the fae creature floated upward. Since Bandemer's office had high ceilings, she could expand to her full seven feet of height without hardship.

The Cassandra continued speaking, consumed with the vision of calculating possible futures, "After observing their teamwork last night, if both wanted the relationship, I believe it would have a 78 percent chance of success during the first year. However, opposition from their families is likely to be a significant factor. As a princess, Brigit's family would expect her to form an alliance that would benefit their court. Logan's family would probably be concerned about the danger of being united with a fae, especially a royal one."

"Fat lot you know about Logan's relations. They have their own problems," muttered Brigit darkly, crossing her arms so she wouldn't choke anyone in the room.

"Since Brigit is a fae Natural and her body conforms to a human shape, sexual compatibility should not be a biological problem."

Having had enough of the speculation, Brigit shouted at Bandemer, "She's your problem! Deal with it." She slammed out of the chancellor's office.

Bandemer was too well-bred to show a smirk, so he settled for a satisfied smile directed at his Doppelgänger. Paul, posing as Darcy until a better disguise could be worked out, was instructed to take care of the banshee.

"M. Darcy, why don't you get our weeping lady settled? I think she'll be a fine addition to our symposium. She can meet up with that venture capitalist who wanted market predictions."

The banshee's form flickered like a faulty light.

"Symposium?" she cried out, but before the two men could explain, she added in her Wyrding predictive wail, "An ancient vendetta will trap a queen."

Bandemer looked like he had bitten into a lemon.

"How many fae queens do we have attending the symposium next week, Darcy?

"Twelve have RSVPed but some invitations are still awaiting a response."

"Try to get this Cassandra to narrow things down a bit will you?" said Bandemer. Feeling a headache coming on, the chancellor waved them both out of his office.

Bane of Hounds

Chapter Four
Pop Quiz

L ogan woke to doggy breath.

"Oh, hey, pup. You're looking better." He sat up, his hands fondling the dog's ears. The Black Dog laid his chin on Logan's bent knee. Soulful, cola-brown eyes stared adoringly at him.

"What about some breakfast? Is your stomach up for something?"

A low eager bark greeted Logan's question. Before he could lift the dog off the bed, the beast jumped down. He bounced in place, wagging his plume of a tail with excitement.

In the kitchen, Logan found Brigit's note about visiting Bandemer to discuss the banshee problem.

"I could have done that. Oh well, she does like to wake up early."

On the counter was a bowl with a lid. Logan looked inside it to find a watery mixture of rice and finely chopped chicken meat.

"I think our needs have been anticipated." Logan gave a silent thanks to the brownie. While she wouldn't want praise, he always felt weird not giving it in some way. Brigit warned him that verbal thanks would cause the brownie to leave in a huff. It was just one of the many things he struggled with understanding about the fae.

Looking down at the wriggling dog, he said, "Let's start out slow, okay, buddy? Just a little taste. First, let's see if you can keep it down."

Logan put some on a plate and set it on the floor. Straightening, he saw a black cat in the doorway.

"How was your hunting last night, Jib?" The púca ignored his question. Instead it turned its back, walking away on stiff legs, tail straight up, shoulders hunched. In the living room, it jumped up on the sofa and stretched out upon a cushion. The cat closed its eyes, pretending sleep.

Clearly, Jib was not happy. It didn't take a genius to know why. Well, Logan would deal with it later. Maybe pick Jib up some catnip or tuna after classes.

When the dog finished, Logan rinsed the dish off and stuck it in the drain rack. While the brownie did most of the housekeeping, she wouldn't tolerate slobs. It's why she left her last employer, Sam, the troll.

Logan ignored the dog's pleading look for more.

"Let's go outside for a walk."

As Logan locked the apartment door, the pup galloped ahead to the elevator. Unlike last night, he seemed to be full of vigor. That was good to see.

"Hm, so you do understand what I said? Can you tell me what your name is?"

The fae Black Dog remained silent. Logan didn't know if the dog could answer. Jib was a True Beast, a fae that stayed in animal shape, but it could talk. Logan didn't know if that was typical of those type of fae. He'd ask Brigit about it.

Downstairs, on the main floor, he led the dog to an exit. The apartment complex had a miniature park at the back for residents. Logan used his pass card to open the electronic gate. The Black Dog dropped his nose to start sniffing everything in his path.

Keeping an eye on the pup, Logan texted one of his class members about missing the study group this morning. He looked over his day's calendar, reminding himself of what he had to get done.

With that out of the way, he read through the emails from the website that Emma Walker had designed for them. Emma was a computer programmer, more accurately a gamer, they had met last year. It was child's play for her to design a website that would filter the many requests for Logan and Brigit's assistance.

After the incident with the library monster, Bandemer

made them both student liaisons. Unfortunately, Chancellor Bandemer announced it through a university-wide email adding that a fae princess and a human bard would be troubleshooting issues among the student body.

Logan and Brigit were immediately flooded with petitions for mediation.

After being so careful about hiding her identity, Brigit blew a gasket about Bandemer outing her as a royal. However, Logan reminded her that with the way fae gossiped, there was no way she could have kept it a secret much longer. Jib had already slipped up several times; calling her princess right in front of Emma, Granite, and Celia. The púca was a blabbermouth.

When he had made a joke about the cat being out of the bag, Brigit pummeled Logan's head with sofa cushions.

Logan believed it was better for the chancellor to have officially announced it. He told Brigit it would stop anyone accusing her of being sneaky or underhanded about her status at Leopold Otto.

It had resulted in one of their few arguments. So it was all well and good for her status to be shouted out from the rooftops but not for Logan? Why did he get to keep his grandmother's status as a goddess a secret?

What seemed to make her the most angry was that Logan had kept his father's blood tie relationship to the Morrighan a secret from her. While Logan could see her point, he found it hard to explain to Brigit that having a goddess as a paternal grandmother wasn't something desirable.

The Morrighan had caused his family a lot of trouble

over the years. Her interference had made him become a bard, something that isolated him from his peers. Generally, his fellow humans were uncomfortable with someone who saw through every little white lie.

The argument ended when they were faced with the outcome of Bandemer's email. The day after the announcement, Logan and Brigit started receiving unwelcome visitors to their apartment. Fae and humans, angered, upset, or frustrated, appeared at all hours. They brought their troubles to Brigit and Logan and often didn't like the answers given.

For a while Granite, a fae eotan and wrestler for Leopold Otto, slept on their couch. The muscular mountain fae specialized in removing the worst offenders by force. He wrestled them down the hallway and threw them down the stairwell.

But Granite couldn't follow them to classes where both Logan and Brigit were often stopped by those wanting to discuss their grievances.

The tangled mess of being inundated with other people's problems resulted in sleepless nights and missed homework. It also produced some hurtful rumors across campus that infuriated Brigit and made Logan feel tired all over. Last spring ended with both of them taking hits on their GPA.

Things had to change. They called a conference of their friends (or bondmates as Brigit called them) to discuss the problem. It was Emma who suggested they set up a website. They could filter the requests using an algorithm. She'd design it and do the programming for free.

For fae who could not use a computer or cellphone, Logan offered his crow friends as go-between messengers. The birds owed him a big favor by losing a bet with him, so when asked if they would help, they were happy to oblige.

Being secretary for Brigit and Logan put them on the inside track of knowing every grievance on campus. The crows loved to gossip and were well suited to their role as gate-keepers. They delighted in dive-bombing those who broke the rules or pooping on the heads of malefactors as they crossed campus.

They took to boasting they were the Kings of Knowledge.

Things settled down, and Granite returned to his dorm. For those still too stupid to get the point, they were now met at the door by the Scot brownie. She shouted at them that the baw's on the slates, and the game was over. They were to take themselves back home before she gave them a skelpit lug!

Those who ignored the brownie's belligerent warning got more than a slap on the ear — they were summarily chased away by a Hairy Meg who gleefully whacked them with a broom as they fled.

As Logan finished with his phone, he looked up to see Brigit walking across the back lot towards them.

"How's the pup doing?" she called out to him, giving a wave.

"Much better than last night. I swear he's doubled in size!"

She came through the gate into the garden area to join them.

"Oh yeah, he does look bigger. He looks more like a dog teenager than a young puppy. That's not unusual with True Beasts — you've seen Jib get panther sized. They tend to wax and wane with their mood or the strength of their soul-magic."

"So he is a True Beast? Like Jib?"

"Well, no one is like Jib — or so it would have you believe. I'm not totally sure yet what he is other than he's a Black Dog. Most of those are True Beasts, and stay in their animal form. We'll find out more as we get to know him."

The dog, who had noticed her arrival, ran over to the girl. He jumped up to place his front paws on her thighs and Brigit bent down to rub either side of the dog's rib cage. The vigorous petting made him fall over on his side, exposing his stomach to her hands as his tail thumped the ground.

"Yes," she addressed her remarks to the fawning dog in a high-pitched baby voice that Logan had never heard her use, "you're a cutie. Just an adorable cutie-pie."

Logan told her, "I'll help you back upstairs with him, but I've got to get running. I have that meeting with Kados Géza. I can't miss it."

Kados Géza was the conductor of the university orchestra. Last year, he insisted that Logan come to him twice a month to improve his music. Since that was essentially a command, Logan had no choice but to comply.

However, Logan wasn't so sure that improving his

playing of the violin was the Hungarian's intention.

Brigit stood up causing the dog to frolic and bark around them, begging for more attention.

"That's enough," said Brigit sternly, "Logan has classes and I've made an appointment to take you to," she looked at Logan and spelled it out, "V-E-T."

Since they didn't have a collar or leash yet, Logan picked up the squirming Black Dog to carry him back inside. The dog spent the ride in the elevator wiggling in Logan's arms, trying to lick his face.

"He never told me his name. He didn't speak at all, only barked and whined."

"Some True Beasts don't have speech," explained Brigit, using her hand to hold the elevator door open for them, as they exited on their floor. "Or it could be the trauma that has him mum. Let's give him time to open up to us. Meanwhile, we need to come up with some sort of name for him."

"So giving him a name is okay? He's not like the brownie?"

"I still don't know how you got away with calling her Mrs. Tiggy, Logan. That was the worst! She must have thought since you were sick you were too pathetic."

Brigit unlocked the apartment door, telling him, "I've never known a Black Dog to be offended by having a name. Let me think on it. Giving a name is an important ritual."

Logan arrived at the maestro's office with a few minutes to spare. From experience, he knew if he arrived late, the door would remain locked. Logan had come late only once.

Their meeting always followed the same pattern.

When the clock hit the exact time for the meeting, the door opened, and Logan would be silently ushered in by Géza. The maestro was a small, wiry man. Since Logan usually saw him on a platform conducting the orchestra, it always surprised him that he could, when they were side-by-side, look down at the man.

Logan wasn't sure how the maestro instilled so much fear and respect in the musicians of the Leopold Otto orchestra. It wasn't like the maestro yelled at anyone. He'd seen him do that only once, when Celia, Granite, and Sibyl interrupted orchestra practice at the auditorium almost two years ago.

Still, he couldn't resist the impression that the short man was a ball of fiery energy, barely restrained. Still waters that ran so deep that they could knock you off your feet if you weren't careful.

Once the maestro was seated behind his desk, he would ask for Logan's written work assigned at their last session. After Logan handed it over, Géza would request him to start a piece on his violin.

Herr Géza never told him what to play. Only that it had to be different than anything Logan had performed for him before and that Logan could not use sheet music to guide him. Other than those requirements, the maestro made no comment about his choice or his technique.

While Logan plied his bow across the strings, Géza read the assignment. When Géza was ready to discuss it, he indicated, with a brown-spotted hand, for Logan to put his instrument away.

So far, no matter how short the piece, Logan never finished any of his music. Today was no different.

The maestro set aside the paper and motioned to Logan who immediately stopped playing. Steepling his fingers, the old man said, "In your evaluation of last week's tale, you believe the hermit shouldn't have spoken his prophecy to the king."

The week prior Herr Géza had told him a story about a king, a hermit, and the hermit's daughter. In the fairytale, a king learned that the hermit's daughter would marry his son. The king promises to raise the baby as royalty and her father gives him the girl. Instead, the king leaves the girl for dead in the forest.

In typical fairytale fashion the girl is found, healed, and grows to be a pretty young girl. Despite the king's actions, she eventually marries the prince.

Hands behind his back, Logan defended his reasoning to the maestro. "If the king didn't know the hermit's daughter would marry his son, he wouldn't have tried to kill her."

"So silence would have protected the girl? Do you think silence would have changed her destiny?"

"I — well," Logan could feel himself stumbling. These sessions were torture. He ended lamely, "I think it would have prevented something."

He hated these sessions with the maestro. They always

made him feel like an idiot, never knowing what to say, and feeling what he did say was wrong. He wasn't sure what Géza wanted or where he was going with his inquisition. Inevitably, in the middle of the night, right before falling asleep he would think of a snappy comeback that was far too late to use.

It was as fun as taking a pop quiz on a subject you weren't studying in a foreign language you never learned.

Géza backhanded the paper he held with his other hand. "You never address the problem in the story that the king, who attempted murder, was not punished."

Logan felt his heart gallop. No, he hadn't. Was he supposed to? Géza gave little instruction on what he expected from these assignments.

The maestro continued speaking as if he had not noticed Logan's widened, panicked eyes, "Preventing the physical hurt of the girl seems to be what you feel is the most important takeaway. Not justice."

"I thought that was the crux of the story, not whether the king was punished." When Géza did not answer, Logan suggested tentatively, "But I wonder if this fairytale isn't more like a Greek Tragedy? The marriage could not be avoided no matter what action was done or not done?"

Herr Géza folded his hands, shoving them forward across the desktop as he began the story. "The king chose to go hunting on a day it rained. In seeking shelter, he meets the hermit. How many stories have the protagonist meet someone that gives them a fated message that changes the course of their actions?"

"The three witches in Macbeth," suggested Logan.

The fluffy white dandelion of the maestro's hair bobbed emphatically. "The king failed to escape his fate, despite having foreknowledge, and taking action. What does that say of free will?"

"In stories, especially those designed to teach a lesson," said Logan, "fate removes choice from the protagonist. In real life, we have free will."

"You think you have a choice?" the maestro's bushy eyebrows climbed halfway up his forehead, indicating skepticism. He gave a harsh laugh, something reminiscent of a fire grate being cleaned. "You hate coming to these sessions, yet you come. How free are you?"

Logan opened his mouth to deny it but stopped. His bard sense that always discerned truth would make the false words on his tongue taste sour. Speaking untruth would fill his mouth with bile. Logan avoided this by not speaking. He decided to temper his reply, skating an outright lie.

"I have a choice to continue my enrollment at Leopold Otto or to leave. I choose to stay. Coming here is one of the prices I pay for that."

The maestro put Logan's paper back on the pile on his desk. Picking up a pencil, he tapped the eraser head on top of it like a baton counting time. Géza's stare was opaque, stubbornly refusing to reveal his thoughts to his protégé.

However, Logan could also keep a stubborn silence. A technique that he learned in childhood. Finally, it was the maestro's impatience that broke. He threw the pencil vehemently down on his desk.

"Still you do not see the big picture—the greater truth. Have you taken any philosophy classes?"

"Intro. It's a requirement."

"Sign up for another one. Whatever you can find still open in the spring semester."

"I'm — well, I don't know if I can fit them into my schedule." The stare stabbed Logan. "Uh, I guess I'll make the time, sir."

Tap—tap—tap. The maestro now thought with his fingers, drumming them on the wood desktop. He stopped. The chime of the clock on his office wall sounded the hour mark. Their session was over.

"Next week I want you to work on a narrative. How would you convince someone, with a quite different worldview than yourself, of something you need them to accept. Make a speech. A convincing one."

Logan finished packing his violin and grabbed the handle of the case, eager to escape. At the door, he halted, looking back beseechingly. "Could you give me a hint? Some ideas?"

The maestro gave a slow tight-lipped smile commonly found on a cobra.

"No need. Your mother will supply you with an idea. Let her know she can attend one of our rehearsals."

Bane of Hounds

Chapter Five
Knight's Gambit

Six hundred years ago, when Paul was a knight, his occupation meant risking maiming or death to serve his lord. Now the Doppelgänger worked for his liege by doing paperwork. While he no longer risked a hard fall in armor from a horse at full gallop, he had to deal with people.

The vote was still out on which was the worse fate.

If he thought the job was beneath him it didn't show on Paul's face. Probably because it wasn't his face.

Last year, injured by a creature lurking in the library, Paul lost his ability to use images from other people's minds to disguise himself. A temporary illusion spell by Celia Rivers let him conceal his real appearance, that of a wyvern dragon, from humans.

Since fae were immune to Glamour it had caused Paul to retreat from tasks that dealt with them. Besides, Celia's spell was only a temporary disguise. When it wore away, Chancellor Bandemer stepped in and gave him a new face to wear. The force of Bandemer's unique magic made it a mask that neither fae or human could penetrate.

Paul was not enjoying the gift.

The Doppelgänger wasn't ungrateful, but he was uncomfortable being stared at when he went about his business. As Bandemer's spymaster, he had spent his life in the shadows. Parading about with a face that drew everyone's gaze was unsettling.

Staring into the mirror that Bandemer always kept in his office as a place to primp before meetings, Paul frowned at the visage staring back at him. He knew his liege had a twisted ironic humor. This Darcy persona was one of them.

"It draws too much notice," he protested.

"What is wrong with being the center of attention?" Bandemer countered, patting Paul on the back, "I'm tired of you trudging about, looking average. Think how that reflects upon me?"

"How can I get my work done?"

The chancellor told him sternly, "My symposium cannot be put on hold until your magic fully recovers. The humans attending will want a human-looking face greeting them, not a two-legged wyvern with feathers and scales."

"But it doesn't have to be this face."

The symposium was the chancellor's baby — a project that had taken three years to develop. The week-long meeting would bring together talented fae and human leaders, in business, government, and the arts. The goal was to form new partnerships between the human lands and the Perilous Realm.

Leopold-Ottos-Universität Geheimetür, Bewachterberg, was the only institution of higher learning in the world that had a unique student body composed of both fae and humans. Chancellor Bandemer wanted the university to facilitate these partnerships, not only for the prestige, but for a cut of the pie.

Bandemer liked to hoard money and people.

The Doppelgänger sighed as he scrolled through the spreadsheet on his computer, showing who had confirmed their reservation. Beings were already arriving at the Hotel Kiburg, and he felt as if he was being shoved down a chute with no escape.

How he hated these public events!

To manage the event, he was assigned an office, with staff. If the face wasn't enough to make him uncomfortable, the glass fishbowl of an office was.

There was a tap at his door.

"Yes?"

A young human woman entered, smiling brightly. They were always smiling at this Darcy face. Ugh. She held a stack of papers in her hands.

"Advance copies of the speeches, Herr Darcy. As you

requested." She set them down on the desk. "One of the speakers, Herr Parkinson, you might want to review."

"Thank you," Paul said automatically, reaching for the documents. "The chancellor is well aware of Herr Parkinson's rather, hm, strident tone and attitude about the fae. Chancellor Bandemer is setting up Parkinson as a counterpoint, and using him as an example of extremism."

The woman gave a head nod and turned to leave. At the door, she paused. "That black cat púca is here again. Should I tell it you're in a meeting?"

"No. That's fine. I have a few moments."

Once Jib discovered Paul had a temporary office for the symposium, the púca kept finding excuses to visit. Jib strolled in, its long black tail high in the air.

When Jib helped Paul in his time of trouble last year, the púca's service voided Brigit Cullen's Debt to the Doppelgänger. However, the púca still found excuses to visit as if Paul still owed it.

Bonds were the building blocks that formed relationships of trust between fae. They occurred through obligations, favors, and sometimes because of perceived slights. The formal system allowed fae to know who to trust and who to kill.

"To what do I owe the honor this time?" asked Paul. The cat jumped up on his desk and stepped into the soft pet bed that was placed next to Paul's computer monitor. Jib settled into the cushion, kneading the material.

"WWWWrrrr," said the cat. "Nothing in particular. I was just returning from visiting Emma Walker and Obake at the library. They've almost finished with helping Anna Burkhalter."

It was Paul who had gotten Emma the job of helping the library restore their database. Jib knew that. Usually, the cat didn't make chit-chat; Paul became suspicious.

Tucked into a loaf on the bed, Jib slit its eyes and purred.

Oh, it was up to something all right.

"Tell me about this symposium."

Paul raised an eyebrow. In all the previous visits, the cat had talked only about itself and its concerns. From these gossiping sessions, Paul learned much about Logan Dannon, Brigit Cullen, and their household.

This question was unusual. Another red flag.

"The chancellor wishes to bring together the fae and humans to foster commercial enterprises. With the advent of technology in the human lands and their love of science, he fears interest in the fae will fade. That human myths and legends regarding us will become forgotten."

"The chancellor wants a new Golden Age," suggested the cat.

There were several periods the fae referred to as a Golden Age in the human lands: when Helen, a siren, caused the Fall of Troy; in the late 1500s when a fairy queen took a throne disguised as a human princess, and the Italians were inspired by fae muses; and the explosion of art and poetry during the 1800s.

"History can and does repeat itself. Don't you think we are overdue for the Wheel of Fortune to spin in our favor?" asked Paul, who was himself also skeptical of the chancellor's plan.

"Shsss," hissed the cat, dismissively, "The fae work best through the creative arts: poetry, plays, paintings, and sculpture. We don't have scientists in the fae world. The Industrial Revolution left us in the dust."

"Celia Rivers graduated as a nurse. And she is a naiad," countered Paul. "Brigit Cullen is studying biology and botany. She wants this change also. The princess could serve as an example to encourage fae everywhere to expand their horizons."

"She gets little encouragement from her mother, the queen, for such an endeavor," pointed out the cat. "I do not see Brigit, as much as I adore her and will serve her forever and a day, setting a new trend."

"Do you not? It might surprise you that the semester after the chancellor announced that a princess was attending LOTTOS, that fae enrollment increased by ten percent. She could set a trend like the king's descendants did back in the early 1900s."

The Treaty of Sigismund, which hid the country for ninety-nine years and a day, resulted in the Bewachterberg king marrying nine fae queens. When the offspring from those unions came to study at Leopold Otto, it set a trend for fae nobility to attend the university. Those not as studious came to live in Geheimetür, forming an upper-crust society.

"It might change the mind of other fae queens, but Queen Elixia is suspicious of humans. There's history there. It was only through my help that the parents of the princess agreed let her stay."

"In that you are correct," said Paul. "Every queen we've contacted, except your own, is coming herself or sending a representative. That's regrettable. The chancellor arranged for a famous human scientist to attend specifically because of Queen Elixia's problem."

"What problem?"

Paul stopped typing his email and looked at the cat. "The problem of your court's grove dying."

"Who told you that?!" the cat hissed, rising to all fours, arching its back.

"You did."

"Oh."

Paul tried to hide his smile. Jib started grooming its whiskers as if it had not been alarmed a moment ago.

"Why should we care about some scientist?"

"Have you not heard of Dr. Sebastian Stuart? I'm surprised at you. I thought you watched a lot of television."

The cat narrowed its eyes, thinking. "Dr. Stuart? He sounds familiar, but I watch a diverse amount of programming."

"Not a fan of the Nature channel? National Geographic? Dr. Stuart was last year's Nobel Prize winner for discovering a bacteria in the heart of a volcano."

"Oh, that Dr. Stuart," replied the cat, still having no idea who Paul was referring to. "How could he help my queen?"

"One of his areas is plant pathology." At the cat's blank look, Paul explained, "That includes the study of diseases in trees."

Digesting this information, the púca suggested nonchalantly, "Perhaps she didn't get her invitation?"

"The invitations were sent months back through the Kelpie's delivery service. Anyway, it's too late for her to RSVP now. Hotel Kiburg is fully booked and the meet-and-greet is tomorrow night."

The púca opened a paw, extending sharp claws. It licked them with an air of indifferent concern.

"Fae can fold a carriage and horses into a walnut shell. Walk through a tree and enter another dimension. A fae as powerful as you are can create another room for her majesty if she decided to come to this little soirée."

Paul dismissed Jib's suggestion.

"That's a waste of time and effort. You already said she wouldn't come."

"I was going to visit her soon to discuss a certain situation requiring her input. I will tell her about Dr. Stuart and the offer of assistance. Just make sure you have her suite ready. Be sure to make it palatial. And decorate it appropriately. She likes French antiques and art from the Impressionists."

Leaving Paul's office, Jib trotted across campus, deep in thought. The púca was conflicted. If this Dr. Stuart fellow could provide assistance with healing the grove, then it was imperative that Jib convince Queen Elixia to come to the symposium.

However, that would mean Brigit would have no reason

to remain in Geheimetür since she was here to learn science to help their trees. If the princess returned to the Perilous Realm, it would solve the problem about the dog, but it also meant Jib would lose a reason to remain in the Human Lands.

It was a mess of a dilemma for Jib quite liked staying in the Human Lands. It was not ready to return home yet.

During Brigit's school breaks, instead of going home, the púca and dryad had roamed about Europe, looking for adventure. This would be Jib's first visit back home in almost two human years.

Jib's duty was clear. It needed to discuss with Queen Elixia the opportunity to meet Dr. Stuart. The health of the grove, the queen's seat of power, was of top importance.

There were several access points across campus that Jib could have taken to step across to the Perilous Realm, but it preferred a direct route to home. For that reason, the púca made its way to a Mother Oak near the university tennis courts.

When Jib met Brigit at Leopold Otto, the dryad had revealed the tree as a direct portal to their court. The first time she left home, she needed a direct access to find her way to the university in Geheimetür. Now, knowing the way, Brigit could create a return portal in any living plant.

Jib sat down on its haunches, contemplating the bark of the Mother Oak. Unlike the dryad princess, the cat couldn't talk one-on-one with the oak.

Still, Jib knew how to pay its respects. It projected mental images of gratitude and well wishes: rain to soak, but not drown the earth; gentle winds to play with her leaves; and a summer without pests in her bark.

In response to its greeting, Jib felt its fur grow warm. Greetings acknowledged, the cat stepped into the tree, passing through the portal. Colors on a spectrum invisible to human eyes flared across Jib's vision, and in three steps, the cat crossed to the other side.

Like many who return home after a long absence, Jib fully expected everything to be the same.

It was not.

The smell made the cat's hackles rise. Jib found itself raising its back in a hostile attack stance. Instinctively, it started growing from cat-size to a larger animal.

To the human eye, the Perilous Realm was silver, white, gray, and black. Or at least that was what Logan described to the púca after his visit to the court.

But to Jib and the fae, it was not monochromatic. Instead, the Perilous Realm was filled with the swirling vapors of riotous color, magic trails left by the fae who lived there. Smells that tickled the nose with rich messages of enchantment.

These vapors identified every fae being's affiliations to another in a weave that made their world sing.

In Queen Elixia's court, where hundreds of beings lived, there were always waves to delight the nose, ear, and eye. As a True Beast, Jib was perhaps more sensitive than others to this complex web.

It was this sensitivity which enabled the púca to identify the Doppelgänger's dangerous Mindbending affiliation at their first meeting. And while Paul's magic and later Bandemer's disguise hid Paul's true face, it could not conceal his aura from Jib.

But Jib was at home and it was all wrong! The land was devoid of anything but musty smells, perfumes so faint that even Jib's powerful nose caught only an unidentifiable whiff.

Where was the laughter, the cries, the teasing voices of its own kind? For signs of habitation, there was none.

The court was deserted. The cat could feel only the stale sighs of sadness.

Where was everyone?

Bane of Hounds

Chapter Six
Queen in Play

Jib ran through the grove of silver trees, dashing around the trunks, while scanning the forest for any sort of threat. As it did so, the cat's form swelled in size, until it became that of a panther.

Emerging from the portal had placed Jib in the outer area of the court's forest. The púca took a path towards where a castle carved out of a mountain was the center of court life.

While Jib ran, it met no one, friend or foe.

As the cat ran it kept the roof of its mouth open to detect any scent trails. Nothing was fresh, until Jib came to the path that led into the cavern. The True Beast did not hesitate; it rushed in, feeling the cooler breeze of the cavern's tunnels brush its fur.

As it traveled the corridors, Jib's paws padded over rock smoothed by countless feet before it. It found the rooms vacant. Some interiors were stripped of their personal belongings, leaving only furniture; their beds bare of linens, pillows, or hangings.

While other chambers looked as if someone just walked away a moment ago. Garments were strewn over the bed; shoes on the floor; and sometimes plates of spoiled food lay on a table.

Nothing seemed out of place, except for the lack of inhabitants.

Finally, Jib came to a branching that gave the cat two choices: go down to the treasure room, or up to the suite of rooms reserved for the royal family. First, the treasure room. It was always guarded.

Jib went deeper into the mountain, searching for sound or smell. But all it heard was the pinging drip of water sliding down the cave's walls to the ground.

When the púca reached the opening of a hall that would have taken one to the vaults, Jib found a strange wall of crystal. Its thick opaque mass hid from view anything on the other side.

Its surface burned with the coldness of a death frost. The cat would be a fool to touch it. It was a protective magic strong enough to kill. It did give Jib courage, for the protection looked like work done by King Ladislas.

Jib backtracked. Running back up the ramp, the cat's mad rush started to slow from exhaustion.

In one moment, Jib wished Brigit was with it; the next

moment, was glad she wasn't here to see this strangeness. Better that she stay in the Human Lands forever than see her home in such a state.

At the branching of the corridor, Jib took the spiral staircase. The steps were cut out of stone, with a worn dip in the middle where centuries of feet had traveled. These stairs would take it to the queen's quarters.

Reaching the last step, Jib heard words spoken by Queen Elixia. "Pack it all. Don't leave a pearl."

At the entrance to the queen's bedchamber, Jib scratched and yowled. The magical tapestry that hung over the opening and blocked admittance was moved aside by one of the queen's ladies.

The cat ran into the room and howled in distress, "Where is everyone!? What has happened?"

Queen Elixia, standing in the middle of her bedchamber, turned abruptly at the púca's entrance. She asked Jib sharply, "Why are you here? What is wrong? Brigit?"

Jib, usually so suave, was confused and frightened. Before it could help itself, the púca yowled, "Brigit got a smelly dog. It's living with us. In the apartment. I can't stand it! Make it go awayyyyyy!"

The last ended in a drawled out, high-pitched, animal scream of despair. Elixia looked at the cat blankly for a moment before she collapsed on her bed, kicking her heels. Her belly-laugh left her gasping for air.

Insulted by the queen's actions, as well as still shaken, Jib's form shrunk to cat-size. It dashed under the bed to hide.

It took a few more moments for Elixia to gain control of herself. Still wheezing, she got off her bed and looked under the mattress to where Jib had fled.

"Now, now," said Elixia soothingly to the orange eyes glowing in the darkness. "Come out like the smart púca you are. I didn't mean to hurt your feelings."

"Everything is wrong!" Jib wailed.

"Yes, things are not good right now," Elixia agreed, sighing. "If it will make you feel better, I will talk while you stay in your safe place."

The queen rose. Elixia talked while she pointed to things she wanted packed by her servants. Her two court ladies were both dryads, but their breeding wasn't as refined as Brigit's: they had long oval faces, and round eyes as big as walnuts with thick eyelashes.

These deviations from the human average identified them as fae. With two years living amongst humans, the púca could see they were a bit odd looking when compared to the human ideal of beauty.

"The disease in our Grove has worsened. King Ladislas has moved the court to Queen Titania's realm for their protection. I'll never live that one down." The last sentence was muttered before she began again. "I'm attending to the last of what needs to be done now."

Jib crept out, only a black nose peeking out. "Leaving the kingdom? When were you going to let me know? Tell the princess?"

"I was going to send a message, but you arrived. Now I don't have to." Elixia rummaged in her wardrobe tossing things out in different directions. "That pile goes, this one does not," she told her companions. The ladies-in-waiting returned to the job of sorting the extensive collection of the queen's personal items.

"Are things truly that dire?" said Jib with a quiet meow.

Queen Elixia spared the púca a glance before motioning to her court ladies to latch her traveling trunks.

"If any remain here when the Grove dies, they shall perish."

"But—" Jib was about to say the obvious, but grew quiet.

A court in the Perilous Realm formed when a female fae was accepted by a wild spirit of power. When the fae and the Elder spirit became bonded, it created the land of the court. How the process happened exactly even Jib was unclear about, as it was considered one of the Mysteries.

However, the púca did know that the two were bonded for life. Queen Elixia's heart beat to the rhythm of the Elder magic that suffused the silver birch grove. If the grove lost the queen, the Elder would survive, but if the grove perished, Elixia would die.

Jib gave a pitiful meow, feeling guilty. Enjoying the freedom and delights of the Human Lands, it had rarely considered what was happening back at court. Worse, Jib knew that Brigit had no inkling the tree's disease had progressed so rapidly.

She would need this news.

But as the queen's adviser, Jib's first loyalty was to Elixia. What could the púca do to help?

During Jib's silent contemplation, Queen Elixia had

moved to her dressing table. She sorted through her extensive jewelry collection, discussing the various pieces.

"His majesty gave me this when he went to Tokyo to consult with a royal dragon." She held up a choker of pearls, each one the size of a magic bean from the Jack-and-the-beanstalk story. "I usually keep them in a safe deposit box in Sweden. Residing in the human lands helps them retain their luster."

Any human object dwelling in the Perilous Realm for an extended time became dull. It was one reason that some type of secure storage lockers located in the human lands were a popular conceit for fae royalty. It kept every human pearl, diamond, and gold locket perfect.

"Very nice, your majesty," agreed Jib as it crawled out from under the bed. The púca came to the foot of the queen's chair. "Now, back to the issue of what's happening around here—"

Queen Elixia was an expert at ignoring what she didn't want to discuss. She picked up a diamond and sapphire brooch and gave the object a pensive, contemplative frown.

"So pretty. But I don't wear cloaks as much as I once did. I will gift it to Saffo since Ladislas gave this to me as a push-present to commemorate her birth."

Queen Elixia gestured to one of her ladies, and the dryad came forward to take it. "Be sure Saffo gets this."

Next, Elixia ran a chain of thin links made of precious metals through her fingers. "Do you think silver and gold can be worn together? I've seen a new fashion in rings which combine both of them."

Consulted, Jib felt the need to give an opinion. It wouldn't do for the court's minister of fashion not to comment. Beside, the púca was well known for its discerning taste.

"Ostentatious pieces are out; Minimalism is in. Simple pieces that hold personal meaning is what all the wealthy humans are wearing now."

"Then I'm happy to say I'm not a human," snapped Queen Elixia. In a peevish fit, she threw the chain back into her jewelry box.

Next, she opened up a box lined with blue satin. Nestled within was a tiara glittering with diamonds and sapphires as large as a man's thumb.

Putting the crown on her head, Queen Elixia gave her reflection a pout, asking, "What do you say, mirror?"

"Your majesty, no jewels could compare with your beauty. They dim in comparison."

"Suck-up," Jib told the magic mirror. The púca had no good opinion of enchanted sycophants. Yes-men were not to be trusted.

However the queen held no such prejudice against enchanted lies. She was always well pleased when receiving compliments about her beauty.

Long used to the fluttering nature of the queen's attention span, the cat needed to regain her attention. The púca jumped to the table and with a swift swipe knocked a perfume bottle off the table. As it hit the carpet, the crystal stopper fell out and the smell of happy tears from a virgin's first love affair filled the air.

The queen jumped up in anger from her stool, exclaiming, "That bottle was my last! And it's not like the human world has plenty of naive virgins nowadays to collect tears from. Their young are all too cynical and world-weary."

Jib would not be distracted again.

"Can we return to what is happening to the kingdom?"

The queen couldn't handle the overwhelming smell. Waving her hand in front of her nose, she left the table.

"Fine, Jib," snapped Queen Elixia. "You want answers? So do I. I planned on visiting the Elder before I left. Since you arrived, you can come with me and see if the Elder gives you better answers than it has me!"

They walked to the Elder in silence.

Elixia was barefoot. She had showered and dressed in a simple pullover white shift. Jib thought she was overdoing the supplicant to the goddess thing, but what did the púca know. For Queen Elixia was the Pythia, the High Priestess, and Jib had never participated in the secret, sacred rituals of meeting the Elder known as the Mysteries.

This would be its first time meeting the Elder directly. Jib was nervously excited, but also a bit frightened.

The soles of the queen's feet were quiet over the stone path that eventually gave way to grass. This area of the glade was only traveled by those of the inner court. Jib had only done so during certain ceremonies, and less than a dozen times in its lifespan.

They had all known of the dying trees; Brigit had run away from home to find a solution. But all of the courtiers felt it was a temporary illness. Jib did not expect this. Not this. Not the collapse of the court itself.

If the Elder died, Elixia's court in the Perilous Realm would fold onto itself, ceasing to exist. It would not be a vacant land where fae could later repopulate. No, it would be a void in the world — a black hole of loss.

Jib's fellow fae would forever be exiles, never able to return. The queen would die with her tree.

The grass and ground felt cool and slightly moist under Jib's paws. They passed trees which shimmered glass-frost-white. None had leaves.

"How is Brigit doing at school?" asked Elixia. The question was so sudden in this quiet stillness, Jib's tail gave an involuntary poof. The cat calmed himself and said in a low and subdued voice, "She is attending classes, passing her studies. She is well content."

"Good. It was my daughter's dream to be there. I'm glad she is succeeding."

After a moment, when Jib couldn't think of any other small talk, it broached the reason for its arrival. "I came to tell you about your invitation."

"What? What invitation?"

"The chancellor of Leopold-Ottos-Universität Geheimetür, Bewachterberg, invited you to a conference. To meet a scientist."

Their voices seemed too loud in such a sacred place.

"Yes, I received it. But I have more important things to do than consort with humans."

They came upon the two slabs of stone, twice as tall as

any nymph or dryad. The blocks of stones stood as sentinels, guarding the entrance to the grove's most sacred place—the seat of the Elder's power.

Jib felt the increased weight of ancient magic in the air; it dampened the mood when you felt so small.

"Now, shush," Queen Elixia told Jib.

She placed the palm of her hands together and bowed to each sentential. Passing into the alley formed by the two gray stones, Queen Elixia placed one hand on either rock, paused a moment in benediction, before proceeding.

Jib could hear a whisper from the sentinels, but didn't understand it.

Next, they entered a ring of trees, seven of them surrounding the Elder, who was rooted in the center. If the Eiffel tower were a tree, it would be smaller than the Elder.

Queen Elixia stood before the Elder. Jib sat on its haunches behind her position, waiting. Her majesty tenderly placed her small hand on the tree, caressing the bark.

She spoke to Jib in a voice that cracked, "Thank you for being my daughter's bondmate. Forget the dog. Go back and be with her. Aid her."

Her hand merged into the bark.

"I have promised the Elder what energy I have left to prolong its life span. Ladislas will visit our daughter and explain my decision to her."

In surprised horror, Jib watched as Queen Elixia merged with her life partner. Stepping into the Elder, the last trail of her dress vanished.

Jib barely had a chance to give a silent meow of grief

when a thunderclap sounded. The ground under its paws shuddered.

Abruptly, the body of Queen Elixia was thrown out of the Elder, her body flying past Jib's position. She landed with bruising force upon the ground, crushing the grass.

Jib yowled, running to her, fearing she was dead. But Queen Elixia pushed herself up, stumbling to her feet as she tried to regain the breath that was knocked out of her.

"What happened?" yowled Jib. Panicked, the cat tried to climb up her dress. She disengaged the púcas claws, lifting the cat so she could cradle Jib in her arms.

"The Elder rejected me! The Elder denied my sacrifice."

"Impossible!"

Queen Elixia gritted her teeth and approached the tree again. She was slapped with a burst of magical energy that sent her and Jib staggering back.

Raising a shaky hand to her temple, she concentrated on the series of images, impressions, and feeling being projected to her from the Elder.

She hugged Jib tightly and said with astonishment, "The Elder wants me to accept that invitation to the Symposium."

Bane of Hounds

Chapter Seven
Surprise Visit

Brigit was dreaming. In this dream, she was standing beside Logan's bed. It was part of an old memory of when he was sick with fever from his stay in the Perilous Realm. She bent over him, the back of her hand touching his hot forehead.

A black cat lay next to Logan's side. She told it, "We have to do something" because dream knowledge told Brigit that Logan would die if she didn't act.

Dream-Jib looked up at her, cocking its head. "You know what to do."

"I don't. I don't know what to do," she admitted to the púca. "Why can't you just tell me, you cursed Trickster?"

From there the dream twisted into something fantastical.

Logan's human skin changed to a brown and gray rough texture. His body morphed to that of a tree's trunk, leaving only a faint impression of his face in the ridges and recesses of the bark.

Brigit had seen humans imprisoned in cloven trees before. It was one of her mother's favorite punishments.

"Stop it!"

She felt a piercing pain like a knife prick her, right above her left breast. Her hand slid over her skin, and under the pads of her fingers she felt the raised outline of a leaf.

Two summers ago, the silver leaf had penetrated her skin, becoming one with her flesh, when she slept with it overnight.

Absorbing organic material within her flesh wasn't new to Brigit. Being a dryad, she could always move within anything made from trees, including books. But it was always her who decided to merge. This leaf had burrowed deep within her, unasked, and refused to detach.

With her fingers still touching her skin, Brigit watched the log rapidly age. Fungus sprouted, darkened, and crumbled. The outer bark flaked away, exposing the cracked heartwood. In moments, it was a crumbled brown mess of decayed tree.

A disembodied voice told her, "Soon it will be too late."

Brigit woke up to the dog licking the wet salt of tears off her cheeks. She was on the couch, having planned on grabbing a quick nap. From the path of the sun outside the windows, it was late afternoon. She'd slept longer than she intended.

The girl yawned and sat up, stretching her back, arms over her head.

"How are you doing, pup? Do we need to go outside?"

While the tail thumped at her voice, she didn't get any sense of speech from him, either verbally or in her head. She caressed his ears, cupping his muzzle in her hands to look into his eyes.

"Will you ever talk?"

The vet check had gone well and Brigit was told to continue what they were doing. His appearance was much better than last night, although his coat was still dry and listless. Maybe they should give him a bath?

Not for the first time, she wished she had a phone. She could text Logan to pick up dog shampoo, a collar, and a leash.

"Ye need to be answering the door."

Surprised by the brownie's voice, Bright replied to the air, "Take a message and I'll get back with them."

"She has the right to be here, so I kinnae turn her away. It will have to be ye that tells her to go."

Hopping off the couch, Brigit went to the door. Through the peephole, she saw a human woman in middle years with dark brown hair. She didn't recognize her. Didn't look the age to be a student. Maybe a teacher. More likely, a tenant in the building.

Sarah Dannon wondered again if her son, Logan, was at home.

Arthur, Logan's father, was at a banking conference in Berlin for the week. Sarah had accompanied him, eager to use the overseas trip as an excuse to visit their only child in Geheimetür. It was only a four-hour flight to Switzerland, and from there, another two hours by train to get to Geheimetür.

In Berlin, when she revealed her plan to her husband, she met resistance from Arthur. "Let the boy be. He'll be back with us at Christmas."

"I'm not going to sit in a hotel room, flipping through the TV channels listening to shows in German."

"You haven't unpacked yet. Or taken a tour of Berlin. There is plenty to do here," he argued.

She gave her bear of a husband a hug. Chin on his chest, she looked up at him and gave him a beseeching smile. "I'll just be away for a few days. You won't even notice I'm gone, you'll be so busy networking with those big bankers."

He was still protesting, insisting they call Logan, when she stepped into the taxi cab that would return her to the airport.

Sarah knocked again. Perhaps Logan was in class? He was such a hardworking boy.

When the door finally opened, it didn't reveal her tall, dark-haired, blue-eyed son with the lop-sided smile. Instead, Sarah faced a short, skinny black girl wearing a challenging attitude.

"What do you want?"

Sarah was unpleasantly bewildered. While she liked keeping others off balance, Sarah was not a woman who reacted well to surprises, preferring her life to be ordered and predictable. Logan's mother checked the number on the door again, wondering if she had made a mistake in the apartment.

"I'm looking for Logan Dannon. This is his apartment?"

"Yes, but he isn't here at the moment. Do you want to leave a message for him?"

With her son's residence confirmed, Sarah crossed the threshold, rolling her suitcase behind her. The girl moved hastily aside, so they wouldn't touch each other.

"Excuse me!" snapped the black girl. She had the type of manner which Sarah immediately found distasteful. Just the type of sarcastic, smart-mouthed girl Sarah had little use for. It reminded her a lot of her niece Evelyn, and not only because both girls had dark skin.

"Is Logan's roommate here? Granite Hillside?"

"Granite? Logan's roommate?"

"I don't see what is so funny, young lady. Where is Logan? When will he be back?"

"I don't know." The girl shrugged with a lazy roll of her shoulders. Her tone was insolent as she told Sarah, "I'm not his mother."

"But I am."

The girl's mouth made a rounded O of surprise. She took a step away to increase the distance between them. Sarah ignored her. She had put the girl in her place and knew herself victorious.

Sarah took the smaller bag off the top of her suitcase. Going to the kitchen, she set it on the counter. She unpacked the food and put it inside the refrigerator.

The girl followed. She now spoke in a more subdued, contrite manner. "I think we may have gotten off on the wrong foot, Mrs. Dannon."

Sarah said nothing. She wasn't the intruder here.

She flattened the empty bag and set it aside. Opening every cabinet, she inspected what was inside, sometimes rearranging its contents.

Sarah felt that old compulsion to set everything straight. She tidied a row of glasses, so all of them aligned like soldiers on parade. Opening a drawer, she sorted the silverware from small to large. These acts of organizing actually increased her anxiety, but it gave her some way to vent her nervous energy.

"There's no need to—" began the girl, earning her a cold sweeping glance. Logan's mother had perfected the look as a way to dismiss encroaching salespeople. It worked its magic and the girl's protests faded away.

Sarah was surprised to see the kitchen was cleaner than she had imagined two young men would have kept it. Perhaps Logan would get his security deposit back after all. Still, it wasn't up to her standards. She would find something to keep her busy until Logan came home. Wouldn't he be surprised!

She retrieved a sponge and soap from under the sink to scrub the counter. The girl stayed in the kitchen watching her which irritated Sarah. Didn't the girl see she clearly was unwanted?

"I'm not sure why you think Granite is Logan's roommate. He isn't. Granite has a place on campus where he bunks down with the rest of his wrestling team."

Sarah said nothing. She wasn't going to show this stranger that how her words troubled her. Sarah distinctly remembered Logan writing to her that he had found a roommate this year. He had used that to justify continuing the two-bedroom in Geheimetür.

Either the girl was lying, Logan was lying, or Sarah misremembered the letter. Surely, she didn't remember it wrong? As self-doubt started, Sarah scrubbed the counter harder, working the sponge around the faucet. Since some of those options were unpleasant to consider, she would believe the girl was lying.

Finding a broom in the kitchen closet, Logan's mother started sweeping the floor. Using sweeps of the broom, she forced the girl out of the kitchen, into the hall. It didn't stop the stranger from commenting, "I don't think you should be cleaning. The brownie doesn't like anyone doing those jobs."

"There is nothing here that couldn't use a bit more being done. Of course, it's natural that a boy wouldn't keep a place as clean as his mother would. But I'm here now, so I'll get the place into tip-top shape while I wait for him."

Sarah bent over to brush the crumbs into the dustpan. Suddenly, the top of the broom handle came down hard on the back of her head. Surprised by the blow, she fell to one knee. Her grip on the stick must have slipped.

Righting herself, she finished brushing the dirt into the dustpan and disposed of it into the garbage can.

Finished with the kitchen, Sarah went to find Logan's bedroom. There, she quickly and efficiently started stripping the bed of its sheets and blankets. Sarah found a laundry basket in the bathroom. Scooping up the bed linens, she dropped them inside.

Next, she pulled down wet towels from the shower bar and threw them in on top of the pile. She'd get a load of laundry done while she waited. There was nothing like the smell of clean sheets to make a home cozy.

"I really don't think you need to do that, Mrs. Dannon," said the girl, standing in the doorway. She had a worried frown on her face and appeared nervous.

"It's dangerous to be doing the brownie's work. Jib's been taking her to see a psychiatrist about her anger issues, because she almost turned boggart some time ago. So we need to be careful about offending her."

What nonsense these young people spoke!

"If Logan has hired a housekeeper," said Sarah. "I'll speak with her later about the quality of her work. As the employer he should dictate the work needing to be done, not her. Regardless of whatever psychological problems she has. I know how to deal with those types, young lady."

If Sarah had to wait for Logan to show up, she'd prefer being busy and of use to him. Besides, she would never show doubt or vulnerability especially to an inferior. She tightened her lips and kept at her work.

Guilt fueled her whirlwind storm of cleaning. Arthur had

discouraged this unannounced visit, wanting her to call Logan before taking the trip. Better yet, why not wait until his conference finished? They could go down together.

But her husband didn't realize, since he was a man, how much she missed her only son. Seeing Logan for the holidays wasn't enough. As it was, last summer she barely saw Logan. He spent most of it with his cousin Evie who was home from college.

Hearing a bang Sarah stopped.

"That's loud. Logan should report those neighbors to the manager."

"It's because you're cleaning. She's warning you. Please stop," the girl said.

"Whatever are you talking about?"

Sarah left the bedroom and returned to the kitchen to investigate where the noises were happening. She found the cabinet doors flying open and slamming shut. The dishes that Sarah had so carefully stacked were spinning in place. As if by an invisible hand, the pots in the lower cabinets were violently shoved out to land on the floor with a loud, ringing clatter.

"Stop. Stop that!" Sarah cried at the disorder. She tried to shove the cabinets closed, but whatever was pushing from the inside was stronger. The door continued to bang wildly back, hitting the wall.

A deep, booming voice made Sarah spin about. A black dog, about the size of a St. Bernard, was standing in the doorway to the kitchen. The beast was unnatural, wrapped in ice-blue flames. Sarah gave out a choked scream.

The creature howled, "An injury of iron will fall, spite will be both tool and cause."

Logan's mother had a rational fear of dogs.

Instinctively, she took a quick step backward, her right foot stepping into a skillet. The pan slid and Sarah's foot went out from under her. She hit the floor, the back of her head slamming against the tile.

Chapter Eight
Double Trouble

L ogan found his mother lying on his kitchen floor with his roommate trying to revive her. For a moment, he froze in shock. Memories of an incident from his childhood paralyzed his panicked mind. He shook off old fears and roughly asked Brigit, "Tell me what happened."

The first aid training Logan had taken back in high school kicked in. He placed his index and middle fingers on Sarah's neck, near her collarbone. At first, his fear kept him from finding her pulse, but when he did, he counted the beats to the seconds using a clock on his cell phone.

Brigit explained that his mother slipped and fell, banging her head on the floor. Logan checked his mother's breathing. That seemed okay.

"How long has she been out?"

"Just a moment! I swear, Logan, it was an accident." Brigit's voice was shaking, and he reached over and patted her hand. His gesture undid her.

"I'm so sorry, Logan. The brownie went crazy, and then the dog came in. He spooked her—"

"She doesn't like dogs." Logan's voice wasn't his own. It sounded remote, far away. The only way he could operate right now was to shut himself down emotionally. Too many flashbacks to the past would just get in the way of caring for his mother.

He was about to call emergency services on his cell when Sarah's eyelids fluttered. She gave a low groan. Putting a hand on her shoulder to keep her down, he reassured her, "Mom, take it easy. You've had a fall. Stay down. Brigit, raise her feet off the ground, like this."

Sarah Dannon's hand fluttered up to her head. She blinked several times as she stared blankly at her son's face.

"Do you know where you are?" he asked.

"Your apartment, in Geheimetür," her voice was slow at first but gained confidence as she went on, "I brought your favorite cookies. Chocolate chip. I picked them up at a bakery before coming here."

She closed her eyes again, wincing hard. "My head hurts."

"Brigit said you fell."

"There was a dog. A black dog. It was on fire. It said things."

"It's okay, mom. He won't hurt you. I won't let him."

78

"My head hurts," she repeated.

"Let's sit you up. Slow and easy." Tucking his arm under her shoulders, he brought her to a sitting position. Brigit let go of Sarah's legs but remained sitting beside them on the floor. Her eyes shuffled between Logan and his mother.

"This girl," Sarah Dannon's pointing finger shook slightly, "she's your roommate, isn't she? Don't deny it."

"Yes, she is. But before we discuss roommates, let's see if you can make it to the couch. The floor is cold. Brigit, would you get some coffee started?"

With assistance and by taking it slowly, Sarah was able to stand. Leaning heavily on her son, they were able to get to the living room without further mishap. Sitting down on the sofa was a relief. Logan examined the back of her head.

"There's a goose egg forming. Will you be okay while I get an icepack?"

Sarah started to nod, but a wave of nausea arrested her mid-movement. She settled for saying, "Yes."

In the kitchen, Logan started assembling an icepack. Brigit whispered, "Do you want me to go? Let you be alone with your mom?"

Logan frowned, concentrating. He lowered his voice, though it was doubtful his mother would hear him. "It would help if you could take the dog away for now. Maybe on a walk or something? It's a long story, which I promise to tell you one day, but dogs make her anxious."

"Yeah, I can do that. I really am sorry, Logan. I didn't—"

"If you say it was just an accident, Brigit, it was. So don't worry about it. I do want to keep her quiet and calm so taking the dog would be a great help. I'll take her over to the walk-in clinic to get her checked out."

Brigit gave him a quick nod. Before she could leave the kitchen, Logan added, "In the bag I dropped in the hall are some different sized collars for the dog and a lead that you can use. But before you leave could you grab me a blanket? And a bottle of aspirin from my bathroom?"

Returning to the living room, Logan laid Sarah backward on the sofa, sandwiching the ice pack between his mother's head and a pillow.

"I'd like to take you to a med center. Get you checked out."

"Don't fuss, Logan. You and your dad are always fussing. I'm not going to break."

Logan said nothing to this. Once his mother had broken. It had terrified them.

Brigit arrived with the blanket. He tucked it around his mother, while asking her, "How did you get here? Where's dad?"

His hand rested over hers and he could feel the wedding band on her finger. It gave him a strange twinge. His dad really should be here.

"Your dad is at a banking conference in Berlin. I thought I'd surprise you by coming for a visit. In all the time you've been here, I haven't seen your school. Or where you live. Or who you live with."

"I'm glad you came. It will be fun to show you around and introduce you to some of my friends."

"Like that girl?"

"Yes, like that girl. I've mentioned her in my letters."

"I don't remember." Sarah pursed her lips with an "I don't agree with this, but will show a silent disapproval" way she had. Instead of voicing her open disapproval, she said, "I thought you were rooming with someone named Granite."

"He's also a friend. But no, I roommate with Brigit."

His mother gave him a weak smile.

"Things are so different with your generation. Sharing an apartment with someone of the opposite sex — doesn't seem right. I'm old-fashioned."

"She's a true and loyal friend. That's what matters to me the most."

His mother gave an owlish stare. "Does she know—?"

The two had never spoken about Logan's bard talents. It was one of many things they didn't talk about, such as his father's mother, the vacation where he was lost on a mountain, or the summer Sarah died.

"Yes, she knows. She's okay with it. That alone makes her an ideal roommate. There aren't many people who would put up with that, you know. It's why I didn't want a place on campus when I came here."

"I know."

When Logan returned to high school following his initiation as a bard on the Snowden mountain in Wales, he discovered his friends were uncomfortable with the changes. He discovered all too well how people couldn't handle the truth.

"Maybe we should call dad?"

"No. Don't do that. I'm feeling better. I'll just take that coffee you promised me, okay?"

Brigit exited the apartment building feeling confused and guilty. With her thoughts elsewhere, it took her a moment to connect the voice with the being speaking. It seemed to be the day for surprises.

"Jib, what did you say?"

The black cat was sitting on its haunches in the middle of the sidewalk, blocking her path. Brigit pulled back on the leash to prevent the frolicking dog from reaching the cat.

After giving Sarah a Bane of Doom, the Black Dog had shrunk back to a smaller size. But it was still bigger than the puppy they had found the night before. Brigit used both hands on the leash to prevent a collision.

"Queen Elixia requests her daughter to present herself."

The Black Dog seemed to hold no ill will at the cat's frigid tones. Instead, he smiled, dropping a large pink tongue from the side of his mouth.

The cat looked away and added reluctantly, "Bring the dog with its disgusting drool if you must."

"I'm not returning to the Perilous Realm, Jib. Logan's mother—" But before Brigit could explain recent events, Jib interrupted her, "The queen is in Geheimetür, staying at the Royal Kiburg hotel. By invitation of Chancellor Bandemer."

The Royal Kiburg of Geheimetür was a well-known local institution. The historical landmark was located on the edge of the original Geheimetür, overlooking the river.

Once a hunting lodge for nobility, the estate gradually sold off the surrounding forest land until, eventually, the town surrounded the lodge. During the 1800s, when Geheimetür became a famous watering hole of the rich, the city was part of the Grand Tour that young men would travel to increase their exposure to art and culture. With the royal Bewachterberg family having an affiliation with the fae, there was a certain panache to staying in the country.

To take advantage of this, the Royal Kiburg lodge was transformed to a luxury hotel. But in 1890, when the country was concealed by fae magic from the world, and the hotel's revenue also disappeared.

The mansion became derelict, and the decay only stopped when it was declared by the state to be a national treasure. In the 1960s, work began on the building. It took several decades and a substantial amount of money to bring it back to its former glory. When Bewachterberg rejoined Europe in 1989, the hotel's restoration was soon finished and it started to enjoy a renaissance.

Many visitors expected a medieval castle, but what they saw was a candy box in the early Baroque style. Or a wedding cake. Or a Christmas tree. Something ornate and embellished until it made your teeth hurt from the sweetness.

Jib, Brigit, and the dog arrived at the bottom of the drive, outside the decorative gates. On either side of the road were brick pillars, topped with griffin statues. Brigit gave a brief shiver looking at the winged lions.

The group started up the hill, passing the extensive gardens. While the Kiburg had sold off most of the land, it did have well-maintained and extensive landscaping. Brigit had never found the time to explore the area and mentally made a note to do so.

Electric cars passed them by on the drive, along with a scooter or two. The Kiburg seemed to be having a full house this week.

Jib was trotting in front of their party, waving a black tail. After commanding Brigit to follow through a portal of the Perilous Realm to the Kiburg gates, the púca hadn't spoken again. Its silence made Brigit suspicious.

"I know you're upset about the dog—"

"The dog is a nothing."

"C'mon, Jib, something is wrong. If it's not the dog, what is it? Your whiskers are out of whack about something. If it isn't the dog, what's rubbing your fur the wrong way?"

They were stopped in the hotel's courtyard, and a crowd, both human and fae, were forced to walk around them to get to stairs leading to the hotel's grand entrance. Brigit and the cat ignored the passers by, while the dog tried to leap on everyone.

The cat stared at her before saying, "I'd like to kill something."

Brigit could sympathize with the cat's mood. She'd often had that feeling herself. "I understand you're frustrated by the dog being in the apartment. What about if—"

Before she could complete her sentence, something hit

Brigit in the back, painfully jabbing her kidney. It was a luggage rack, being pushed from behind by a hotel staff person. Hitting Brigit caused the wheeled cart to sway, the wheels twisting. A hatbox and a small overnight case resting on top of a stack of suitcases fell to the ground.

The stout woman who was following her luggage snapped an insult at the staff person. "I thought the Kiburg was known for luxury and well-trained staff. Apparently not!"

The woman was as round as a tomato and her outfit did her no favors. She wore a green satin hoop skirt styled from the 1860s, and a crimson stovepipe hat with a taller feather dyed pink. Her hands held a creamy fur muff.

"It's not his fault," explained Brigit, picking up the hatbox and case. She put them back on the tottering stack of luggage. "I shouldn't have been standing there like a statue."

However, Brigit's attempt at reconciliation fell flat. The woman's furry muff unwound itself, changing to a small tan dog with a black muzzle and round bulging eyes. It snarled at Brigit, "You certainly are to blame! Move out of the way of your betters, dryad."

Startled by the transformation, Brigit jumped back. The Black Dog at her side gave a deep woof of warning to the newcomer, causing the pug's eyes to roll in derision.

"A harbinger? Here? What impudence!" the small dog yipped shrilly. "Who allowed such scum to be here with decent fae folk?"

The woman simpered something soothing to her dog

companion. Her tone showed that the dog was the master, for he ignored her. His jet-black eyes examined Brigit with clear contempt.

"I will lodge a complaint with the Chancellor over this Bane hound. Bandemer would never countenance such a creature."

"As one that actually knows François Auguste Bandemer," sneered the black cat, "the real question is why a fae of such delicate refinement as the chancellor would invite a flea-ridden mutt of uncertain pedigree like yourself to Geheimetür."

The púca turned to Brigit and said, "I think we need to call animal control and have this thing checked for rabies."

"Jib," Brigit murmured a cautionary warning to the cat under her breath. But it seemed Jib did want to kill something, and the newcomer gave the perfect excuse for picking a fight.

From the safety of the woman's arms, the dog taunted them, "There is a treaty of parley in place for this conference, but I haven't signed it yet."

The pug gave a false lunge forward as if it was about to attack them. Its movement made the Black Dog beside Brigit jump excitedly, giving deep woofs. Brigit hauled him back.

However, she couldn't stop Jib and this faux threat was too much for the púca. The black cat grew to the size of a panther, flames of orange and red licking its black coat.

The púca hissed, "A treaty does not bind me either. Take me if you dare, flea-rag."

Chapter Nine
Cat Fight

Those of the Perilous Realm were no strangers to fighting. To adhere to the Laws of Civility, there were certain rules that a duel needed to meet.

For example, as Jib's bondmate, Brigit needed to introduce them so if bodies resulted, the appropriate court could be informed. The dryad shouted to the female fae, the round tomato woman, "Court?"

"Court Tinlaxi."

The dryad didn't recognize it. As far as she knew, her court held no alliance with that queen. She shouted back over the growling and hissing of dog and cat, "Court Elixia."

The Black Dog was now leaping up and down, barking hysterically, at the two beings preparing to do battle. Unlike Jib, their opponent had not changed size when it leaped to the ground. This worried Brigit for why did the small dog think it could take on the larger cat? She knew fae were never as they physically seemed. She guessed the creature was concealing a trick.

Jib, with arched back and puffed tail, was circling with the tan dog, as the two sized each other up. As they moved in the dance of war, the two traded insults, each more grandiose than the last.

"Fish breath, go catch a mouse and perhaps you'll win," growled the dog.

"I think I saw someone throw a stick. You better go chase it, lickspittle," the cat hissed back.

"Armor!" the dog barked gruffly. In response to its command, the short tan hair became sheets of steel plates, black-gray in color. Its magical affiliation must be metal. Jib would find it hard, perhaps impossible, to pierce that armor.

Paul and Chancellor Bandemer were standing in the best hotel suite Royal Kiburg provided and arguing about the conference. The set of rooms gave a superb view of the river and the skyline of Geheimetür. It would be the chancellor's temporary headquarters for the symposium.

Despite it being mid-October, the chancellor wore an outfit from his summer wardrobe: a silk frock coat of lilac, yellow waistcoat, and ribbons of spring green. He would change to the darker colors of his winter wardrobe on November 1st. This was the rule set out by the court of Louis XIV of France in the 17th century, and which Bandemer followed with the precision of a Swiss clock.

He looked like a pretty summer butterfly.

"I'm already exhausted," said the Doppelgänger, in a voice ringing with discordant, chiming bells. "When this conference finishes, I plan on taking a long vacation."

Bandemer frowned at his companion. During their long acquaintance, he had never known Paul to take time off from what he considered his duty.

Since temporarily losing the use of his Mindbending talent to imitate another person, Paul seemed to be having doubts about his competence. The confrontation in the library was probably the first in over a century that the Doppelgänger had lost.

All would be fixed by getting back on the horse that threw Paul. Work was the antidote here. It was why he insisted on Paul managing the symposium. The Doppelgänger would be too busy dealing with other people's problems and would have no time to dwell on his own.

Paul's hesitancy must be because, without his ability to hide, the Doppelgänger felt vulnerable. A turtle without its shell. Not the best mindset when you are about to meet dozens of strange fae with unknown loyalties.

Paul's doubt could turn into depression. It was never safe for a Doppelgänger to grow morose.

"We will speak of vacations later," Bandemer said firmly.

He rested his long white fingers on the window sill and looked down into the elaborate court gardens. Being late fall, the topiaries and sculptures were now the highlighted features.

"For now, we need to focus on the scientists, celebrities, business leaders, and fae nobles arriving for the symposium. They will all need to be greeted and made to feel they are special."

Bandemer felt keeping busy was the best sort of medicine especially if it included sampling wine and gourmet food, while attending parties wearing his latest finery.

"I don't expect many complaints from the humans — they will be content with what we provide," Bandemer said, scanning the clear blue skies outside the window, "But you know how our kind, even on a good day, will jockey for position, trying anything to increase their status."

"I don't want my real self revealed to any human," Paul said, his bell-like voice more dirge than a jingle.

Bandemer turned and gave Paul's disguise a critical going-over. The Doppelgänger's true form was a wyvern—a two-legged dragon with wings. He had a beak, pointy ears (in fact feathered tufts), and beautiful feathers of blue and gold across his breast that changed into scales along his tail. All that was hidden from fae or human by the chancellor's powerful spell.

"No one but myself will see you as you really are," Bandemer reassured him.

"Except for Logan Dannon."

"Of course! That goes without saying. No fae Glamour or spell-work would hide the truth from a bard."

Bandemer could never figure out why Paul had such an aversion to humans seeing him as a wyvern. Maybe it was because when the Doppelgänger appeared as-is, humans either fled in terror or wanted to touch him. Like most fae, Paul disliked being touched by strangers.

"Stop sulking. My enchantment is foolproof."

Paul protested, not for the first time. "I'm stuck with this face until the wound to my Mindbending talent fully heals. It's uncomfortable. And this silly name you've saddled me with draws too much attention."

It was probably the closest that Paul had ever gotten to voicing a criticism of his liege.

"I think you're just uncomfortable being an object of interest. Why struggle against it? Enjoy the attention. Did I tell you that Anna Burkhalter asked me at the last staff meeting who you were?"

"She's more soldier than librarian," said Paul. "She was probably wondering if I was a security risk."

"So cynical," chided his liege. "You can be attractive both as a wyvern and a man."

Bandemer saw nothing wrong about being admired by women, and the fawning that came from being beautiful.

"Why did you make this form so attractive? And that name? Darcy. Ridiculous! Both have given me nothing but trouble."

"You cannot hide forever in your warren, licking your wounds. You need to get out and about. Meet people. This despondency isn't healthy, especially for one such as you."

While Doppelgängers were from a powerful Fae Sept, their magical affiliation of Time and Memory ostracized them from the fae society which both feared and envied them. This combination often made them painfully shy.

From their long acquaintanceship, Bandemer knew Paul, like all Doppelgängers, was prone to depression and melancholy. Faced with futures that could go in any direction, while remembering all of their past, a Doppelgänger's mind sometimes lost its mooring.

To combat this weakness, Doppelgänger used significant events or bondmates to secure themselves in a time stream. Bandemer was Paul's oldest Anchor, a term for a person (or place in time) that, due to its importance, the Doppelgänger could use to keep himself sane.

However, the depth of their relationship didn't mean Paul agreed with everything Bandemer did or wanted. Paul suggested, "Perhaps we can get Emma Walker to help at the conference?"

Bandemer waved away Paul's suggestion, shaking his head.

"She's still assisting Burkhalter at the library."

Bandemer liked collecting people, especially those that could be of use to him. The fact that he had given the girl a job which would keep her close made Paul make a mental note to warn Emma of Bandemer's interest. It was the least he could do for the human.

"I wish I had cut that creature's head off myself," said Bandemer, letting his aggravation show. "How dare it show its ugly face here, hurting my Doppelgänger and attacking my librarian."

Something flashed down below, and Bandemer crooked a finger at Paul, gesturing for him to move closer so he could take in the window's view.

"Look. Down there," the chancellor pointed. "See. An altercation is already happening between our fae guests. You being here is essential."

Paul looked down to where Bandemer gestured. An unnaturally large black cat and a small tan dog were circling each other in the courtyard. A crowd of fae were forming around the combatants, some seemed to be laying wagers as purses were being opened and gems exchanged.

"I wonder who will win?" mused Bandemer, adding in French, "The *petit chien* or the *bête noire*?"

Paul didn't answer the chancellor. He was already running out the door. Seeing him rush away made Bandemer chuckle.

"See, having a problem cheers you right up, *mon ami*."

Paul didn't wait for an elevator but ran down the stairs. Running full-tilt through the lobby, his hip collided with a hospitality cart.

"Excuse me!" he grabbed two pitchers of water from the trolley and continued his sprint. Seeing him, the Kiburg doorman held the door open as Paul rushed through. Shoving past the people standing on the steps watching the altercation, Paul saw Brigit.

Ah. The black cat hissing and spatting was Jib, the púca.

He didn't know the armored dog by sight, but assumed it was an invitee to the symposium. Regardless of who they were, tempers needed cooling.

He pitched both jugs at their heads, water spraying towards them in an arc.

The cat yowled, ears sideways, and retreated behind Brigit. In a moment, Jib was reduced to the size of a shivering house cat.

The dog was hopping mad. It jumped up and down in a fury. "An insult! How dare you!"

"Identify yourself," demanded Paul sternly. The Doppelgänger was calm in the face of the dog's anger and the crowd assembled around them.

A female fae wearing a hooped skirt and a ridiculous hat told him, "His royal highness, Prince Fidalo of Queen Tinlaxi's court."

Paul, who had the burden of a photographic memory, recognized the name from the list of fae invited to the symposium. "You have broken the treaty of parley."

"I didn't sign it," snarled the dog. The dog changed the focus of its attack to Paul. He started circling the Doppelgänger, looking for a chance to attack the new enemy.

Fae were always the same. Paul would have sighed, but was more irritated than aggrieved. He patiently explained the trap the chancellor had laid for those fae who attended the symposium.

"The fine print on the invitation clearly outlined that your RSVP signified acceptance of the treaty. An inability to read does not exempt you from the law of Bewachterberg."

"What about the púca! It started it!"

"I'm not here for the symposium, and I never personally received an invitation," meowed Jib meekly, but with his gleaming orange eyes showed his lack of contriteness. The cat's fur was dry, since the púca had used its Fire element to dry its coat.

The dog lunged at Paul — lips pulled back in a viscous snarl.

The Doppelgänger might be temporarily unable to imitate faces, but he was not without the ability to manipulate Time. He froze the dog in mid-air, wrapping the creature's actions in a time eddy loop.

There was a gasp from the crowd, which changed to whispers. Time-shaping was not a common magic, and Paul received many wide-eyed stares. Smarter fae in the crowd started sneaking away.

"When the prince regrets his actions, I will release him," Paul told the dog's companion from Queen Tinlaxi's court. To the crowd, he said in a loud voice, "Any attempt at violence at the symposium by human or fae will not be tolerated."

Paul turned on his heel and started back toward the hotel entrance. Brigit ran up beside him, dragging a Black Dog on a leash. Jib trotted at her heels, tail high.

"That was pretty cool, Mr. Darcy, or should I call you Paul?"

His magic signature had revealed Paul to Brigit. He gave a silent sigh. Was he to have no peace? Hiding in plain sight wasn't working out very well, was it?

He ignored Brigit's question and instead told her, "Your mother, Queen Elixia, is in suite 507. We've made special accommodations for her, as Jib requested."

"As Jib requested?"

The dryad turned to the cat and demanded that it explain itself. While Brigit and her companion argued in the lobby, Paul made his getaway.

Chapter Ten
Doom and Gloom

Brigit knocked gently on the door to her mother's hotel room. She took a deep breath, trying to calm herself. She was anticipating a brawl. Her mother would push some agenda, and she would need to fight back in order to survive.

One of her mother's bodyguards opened the door. He bowed and waved her in with a sweeping gesture and a murmur of, "Your highness."

"Darling!" Her mother's perfume, a floral scent with undertones of tender-spring-love, filled Brigit's nostrils. It brought an aching sense of memories from home, causing the young woman to blink back tears.

It would be easy to become sentimental, for Brigit hadn't been home for some time. But a soft mindset was the worst to have when facing her parent. Elixia had a flamboyant and powerful personality that often swept away lesser beings.

"Mother, what a pleasant surprise."

"Is it? I hope you speak true, dear daughter."

They greeted each other with the traditional touch of palms. It showed trust, as well as that the other held no weapons.

"Where is my envoy?"

"If you mean Jib, mother, the púca is off having a pout."

This got raised eyebrows from her mother but she kept her pleasant smile and asked, "I see you've brought a friend? Does the Black Dog have a name?"

"Not yet. I'm working on it."

Brigit moved away, maneuvering so she was between her mother and the dog. She ignored her mother's question and took in the luxurious surroundings.

Queen Elixia's rooms were elegant with high ceilings, detailed crown molding, and an intricate wallpaper of birds and vines. Brigit thought she saw the hand of the chancellor in the design for the furniture—two chairs and the sofa were all from the period of Louis XIV. Monet's Water Lilies hung on one wall.

The place held everything the queen admired and she had made herself at home. Silk robes, hand-painted scarves, and feathered hats were scattered everywhere. A group of shopping bags with the names of expensive labels were in the corner.

Across from where Brigit stood were a pair of double doors. These probably concealed the bedroom and private bath.

The bodyguard who had greeted Brigit was now in the kitchen. He started doing a routine test for poison in the food using a spoon made of unicorn horn. It would turn purple if it detected any dangerous substance. Considering the plethora of unicorn horn testers that fae royals liked to use, it was no wonder the beasts were no longer making their whereabouts known.

"Would you like a drink, my dear? Cricon makes a mean cocktail."

Before Brigit could prevent herself, she asked bluntly, "Whatever are you doing here, mother?"

"I've been invited. Some at Leopold-Ottos-Universität Geheimetür know the importance of a queen." Elixia sipped the drink handed to her by Cricon. Her kaleidoscope eyes with shades of pinks, blues, and oranges peered coyly over the glass rim at her daughter.

Before Brigit could demand a better answer from her mother, there was a knock at the door.

"Chancellor Bandemer and Mr. Darcy," Cricon announced.

The queen's hand was kissed. Hearing the French phrases of adoration given by the chancellor, Brigit rolled her eyes. Raised at a court of the Perilous Realm, she had heard enough outrageous butt-kissing lies to last multiple lifetimes.

Although, she reluctantly admitted, Bandemer's spiel was very smooth. It was never so outrageous that his compliments couldn't be accepted by a generous mind or denied by a suspicious one.

"My daughter, Brighid Holly."

"I prefer Brigit Cullen. Besides, mother, the chancellor and Paul know me already. No need to introduce us."

Brigit crossed her arms, showing them she wasn't as welcoming as her parent. Flaunting court etiquette by not touching hands paradoxically showed that Brigit was of a rank to get away with such a breach.

"I hope you read the fine print on your invitation, mother," Brigit warned her, giving Paul a dark look. "There seem to be rules in place you might not be aware of."

"Look very closely with a candle," Paul explained. "Some print was written with invisible ink. A proprietary blend of lemon juice and gargoyle urine."

Her mother turned away from her guests, to give her daughter a scorching look. She silently mouthed the word "behave" before walking past Brigit to where trays of food were displayed on a side table.

With the graciousness of a queen, Elixia told her guests, "Please feel free to eat anything you wish. It's been thoroughly checked by my staff."

"Thank you, your majesty," said Chancellor Bandemer, "but I cannot tarry. We have much planning and organizing to do. Other guests, of lower rank, to greet. But I wanted to be sure to welcome you to our little symposium. Dr. Stuart should be arriving in the morning. Darcy will arrange a private meeting for a personal consultation about your problem."

"Your problem?" demanded Brigit of her mother.

"The Grove. Or have you forgotten why you ran away from home?" said the queen. "We may need new alliances to help the Elder."

"So you're finally taking it seriously?"

"I've always taken it seriously," said her mother, the colors in her eyes swirling.

"Not that I could see," muttered Brigit. To the chancellor, she asked, "Dr. Stuart? Are you talking about Dr. Sebastian Stuart?"

It was Paul who answered, "Yes."

"What a lucky chance, but color me suspicious," said Brigit, her eyes narrowing. "I wrote to him last year about this very problem. I never heard back from him but suddenly he appears here, along with my mother. How curious."

"Exactly," said the Chancellor, who had decided to take a glass of champagne from Cricon. "Dr. Stuart was specifically selected because of your interest in him, Mlle. Cullen."

"But how did you know about—?" Before they could answer, Brigit slapped a hand against her thigh as the answer revealed itself to her. "Jib. That cat is such a blabbermouth."

"It's interesting you immediately believe the púca divulged the information," noted Bandemer. "Why not the human, Logan Dannon?"

"Because Logan would never reveal a confidence. He knows when to keep his mouth shut, unlike a certain True

Beast." Brigit turned to her mother and asked her sharply. "Why isn't father here? He should be, if you are making negotiations."

"Don't get your leaves falling," said Queen Elixia to her daughter. "I will make no promises without due consultation. I'm simply meeting people who could do our folk good. And shopping."

As a horrible thought crossed the queen's features, she asked Bandemer in a panicked voice, "The schedule will allow time for more shopping, correct, chancellor? I would hate to have wasted my week in all talk!"

"Don't drop your leaves, mother," quipped Brigit nastily.

Bandemer soothed the queen's panic, reassuring Elixia that the schedule allowed plenty of time for leisure activities.

"As long as you have an account set up with a local bank to act as surety, there will be no difficulty in buying your heart's desire."

Queen Elixia stiffened in displeasure at Bandemer's words. "Of course, I have established funds at a human bank. I am not a country boggart falling off the tailgate of a farmer's wagon."

The queen set down her drink, picking up a fan. She jerked it open with a practiced flick of her wrist to furiously fan her flushed cheeks.

Bandemer said in a apologetic tone, "I beg pardon. It is just some fae think humans will still take fairy gold that turns to rotting leaves in the morning. Some of the attendees are experiencing Bewachterberg for the first time and their etiquette is outdated."

"There will be no problem with our finances," Queen Elixia said firmly. "I might not frequent the human lands often since that incident with the bard, but I know how to set up a bank account."

As fast as a rabbit's heartbeat, her fan transformed into a black credit card. Bandemer gave her a low bow of respect.

Paul changed the topic of conversation. "Your daughter has quite an interesting pet. I have never seen a harbinger in the role of a companion."

"Logan and I found him last night. Some foul person dumped him into a trashcan. He barely survived." said Brigit, claiming ownership. At her words, the dog's brown eyes gazed at her worshipfully. She told Bandemer, "You might want to think carefully, chancellor, on how Geheimetür treats its fae population. The poor thing would be dead now if we hadn't found him in time."

Everyone stared at the dog. As if in response to their attention, it suddenly started to grow in size. Brown eyes turned to blue-ice chips. A gas-blue flame licked its black coat. In a vibrant, prophetic voice, the Black Dog spoke:

"The hound of death hunts a noble prize; When the glass turns, who falls, so others rise?"

In the stunned silence that followed, Brigit's mother said, "That is why I've never allowed a dog at home. Between their stinky breath and the omens, one simply can't have them about."

At her words, the dog shrank in size, and the blue flames disappeared. Tucking his tail, he crawled under the French Provencal sofa, leaving only the tip of a tail showing.

"Mother!" cried Brigit. "You've hurt his feelings."

"Dear, you can't let sentiment influence you. No reasonable person keeps a harbinger. It's simply not done."

Bandemer said, "Do not be so harsh upon the Black Dog or your daughter, your majesty. At least, with the dog speaking its Bane, we have a fair warning of a future disaster."

In a contemplative tone, the Doppelgänger repeated the Black Dog's prophecy: "*The hound of death hunts a noble prize; When the glass turns, who falls, so others rise?*"

The queen nodded her head sharply, pointing at her daughter. "See! It is just as I said, the dog is hunting someone. Get rid of it, and the problem is solved."

"It's not as simple as that," said Paul. "I do not think the dog is actually hunting. That would be a literal translation of the Bane and it is a well-known fact that fairy magic is tricky and never to be taken at face value. The Doom or Bane is not about itself. Thanks to your daughter, I recently had a long conversation with a banshee about this very thing."

To forestall a discussion of her activities, Brigit quickly interjected. "But, I do think you are right in one way, mother. You should go home immediately. I'll meet Dr. Stuart and report back to you and father about what he advises."

"You are not my envoy, Brigit, but my daughter. I shall do as I please. And I do not please to go home just yet."

Bandemer was stroking the edge of his jaw with the back of his forefinger's fingernail, indicating a thoughtful mood. "You all have assumed that the prophecy means Queen

Elixia. That may seem logical, as a Black Dog's Bane is given to the person who it concerns, but there are others here that could be the target of his prophecy."

"I'm a nobody, so I doubt I can fall from any height," pointed out Brigit.

"But I am not a — as you put it — a nobody," said Chancellor Bandemer. He grimaced distastefully as he flipped back the lace of his cuffs. "This Doom could describe an incident meant for me."

"That's true!" exclaimed Elixia. She picked up a small round canapé made of puff pastry called a *vol-au-vent*. Stuffed with a blend of goat's cheese and herbs, its taste was delightful. She popped it into her mouth, happy to know someone else could be Doomed.

"The chancellor is correct," said Paul. "The Black Dog spoke after we entered the suite. Its Bane could be addressed to the chancellor, the queen, or even myself."

Bane of Hounds

Chapter Eleven
Mother's Helper

After being checked by a doctor, Sarah Dannon spent the night at his apartment because Logan insisted. She took his room while he slept on the couch. Thankfully, there was no dog or a smart-aleck girl to contend with.

The next day, after a rest that did some good for her aching head, Logan helped Sarah to her hotel. She had already paid for one night that she hadn't used and insisted on not wasting any further money.

They traveled to the Kiburg via a private electric taxi because Logan felt it would be easier than the public bus.

They talked about what they would do in the afternoon when Logan was available after class.

The vehicle pulled into the Kiburg's drive, passing between the pillars with their griffins.

"What in the world is that?" Sarah pointed at the strange sight of a small dog floating in mid-air at the front entrance where the taxi had stopped.

"Probably a street magician doing a trick," her son said. With his arm under hers, he hustled Sarah out of the taxi and into the lobby before she could get a better look at the floating dog.

Sarah had booked a room far in advance and Logan had checked her in yesterday so she didn't lose her reservation. The front desk was busy for it seemed there was a convention starting on Monday. The hotel was filled to capacity.

"Maybe we should look at some place quieter?" Logan asked her. He noticed the large group of fae in the lobby, and knowing his mother's nature, wondered if it wouldn't be better for everyone that she be elsewhere.

"I'd rather take my chances here. Geheimetür doesn't seem to be that big of a city. As it is, I only got a room here because of a last minute cancellation. I didn't know this town was so popular. It looked small on the map."

Logan and Sarah waited in the hall for an elevator. It dinged and when the doors opened, they politely stepped back. Upon seeing who exited, his mother whispered to him, "Isn't that your roommate?"

"Yes," said Logan, surprised.

Brigit was with her mother. They were flanked by two large beings, obviously bodyguards, wearing dark green suits.

Logan noticed that Queen Elixia wasn't wearing Elizabethan garb like the last time he had seen her in the Perilous Realm. Instead, she was dressed in a modern business power suit with a short skirt showing off long, shapely legs. The fabric was a shimmering medium blue color with a hint of orange undertone, setting off her brown-green-gray skin. On top of her head, nestled into a smooth braid of black hair, was a diamond and sapphire tiara set in silver.

As Brigit passed him, she gave him an urgent whisper for his ears only, "The lobby in ten minutes."

Logan gave a quick nod and quickly steered his mother into the elevator. As the doors closed, Sarah asked him, "Why was that woman wearing a tiara? Is that a German thing? Are they having a costume party here this early in the morning?"

Logan pushed the button for his mother's floor.

"That's Brigit's mother. She's a fairy queen."

"Oh. I didn't know your roommate was fae."

The tone she used upon voicing this discovery didn't encourage conversation so the journey to her door was in silence. Inside the hotel room, Logan set Sarah's luggage on the rack while his mother explored the small room.

Sarah took a moment to peek through the drapes. Her view didn't show the front of the Kiburg, so she didn't see the floating dog or the magician. She'd go take a look at it later.

"I grabbed a brochure in the lobby," Logan said, handing her a folded map, "for a historical tour of Geheimetür. It takes you through some of the oldest historical buildings of the city. And visits a museum."

Sarah wasn't going to be sidetracked so easily. She wasn't a child to be distracted by a toy.

"Whatever is going on here, Logan? There were some extraordinary people in the lobby. I thought it was like — I think you kids call it a con — where you dress up in odd outfits. But it's not Halloween yet."

"Those weren't outfits, mom. Those were fae creatures from the land of fairy. They call their country the Perilous Realm."

At the creasing of her forehead, Logan felt the burden of his mother's unspoken disapproval squeezing his heart. Living away from home made it easy to to forget how she would purse her lips or frown her unspoken criticisms. Well, this was just a short stay. He would manage. Somehow.

"Bewachterberg has a long history with the Perilous Realm. In 1890, the fae hid the country away until 1989 to protect the people from two world wars. You often see the fae in Geheimetür. Some attend the university."

"What an odd place. Nothing like home. I can't think why you would go out of your way to come here for your education. Perhaps you should transfer back to somewhere in the States. Somewhere safe from these creatures."

Like some Americans, Sarah Dannon was insular in her knowledge about Europe. She also felt superiority over anything that wasn't American.

Logan tried to keep his voice upbeat. He didn't want to get into another argument about where he was going to college. Not for the first time, he thought about calling his dad despite his mother's orders.

"I like it. Leopold Otto is different. Unique. There's no other place like it. There's always something new happening."

Sarah looked out the window again. The mountain peaks topped with snow were beautiful. She said in an offhand way, trying to make her question appear nonchalant. "I thought it might have something to do with your grandmother. She put you up to coming here, didn't she? She's always trying to take you away from me. Make you hate me."

Logan reached out and hugged his mom. He knew she fretted about his father's mother. She was an obsession of Sarah's.

However, she was right about one thing, when it came to the goddess Morrighan, it was not wrong to second guess anything you thought was fact. The Morrighan could be underhanded when it came to getting what she wanted. Case in point was what happened to him when he got lost on the Snowdon mountain.

"I haven't seen her since we were in Wales," Logan reassured Sarah. "Give the place a chance, mom. You might like it. And if this hotel doesn't work you can always bunk at my apartment instead."

Logan laid the pass card to her hotel room on the dresser, next to the television.

"I have classes this afternoon, so why not take this tour? We can meet up for dinner at this great Italian restaurant I know. We can talk over plans for the days you'll be here. The maestro said you could sit in on one of our rehearsals if you like."

Suddenly, his mother smiled, pleased. It relaxed her face and made the lines in her forehead fade away. She looked friendlier and younger.

"I'd love that. That would be wonderful."

Logan raced down to the lobby. He didn't see Brigit until she poked her head around a column and hissed at him. The Black Dog was happy to see him, leaping and jumping around Logan until the leash required an untangling.

"What's going on?" asked Logan, "What's your mother doing here?"

"I could ask you the same."

Brigit waved him to follow her and the Black Dog. They went down a hallway, turning into a more narrow passage. Finding a carved wooden door, Brigit passed her hand over it and the lock unlatched. They entered a private area marked for employees only.

"Come in here so we can talk privately."

The door revealed a tiny room functioning as someone's office. Thankfully there wasn't anyone at their desk. Between Logan, Brigit, and a dog that kept wanting playtime, the room didn't seem very spacious.

"How's your mom doing?" were Brigit's next words.

Surprised, Logan replied, "Doing okay. I got her checked out last night, and the doctor said she's fine. I kept her with me last night to make sure, but mom insisted on coming here and staying at the hotel room she booked months back."

Because of how small the space was, the two were standing very close.

"I don't think my dad knows she's here in Geheimetür. She refuses to let me call him."

"I don't think my father knows my mother is here either!"

"What do you mean?"

"No one said anything to me about her coming to this symposium. I thought it was strange so I used the magic mirror father gave me last year. My dad didn't answer, but some of my sisters did. They gave me vague, evasive answers. That's a sure sign that something is up."

Logan was an only child and didn't understand so Brigit explained.

"A large family like ours, we carry tales. The fae love to gossip, so it's weird to be told by your sister to talk with mother."

"Maybe you're overreacting?"

Any other male would have gotten a scathing that would have blistered their ears. Brigit only gave Logan a grimace and a shake of her head. "No, I'm not. My mother is not telling me something and my sisters are definitely in on it. When I try to talk to her, mother ignores me. Her behavior isn't normal."

"How exactly?"

"Pleasant to be around. No mood swings. Even-tempered. Agreeable."

"You're right," Logan agreed, saying slowly, "That doesn't sound at all like your mom." Realizing how his words might sound, he added lamely, "You know what I mean."

"Exactly!" Brigit came even closer as if she feared they would be overheard. Logan naturally put his arm around her waist. "I've also sent word to my dad through the trees. My messages keep bouncing back, undeliverable."

The fae had several ways they communicated: air, water, and oak. Logan wasn't sure how they all worked, but this didn't sound good.

"Have you tried the water way — send a message by the Kelpie?"

"I haven't had a moment to get away to do it. My mother's been keeping me on a tight leash. Even now, I shouldn't be away very long." Brigit paused before saying, "I think Jib knows. The púca's been avoiding me. Have you seen it?"

"Jib came by the apartment this morning. The púca said it would stay as long as the dog was gone."

Brigit and Logan instinctively looked down at the Black Dog, who was trying to squeezed between them, wriggling to be as close as possible.

"He seems bigger than the last time I saw him," mused Logan.

"He is," Brigit agreed. "I didn't have time to tell you, but he predicted your mother's accident."

"What?!" Logan exclaimed in surprise.

"He's a Black Dog. They are harbingers. They predict things. When they issue a prophesy it's called a Doom or a Bane. Although technically, they sometimes can help — but usually what they say is all gloomy news about the future."

"Like the banshee?"

"Kinda, but they aren't tied to families, as far as I know. Usually, they are linked to a place — a spirit of place — what is called a genius loci. Remember when I told you about that summer I met a water nymph tied to a spring? It's like that."

Logan thought over what Brigit said, and reluctantly asked, "What did the dog say? About my mom?"

"*An injury of iron will fall, spite will be both tool and cause.* Then she stepped into the frying pan and slipped, hitting her head."

After a moment's silence, Logan said, trying to be upbeat, "Well, she's okay now so no real harm done. And at least he's talking. He must be feeling better."

"Yes, but he's only speaking Dooms."

"Plural? So he said another one?"

"When I was with my mother, Bandemer and Paul arrived and he said this: *The hound of death hunts a noble prize; when the glass turns, who falls, so others rise?*"

The words put a shudder through Logan. His vision dimmed and went gray.

"Are you alright? Logan!" Brigit put her arms around his waist. Holding him up should have been hard for a small being like her, but because she was fae, she had twice the strength of a human of comparable size.

As his vision returned, Logan let out a deep breath, "I'm okay, just—well, bard thing—anyway — I think this Bane is really serious."

"No kidding. Frost on the pumpkin, Logan, we are in the deep end of it again."

Facing each other, they were now openly holding each other. Logan became very self-conscious of the privilege. Brigit like most fae didn't generally initiate touching. But the night they had been hunting the banshee she had seemed happy enough to allow him to hold her.

With the intimacy of being alone in what could pass as a closet, they were both aware that this was somehow different.

Logan was very aware of how much Brigit was female. He could smell the outdoorsy, sweet and fresh smell to her — like a wildflower. Brigit's head was right under his chin; it felt natural to draw her closer.

"Where do we stand among all this?" Logan asked, his breath gently stirring her curls.

"Stand? Well, together, of course. As always. We're bondmates after all."

Logan looked down into her eyes. They were very dark and he was unsure what emotion they held. He asked her seriously, "Only Bondmates? It feels like something else nowadays."

She wet her lips with her tongue, nervous under his stare. Or perhaps it was because as he spoke, her fingers came up to touch his cheeks.

"Everyone else seems to think so."

Their breath was so close they shared the same warm air. Both were oblivious to the dog chewing a notebook on the floor.

"But what do you think?"

Logan's lips were so close that all Brigit needed to do was rise on her tiptoes and give him the answer.

Before Brigit could do that, the door opened. Since they were both leaning on it, the couple sprawled onto the ground still embracing.

Standing over them, hands on hips, was Queen Elixia.

"Mother!" Brigit's complexion might be able to hide a blush, but Logan's coloring wasn't as lucky.

"Come along, sapling!" her mother barked, "No, leave that troublesome dog with your bondmate. The bard can be of use for once."

Logan watched helplessly, the dog licking his face, as Queen Elixia's grabbed Brigit's wrist to drag her away.

Bane of Hounds

Chapter Twelve
Pomp and Ceremony

Elixia was stronger than she looked and Brigit wasn't able to free her wrist from her mother's grip. Only by dropping her dead weight on the floor like a toddler did Brigit get her mother to stop dragging her through the lobby of the Kiburg hotel.

"Get up and act your status!" snapped Queen Elixa.

"Let go of me or I'll—"

"Or what?"

The Castle Kiburg was built of stone, but the interior support was a timber-frame structure. It and the wooden doors started vibrating, making their argument very public.

Both fae and humans stopped to watch. Becoming aware of the interest they were attracting, Elixia hissed, "You're making a scene."

"You like scenes, don't you?" Brigit got up from the floor, her wrist finally free. She rubbed her fingers over the redness that promised to become bruises.

"What I don't like are daughters who think they know better than their mothers!"

"Four of my sisters let you determine their paths in life. I'm not going quietly to whatever fate you've picked out for me."

"Now is not the time—"

"It's never the time with you, mother," said Brigit coldly. This was why Brigit had run away from the Perilous Realm. No one ever listened to her. No one cared what she thought, or what she wanted.

Mother and daughter were standing very close to each other, almost nose to nose. Their conversation was now a series of retorts conducted in low angry sentences which crackled.

"Fine!' her mother said, pointing her finger at Brigit. "You want to know what time it is? It's time for you to protect yourself by gaining the most powerful alliance possible. A marriage gives that. Otherwise, I won't be able to protect you."

"I'll protect myself," countered Brigit. Her mother gave a bitter laugh.

"You don't know the first thing about the forces that will come after you, a princess of a queen who lost her court."

"What?" Brigit reared back in surprise. She frowned and demanded, "What are you talking about?"

Queen Elixia leaned close enough that her breath warmed the tip of her daughter's ear. She whispered, "The Grove is dying. We are near the end of our resources. Now is not the time to play with a human's heart. Save that for when you are safely married."

Pulling away, Queen Elixia gave a told-you nod at Brigit's shocked face. "Exactly. So now you know where things stand. It's time you stop acting like an infant and do your duty. Look over there, at that young being with his fine antler rack. He's been watching us and seems taken with you. Let's go find out what court he hails from."

Her world spinning as her mother's statements sank in, Brigit looked the direction her parent directed. Standing in the hotel's lobby was a tall, elegant fae male with dark straight hair tied in a ponytail and long, narrow face. He wore a yukata, an informal kimono, in bright blue with a red geometric pattern. The narrow belt, or obi, was black.

"Torfa? That dilettante?" Brigit scoffed at her mother's recommendation. "I met him last year at a library opening. He's from Queen Summerblossom's court. I'd rather marry a goat."

"Doesn't he look debonair?" The arm that Queen Elixia tucked over Brigit's elbow was a steel band that stopped her from leaving. "He must have some consequence since his queen sent him to this symposium. Why don't you introduce us?"

Still trying to recover from her mother's earlier words

about their home in the Perilous Realm, Brigit reluctantly
did as she requested.

Torfa was as effortlessly graceful as Brigit remembered.
He bowed his antlered head at their arrival, paying respect to
a fae queen. Since Queen Elixia was not his liege, he did not
touch palms. It seemed Torfa had been sent by his queen to
attend in her place.

The knowing smirk he gave Brigit made her want to
throw a chair at him, but she restrained herself. His words
were polite enough, "My liege has questions for these
humans."

"Like?" asked Brigit, who wasn't one inclined to play
games.

"About the destruction of our courts. By humans."

Queen Elixia gave such a high pitched, hysterical laugh,
that heads, and eyes without heads, all swiveled to watch
their small group. Being in the Kiburg right now was like a
fishbowl.

"Behave, mother," Brigit replied to Elixia. To Torfa, she
asked with false sweetness, "What do you mean about
courts being destroyed? Explain yourself."

"Courts have vanished from the ley lines." Torfa meant
the psychic mooring lines, connecting the Perilous Realm
courts to form the fae network of territories. "We've had a
few refugees from these kingdoms, seeking citizenship
under my Queen Summerblossom. They all report the same
thing. A human visited their court, and soon after, their land
started to die."

At these words, Brigit's hand flew over her heart to touch

the leaf. Queen Elixia seemed to grow taller than her high heels would have warranted. The queen demanded, "Which courts?"

"Court Ambrosia and Court Selena. Nothing remains of their lands."

Brigit gasped, her hand covering her mouth. "Selena is a Black Dog court."

"This has significance?" Torfa asked.

"A few days ago, I found an abandoned Black Dog, a puppy. He was poisoned with wolf's-bane," Brigit explained. "But he hasn't spoken, except for prophesying some Dooms. I don't know where he came from or what happened to bring him to Geheimetür."

"I would like to meet this Black Dog."

Brigit gave a defiant glare at her mother, as she told Torfa, "He's with my bondmate, Logan Dannon, a human. I'll talk with him. We can arrange a meeting."

"Tonight. This is an urgent matter. My room is 217."

Before they could discuss it further, a human holding a clipboard came up and interrupted their gathering.

"You're too showy. We need you out of the shot."

"What?" asked Brigit, irritated at being interrupted.

"Antler-boy. You are distracting from the shot. Dr. Stuart is about to arrive, and we need to clear the lobby."

Caught up in their drama, the trio hadn't noticed the invasion of a film crew. Three people with clipboards and headsets were arranging people along the row or asking others to leave in the lobby. Lights were being set up on tripod stands, and two men with camera equipment on their shoulders were roaming about, trying to decide angles for filming.

"Do you know who you are speaking to, young lady?" demanded Queen Elixia. But before a fight could break out between them, Brigit intervened, "What is this all about? We knew Dr. Stuart," she gave her mother a pointed look, "was coming. We want to meet with them. But why the film crew?"

"It's part of his latest documentary. If you want to remain," said the woman in a tone that clearly said they shouldn't, "you need to sign this release."

Torfa laughed. "I'm gone, ladies. No one uses my image without paying me my fee. I have my brand to consider. I'll see you later, beautiful," he told Brigit.

As Torfa sauntered off, the skirt of his robe flared dramatically behind him. Catching a whiff of an Air spell, Brigit muttered, "Show-off."

Meanwhile, her mother scribbled on the release. The film person moved away to the next being demanding their signature or removal.

"Why did you do that?" Brigit asked her mother. "I don't want to be filmed."

"Don't worry. I didn't sign it with my real name, so the contract means nothing."

The woman with the clipboard called the crowd to order, addressing them all.

"Dr. Stuart will enter through this door," her clipboard pointed to the front door where the doorman politely listened for his cue.

"When he enters, you can call his name and wave your signs. Limit your clapping as it messes with the recording audio. Stay in place so the camera can capture your faces. No one is to approach Dr. Stuart. Do not touch Dr. Stuart. Do not ask for autographs. We will be here throughout the symposium and we will have a table where you can get signed copies of his book and movies."

"I thought this Dr. Stuart was a scientist?" Queen Elixia asked her daughter. "I didn't know these scientists were so admired."

There was another call for silence. Final instructions were given by the woman right before they heard excited shouting from outside. The Kiburg doorman did his duty, and a camera operator walked in backward with her lens pointed at who was entering.

"Hm, decidedly not the skinny stick of scientist with thick glasses that I was imagining him to be," murmured Queen Elixia.

Dr. Sebastian Stuart was unlikely to be pointed out in a room as a world-renowned scientist. He was a big man, with broad shoulders and a flat stomach. He had short blond hair that was whitened from exposure to the strong sun of the equator and a square tanned face. His light blue eyes were so bright that their shine was visible from across the room.

"Not quite what I imagined either," Brigit confided to her mother.

After stopping for a moment to hold a pose in the lobby, Dr. Stuart started greeting those standing along the wall. This was about two dozen people, all of them humans, who didn't seem the geek fan types to Brigit. When one of them stepped out of line and touched Dr. Stuart on the arm, it all came to an end.

"Stop! Stop filming," Dr. Stuart told the crew, and the clipboard lady materialized at his side.

"I told you not to touch him," she barked at the offender who replied sheepishly, "I'm sorry. I got caught up in the moment."

"Get back in line, all of you. No, not you. Out you go. We aren't paying for those who can't obey orders."

The bystanders were all shuffled about, the taller in back. The less attractive ones were given signs to hold so their faces weren't as visible. During all of this, Dr. Stuart stood with a pained expression on his face, arms crossed, waiting.

"Let's start again," said the director of the documentary.

Dr. Stuart turned on his heel and left the lobby. The door closed behind him. Everyone was told to be quiet again. Clipboard lady spoke into a handheld walkie-talkie, and the scene began all over again: the crowd outside cheered, the door opened, Dr. Stuart entered, and his paid fans went wild.

Once the filming of his arrival was done, cameras moved away, and the person holding the boom mic took a break. The crowd filed outside, making their way to the film van so they could get paid. A makeup person rushed forward to powder the sweat off of Dr. Stuart's wide brow.

Knowing he was vain made Brigit feel comfortable. She had plenty of experience being around narcissists.

"A pretty little show," said Paul the Doppelgänger from

behind them.

"But aren't we all about the drama?" mused Queen Elixia. "Maybe Dr. Stuart has some fae in him? He certainly has enough charisma to make one think so."

"Mother," warned Brigit, thinking of Elixia's recent comment about playing with humans after marriage.

"Anyway, Paul, I'd like to re-introduce you to my mother, Queen Elixia. Mother, this is the chancellor's Doppelgänger, who, for some reason known only to himself, is going by the name Mr. Darcy."

"A Doppelgänger? I've always wanted to meet one. But am I safe with you?" Queen Elixia said this in a coy flirtatious tone.

"Of course you are, Queen Elixia. I am here to protect everyone at the symposium, including yourself. Unless you have plans to attack Chancellor Bandemer?"

Brigit asked him abruptly, "When are we going to meet this guy? This Dr. Stuart?"

"The chancellor thought you'd be eager to discuss your problem. I have a room reserved for the three of you to discuss the situation with your grove privately."

Bane of Hounds

Chapter Thirteen
Round Table Talk

The tension between royal mother and daughter was about to spoil Paul's careful plans. Brigit Cullen was sitting as far from her mother as a round table would allow. Paul could see the rigid lines of contracted muscles in Brigit's forearms as she kept her arms crossed over her chest.

Meanwhile, Queen Elixia sat ramrod straight, her hands gripped together in her lap.

While they were waiting for Dr. Stuart to arrive, the two had continued arguing about a fae named Torfa. Paul had no idea how to intervene. His one attempt at trying to calm them had resulted in a blast of cold magic being thrown at him by both mother and daughter.

The cloud didn't harm him, it was only an unpleasant puff, but it was a clear warning for him to back off.

Brigit narrowed her eyes and tightened her mouth as her mother continued her condescending narrative, "Humans are fine for a playful interlude, but it's time to grow up. All of your other sisters are established—"

"I'm not entering an arranged marriage like Saffo and Dianne."

"Saffo was able to establish a court! Are you telling me that match isn't successful?"

"She's married to a toad!" here, Brigit turned to Paul, telling him, "Literally, a toad."

"What about Dianne's bond partner? He isn't a frog! Handsome, well-connected, a gentleman—"

"With a bossy mother," Brigit slapped her palm down on the table for emphasis. "Her mother-in-law, the queen, controls everything Dianne does—what she eats, what she wears. It's like being in prison, despite all the jewels and gowns. Not what I would call a happy union. If they lived in the human lands, I'd plan an intervention."

"Happiness? What does that have to do with it? You're a princess. You marry to establish yourself, to build alliances."

"Ha! That's rich coming from you! You and dad were a love match."

"Because I established my court. When I started my Questing Journey no one knew how that would turn out. Most die in their attempts to find a genius loci that will bond with them. I was three years younger than you, and the Perilous World was much richer with magic. It was a wild dangerous place then. With the way things are—"

Brigit leaned forward over the table, her fists clenched. "The way things are? I didn't know how things were until an hour ago when you dropped your little bomb on me. Why didn't you tell me all of this earlier? You should have called me back home so we could—"

At this fortuitous moment, there was a knock on the door. Paul stood up to open it.

"Dr. Sebastian Stuart."

There was a moment of silence heightening the drama of his entrance. Being the chancellor's dragon, Paul saw many dramatic entrances. He'd give the man a score of seven out of ten on this one, mostly due to Stuart's presence.

The scientist was a bear of a man: over six feet tall, a moving mountain. He filled up the small meeting room and dwarfed the petite Brigit. Even Paul felt a bit smaller by the presence of the human. But the Doppelgänger put his feelings of inferiority aside. He would think over this later. Right now, the air teemed with enough magical tension as it was.

"Your Majesty, your Highness," Dr. Stuart acknowledged the queen and princess during their introductions. Unlike Bandemer, he didn't kiss hands but instead did a short military bow that required no touching.

The scientist took his seat, and the hotel chair strained under his bulk. Paul would have liked to have called him fat, but the scientist was just muscular. Stuart was almost as big as that wrestler, Granite, Brigit's bondmate and a fae eotan.

"You may know Dr. Stuart from his documentaries," Paul began, only to be interrupted by Brigit's eager, "Yes. I'm aware of his work."

Brigit's attitude had changed from aggressive to interested when the famous man entered the room. "It's a pleasure to meet you, Dr. Stuart. You may not remember the name Brigit Cullen, but I wrote you a letter last year."

"Indeed, I do remember it. When I received the letter from Chancellor Bandemer, I knew the symposium would be a good opportunity to meet with you and offer my assistance."

"Explain. How you can help us?" asked Queen Elixia flatly, showing a borderline dislike for the human just on principle.

Paul, still standing with his hands clasped behind his back, gave the details, "Dr. Stuart explores diverse environments located in remote areas across the human lands. He examines ecotones, where biological communities come together. Being interested in extremophiles, Chancellor Bandemer thought he might be a good choice since the Perilous Realm is also a unique environment."

Brigit's dark eyes gleamed with excitement. "He's studied bacterial life inside a volcano, mother!" She practically bounced with excitement, but Queen Elixia made a skeptical noise even though Brigit added, "He's good, mother. I think Dr. Stuart could help us."

"Why don't we discuss the problem, heh?" said Stuart.

From Elixia's demeanor, you would never imagine she had been shouting at her daughter just moments ago. On the contrary, she was everything a queen should be: remote, gracious, and frosty.

She had the attitude of a prospective employer interviewing a candidate they don't quite feel would work out, but is the son of the boss so an interview was required. "Tell me about your experience."

Stuart took charge of the room. He gave hair-raising details about his research: rappelling into the mouth of a volcano to collect samples; an avalanche that left everyone but himself and one other dead; and the experience of being bitten by a poisonous snake in the heart of the Amazon.

"Climbing a Norwegian glacier to study the bacterial life in an isolated lake underneath the ice, we lost my fellow scientist Hans Haugen when he fell into a crevasse. But my quick thinking saved his journal. I gave him a posthumous credit on the research paper I published about it."

Paul's desire to punch the blowhard was growing. Probably the fact that each of these stories was true made it even harder to bear. However, dislike or not, if the man had answers for the queen, Paul would ignore the grandstanding.

While the exciting adventures might have made the ladies gasp, it was his research that made Brigit nod her head. Much of it involved the pathology of disease in organic material subjected to bacteria.

After some time describing his research, Dr. Stuart asked Brigit to update him on what they knew at this point about the disease affecting the trees in the Perilous Realm.

"I've run tests and examinations myself. The disease in our trees does seem like an infection of some sort. Not a fungus or an insect attack."

Queen Elixia's face did not reveal her thoughts as she said, "I do not see how you can help us. Magic and science do not work well together. They negate each other. Believe in science, and you cannot believe in magic."

Of those in the room, only Brigit was willing to contradict the queen directly. She'd been doing it all of her life, starting with a toddler's first screamed "No" when faced with a bowl of prune pudding.

"Don't you see, mother? We need a systematic approach if we want to discover what is killing our trees. Science provides that framework. Once we figure out what is happening, we can make a plan to counteract it. Even if it is rooted in magic, the Perilous Realm still must obey logic."

Her mother gave an exasperated snort. "Do you think a microscope can see magic? What nonsense!"

"Not the magic itself, but the result!" protested her daughter. "If we examine the symptoms, we might find the cause or at least some treatment we could try."

"Perhaps we should take a step back," suggested Stuart, calmly. "I can't say I can help until we discuss the problem in depth. What are the physical symptoms?"

Brigit leaned forward, her arms on the table. "Our trees grow very slowly in the Perilous Realm. So we didn't notice immediately that the Elder wasn't producing offspring. The saplings that were already growing became stunted. Now, the withering has moved to the mature trees. They are producing no offspring, and their leaves fail in the bud."

"Magic?" suggested Paul. "A death spell or hex?"

Queen Elixia scoffed at the Doppelgänger's suggestion but was too aware of her nobility to roll her eyes. "Do you think that wasn't the first thing we checked? No. Whatever the cause, it is not magical, or if it is, it's too subtle for detection."

She frowned at Dr. Stuart as she added, "Besides, should we trust any humans?"

"Don't be so biased, mother."

Elixia countered, "How can you say that, when Prince Torfa just told us that alarming news? It has me re-thinking what is happening to our grove." She paused and said in a dramatic stage whisper, "We have been told there are humans destroying our courts."

This did not provoke the shock Elixia hoped for as Paul responded calmly, "Chancellor Bandemer is well aware of this. He plans on—"

Queen Elixia said vehemently, "He can plan all he wants! Meanwhile, my Elder is dying."

"Mother, we haven't had a human visit since before I was born. Other than Logan. I doubt what Torfa said applies to us—"

Elixia angrily cut off her daughter. "You don't know what vile treasons those creatures are capable of committing. That first bard had guest-right and yet murdered his Lifemate. One of my ladies-in-waiting. My sister! To gain their ends, humans will plumb the depths of any evil."

"That happened long ago, mother. Stop painting all humans with the same brush. This is the real reason you refuse to like Logan."

Before her mother could speak again, Brigit returned to discussing the problem with Dr. Stuart.

"Our Grove is similar to the aspens found in North America. It's a singular organism, bound together through the root system. Each tree is a clone of another. For a new one to emerge from the ground, the conditions need to be right—"

Queen Elixia reached across and gripped her daughter's hand, the intensity of her grip and her expression silenced Brigit. "Stop. We do not discuss this with humans. And if we did, I will decide when and what."

Brigit bowed her head and acknowledged her mother's command with a subdued, "Yes, mother."

It was the first time Paul had seen the girl treat her mother like a queen.

The table was quiet for a moment before Brigit began speaking again in a more subdued voice, "I've taken samples and examined them using lab techniques available here in the human lands. I've tried to see if anything would grow in Petri dishes, but there were no definitive results. None of my research has shown evidence of insects, fungus, mold, or bacteria. I've reached a dead end with what I can do. Perhaps you can help me find a new direction? What I could do next?"

"I would like to review what you have done so far. I

would assume there are lab facilities on campus we could use?" Dr. Stuart asked Paul.

"Yes," the Doppelgänger said, "the chancellor extends all of our resources to help Queen Elixia. Her husband, King Ladislas, is brother to Queen Titania."

Queen Elixia seemed irked with Bandemer's man mentioning her sister-in-law. She explained frostily, "My lifemate is visiting his sister while I attend this conference."

The queen stood up, clearly ending the meeting. "Work with my daughter, Princess Brigit. She knows what a human needs far better than I."

Brigit eagerly told Dr. Stuart, "I want to meet as soon as possible. Can we do it tomorrow morning?"

"I won't be available until the day after as I'm a keynote speaker. Perhaps you can bring your notes to the luncheon? Let me have a chance to review your research?"

"That would be awesome."

The party broke up, and Brigit, with a happy smile on her face, touched the leaf embedded in her skin.

"We will cure you. Don't worry."

The meeting broke up and Brigit was the last to leave the room. She cupped her hand over where the leaf rested in her skin and whispered to it, "Everything is going to be okay. You'll see."

The leaf tried to warn Brigit. But their union wasn't complete, and the dryad didn't understand the message.

Bane of Hounds

Chapter Fourteen
Queen's Wayward Attack

That evening Jib sauntered into Queen Elixia's hotel suite, with tail held high.

"Where's the princess?"

"She gave me a headache. I told her to go and enjoy the mixer downstairs. What are you doing here?"

"The dog returned to the apartment," spat out Jib.

The queen was standing in her bedroom as her ladies-in-waiting spread towels across the bed. When they finished, the queen shed her robe and laid across them on her stomach. Her two dryads moved forward, one on either side. They held a crystal bottle and poured the oil it contained into their palms.

"Amuse me, púca," commanded Queen Elixia.

Unlike her dryad daughter who claimed many trees as her friend, Queen Elixia was a nymph. Her essence was tied to one tree and to be very far from the Elder drained her. The oil which her ladies massaged into her smoky green skin would help mitigate some of that exhaustion. A fragrance of lemons and rosemary filled the room.

Meanwhile, Jib found a spot on a pillow near her head and started recounting all the gossip it had collected over the past year from traveling the campus of Leopold Otto. Some of the stories made the queen laugh, which was the cat's purpose.

"Why humans think a circle of mushrooms would get them into the land of fairy is beyond my understanding! That portal was closed a long time ago." Elixia gave another giggle.

Jib watched his liege with a critical eye: her energy and magic aura had improved. She looked rested and not so drawn and dry as she had been when they first arrived at the Kiburg. Contented with his majesty's change of mood, Jib smugly groomed its whiskers.

Finished, her two ladies drew a clean sheet over Elixia's back. They dimmed the lights and retreated from the bedroom, closing the connecting doors to the suite's living area.

Nestling her head into a pillow, Elixia was almost asleep when Jib asked her, "What's with your staff? They seem to be fawning more than usual."

"It's Brigit," Elixia yawned, half-opening her eyes. "After that Black Dog of hers issued his silly Doom, the girl questioned all my ladies-in-waiting. Even Vica, whom she's known since a child. Brigit told my security detail to do push-ups and run the stairs while she evaluated their fitness. I don't understand why they didn't run away. Instead, they strut about, chests puffed out, looking for danger under my bed."

"It feeds their self-importance," Jib said. "Makes them think that being on an Honor Guard is important. Not just a display to satisfy a royal ego."

"Whatever the cause, I do like the result," admitted Elixia. "Their uniforms look much smarter: coats ironed, and boots blacked to a shine — something I could never convince them to do back home."

"That is probably due to the hotel concierge," said the cat. "The Kiburg has a long list of services."

While they were private now, it was clear her majesty wasn't going to discuss the situation with the Perilous Realm. The púca switched tactics. "Why did you send the princess away?"

"She needs to mingle more with her kind. The child has been far too much with humans. It's time she thinks about her future."

Jib gave a quick flick of its black tail. "By future, you mean—?"

"Alliances, bond partners, a lifemate."

"I did not realize the princess was shopping for a

lifemate. She has made no indication to me, and everyone knows I excel at matchmaking."

"It doesn't matter what she or you want. That can't be left to chance. Her parents need to arrange it."

Exasperated, and with her sleepiness vanished, Queen Elixia got up from her bed and threw on a white silk nightgown. Over that, she pulled on a spider-silk sheer robe with white feathers on the collar and cuffs. "There are many important young fae here attending this symposium. It's like a shopping mall filled with potential mates! She'd be a fool not to spend some effort checking them out."

Jib's whiskers quivered. "Do you, by chance, have a shopping list of who our princess should consider?"

"Tarkula, he's from a court in the Perilous Realm that touches the Russian steppes. Very dashing. What a mustache! Then there's Serio; his court is in South America. Not as handsome, but he's adamant about protecting the rainforest. That should appeal to Brigit. Also, there's a young stag, Torfa, from Summerblossom's court. It seems they've met before. There's tension between them. That could develop into something more."

"I see," replied Jib, and indeed it did. "All of your choices are fae beings."

"Of course."

The cat knew how to use the pressure of silence. Given the queen's temperamental and emotional nature, it didn't take long before the púca's wide-eyed orange stare discommoded her.

"Yes, and what is your point? They are from acceptable

courts, with powerful connections. I have not asked if she prefers antlers or ram's horns, but I do know she likes male beings with dark hair."

"Dark hair and blue eyes. And human."

"No," the queen contradicted the True Beast sharply, shaking her finger at the cat. "Do not bring up that possibility with me, púca. I will not have it."

Jib tucked its front legs under its chest, making a loaf form. With half-closed eyes, it mused, "I think our dryad princess is far too young to be settling down with any type of partner."

The queen frowned at the cat. She unconsciously mimicked her daughter's favorite pose by crossing her arms.

"As it stands, I want to see her settled. If the grove is lost, she will be vulnerable without a court. Yes, Ladislas can claim protection at his sister's court, but since Brigit released Queen Titania's favorite swan from his enchantment, she is not one of her aunt's favorite nieces."

"She could seek out one of her sisters."

"They love her. But they quarrel. I don't think Brigit would stay long with any of them."

"If she needs protection, look closer to home," Jib advised. "Specifically, to her residence in Geheimetür."

"That is a poor jest, púca. A human for an alliance? How could a human protect my girl from fae who want to take advantage of her situation?"

"A human who is a bard. And quickly expanding his powers. With my assistance, the two should be able to stand against any grab for power."

Queen Elixia shook her head again, refusing Jib's offer.

"If I fall, my enemies, and others, will see her as good sport. Something to hunt, either to capture or to kill. From what I saw earlier today it is past time to separate them."

Elixia sat down in an upholstered chair, clasping a pillow across her stomach.

"When Ladislas visited last year, he warned the boy off. But I can see he made a muck of it. Threatening to kill the human was absolutely the wrong tack to take with Brigit. She always does the opposite of what we advise."

Jib watched Queen Elixia as she nervously readjusted her nightgown, fussing with the feathers.

"The best way to deal with this bizarre situation is to show her what she's missing from having a normal fae relationship. Introduce her to potential partners who outshine this insignificant human. She can't help but compare and Logan Dannon will naturally come up lacking."

The queen obviously did not know the full story about Logan and Brigit's relationship. Jib informed her, "Did you know he brought her candy? From his home? Tree candy."

Queen Elixia's mouth fell open in astonishment. Her hands fluttered in confusion.

"He's giving her gifts of food?" She demanded, "How did she receive them?"

"With happy tears."

Jib was also part Trickster, so the púca slyly told the queen, "Did you know that Logan's mother is staying at this hotel? She's in room 319."

Sarah finished her email to her husband sharing what she had seen today. The Geheimetür tour was fascinating, and the campus grounds of Leopold Otto certainly were beautiful and impressive.

She did not mention the fae girl. Best to discuss that in person with Arthur.

There was a knock on the door. Sarah left the desk to peer through the peep hole. It was the fae woman Logan had identified as his roommate's mother. She wasn't wearing a crown anymore but looked to be in a white nightgown with a robe edged in white feathers.

Without Logan's hard-earned knowledge of how dangerous the fae were, Sarah opened the door and invited Queen Elixia across the threshold.

The queen came with a bribe to get Logan Dannon out of her daughter's life. Although Elixia preferred calling it a gift.

"I don't think we've been introduced? I'm Brigit Cullen's mother, Queen Elixia."

"Logan's mother, Sarah Dannon."

Elixia walked further into a hotel room that was nothing like her own. She could barely contain a shiver of distaste at the smallness of the chamber. Very drab. Though, for a human, it was probably serviceable enough.

"Just a little present between mothers." Queen Elixia set a gold chest on the table. It was about the size of a woman's jewelry box and contained an appropriate amount of gems to remove an undesirable human from an entanglement. Elixia knew how much was needed for fae queens often gossiped about the going rate to separate their offspring from unworthy partnerships.

The woman said nothing, causing Queen Elixia to observe her more closely. Logan's mother might only be human, but Elixia saw the dark purple haze, almost smoky, that surrounded the woman. Hm. A powerful will. However, Elixia couldn't discern any magical affiliation. Then again, most human magic was invisible to the fae eye.

Elixia said, "How strange that we haven't met until now."

"Until I arrived in Geheimetür, I didn't realize your daughter was my son's roommate."

Elixia had to admire Sarah's demeanor. The cutting aloof coldness was admirable. She'd have to copy it next time she dealt with Queen Titania, her annoying sister-in-law.

Sarah Dannon gestured to the only seat in the room, and Queen Elixia took it while the other woman primly perched on the corner of the bed. This put them uncomfortably close. So close that either could attack the other quite quickly. Elixia hid her nervousness behind condescension.

"I thought we should talk about our children's relationship. Quite honestly, I cannot accept this alliance. It does neither of them any good."

Sarah Dannon let out a sigh of relief. Smiling, her features were warmer and appeared younger. "I'm glad you agree with my thinking on the matter. It is completely inappropriate for them to be together. Logan gave me the impression he had a male friend staying with him. That I would have accepted. But a fae girl? No. Out of the question."

This was news! Problem solved. Certainly, Jib should have told Elixia that Logan was attracted to his own sex. What a Trickster that púca was. It always had to have its little joke.

Queen Elixia stole a glance at the gold box. Perhaps with a magical sleight of hand, she could steal some of the gemstones before leaving?

"Is your daughter a student at Leopold Otto?"

"Yes," Elixia said, forcing herself to relax into the back of the chair. "She is studying biology and botany. The human sciences."

"You must be proud of her."

"Not really," mused the queen, who didn't understand her daughter's desires and dreams in the slightest. "She ran away from home to attend Leopold Otto. Because of the country's Treaty of Sigismund, she was able to gain entry into the university without our knowledge."

"I'm sorry," said Sarah, giving a little self-conscious laugh that rang false, "but I don't know what the Treaty of Sigismund is. You see, Logan chose this university. I thought Bewachterberg was just another European country like Germany. The history tour I went on this afternoon mentioned it in passing but didn't explain what it was."

Elixia was surprised. She assumed everyone would know

the history of the country and its long association with the fae. She summarized the event: "The King of Bewachterberg was told by an oracle that his country's sovereignty would dissolve because of conflict and wars. Your World Wars. He signed a treaty with the fae, and after wedding nine of our queens, in exchange we hid the country for 99 years and a day."

"Excuse me?" Sarah choked on a surprised cough. "He married nine queens? What year was this?"

"By human evaluation, it was 1889."

During their discourse, the smoky purple of Sarah's human aura had become turbulent. In case Sarah was preparing for an attack, Elixia rubbed her forefinger and thumb together to awaken her powers.

Elixia continued as if she hadn't noticed the change in Sarah, "The marriages formed a strong bond between our lands. It's why Bewachterberg has a substantial number of fae here. Nowhere else compares to it. Well, maybe Ireland. Or Japan. But nowhere else, I assure you."

"I see. I didn't realize all of this when Logan decided to attend Leopold Otto. It doesn't seem an appropriate place for our son. I'll discuss this with his father when I see him next."

Sensing that their conversation was near an end, and her goal was achieved, Queen Elixia rose to take her leave. "It would probably be wise to take your son home. His bard nature makes it dangerous for him to reside in Bewachterberg."

"Excuse me?" Sarah's voice rang out like a hammer

hitting sheet metal. She stepped in front of Elixia, blocking her progress to the door.

"The fae fear and despise bards," explained Elixia as if she was talking to a simpleton. "Only by the merest chance was Logan able to best my husband in a riddle-game and thus save himself from being sealed alive in a cloven tree."

Queen Elixia let contempt color her speech. "He's already gotten into trouble here and almost killed a librarian. I heard she was hospitalized."

The human's face grew an interesting shade of white, supplanted by red.

"How dare you accuse my son of hurting someone! I don't know what incident you are referring to, but my son would never harm anyone, least of all a librarian!"

"It is comforting to know that human children keep their parents in the dark as much as the fae offspring do."

"Now, I understand why your daughter ran away from such parents" snapped Sarah Dannon. "It almost makes me sorry about evicting her from the apartment we pay for."

"What do you mean by that?" demanded Elixia. The queen was so upset by Sarah's words that she lost track of the spell she was using to steal the jewels from the gold casket.

"What I mean is, the apartment where your daughter lives is paid for by me and my husband. My son's name is on the lease. Your daughter's is not. She is a squatter. I will evict her as soon as possible."

Bane of Hounds

Chapter Fifteen
Lover's Tryst

When Brigit escaped from her mother she went downstairs to the front desk and sweet-talked one of the hotel staff to send an email to Logan. She needed him and the Black Dog back at the Kiburg so they could meet with Torfa.

Normally, Brigit would have gone herself to pick them up but her mother had warned her not to leave the hotel. It was a royal command. Her mother would know if she disobeyed and it wasn't worth the argument it would make.

She talked with a few other fae hanging around in the hospitality suite before deciding she better go visit Torfa.

Brigit was surprised to find Torfa alone. She'd thought

he'd have an entourage, a group of hangers-on, but it was only him. He welcomed her into his room with a sweeping bow.

"Hello, gorgeous,"

"Hello, Torfa."

The prince was wearing a gold jacket with a Mandarin collar. The glittering fabric was embroidered with a scroll of black vines. Around his neck was a blood-red ascot tie that was tucked into the open v of his black satin shirt. Torfa's harem pants bagged around his thighs but were tight around his calves, bringing attention to his bare feet.

"I've asked Logan to join us. He should be here soon."

"Have a seat. Would you like some wine?"

"No."

Waiting for Logan was irritating as Torfa kept trying to hit on her. He was handsome enough, Brigit supposed, but she wasn't going to get involved with someone like him. He was just the type of arrogant court fae she spent the last decade avoiding at her mother's court.

Besides her interests lay decidedly elsewhere.

"Can we stop discussing the delicate beauty of my eyes and the whiteness of my teeth? I'm not a broodmare."

"Why? Do my compliments make you uncomfortable?"

Although his hotel room was comfortable and part of a suite, it was nowhere near the opulence of her mother's. She twitched back the curtains and saw his view faced the front. The fae dog was still suspended in the air. The Doppelgänger must want the message of behave or else to be clear to the fae at the symposium.

Torfa materialized behind her, his breath warm on her neck as he said, "There's the little doggie that displeased our chancellor."

Torfa was, as usual, pushing the social boundaries, literally and figuratively. The fae were notorious for taking advantage of each other, and at this close range he could easily maim or kill her. As someone who adhered to a strict line of duty and Balance, it annoyed Brigit. She couldn't imagine being locked into a bonding with one such as he.

"Back off Torfa; I only let dogs slobber on me. Keep six feet between us unless you want a tree to fall on you next time you enter a forest."

Torfa gave a good-natured laugh as he back-stepped, hands up in surrender. "Who knew a dryad would be so prudish."

"I have standards. And you don't meet the lowest mark."

The forest prince didn't seem hurt by her remark. He went to the bar in his room and poured himself a drink. "Have you told your mother that? She's been shopping a union for you all around the conference. From what I understand, it's highest bidder takes all."

The chair in the room, made of solid wood, flew up and hit Torfa on his lower back. The feet struck his kidneys hard making him bend over double. He dropped the glass and the spilling liquid stained the carpet.

"Next time it will be your antlers. Go rut in the wood with your does, forest lord."

Once Torfa had regained his breath and dignity, he lifted his rack high and, with a sneer, told Brigit, "You need to speak with Queen Elixia. It seems you and your mother aren't in the same castle."

"My mother and I are not your concern."

Luckily for them both, there was a knock at the door. Feeling relieved, Brigit opened the door and the dog bounded forward, jumping all over her with happy enthusiasm. She buried her face in his fur, thankful for their arrival. She would have hugged Logan too but she wasn't going to give Torfa more to gossip about.

"This is the Black Dog you were telling me about?" asked Torfa, his angled eyebrows rose higher.

"Yes," said Logan, who, sensing some tension in the air, came closer to where Brigit stood.

"He seems young to be in the Human Lands."

"I agree, Torfa," said Brigit. She explained to Logan, "Fae children aren't allowed to visit the Human Lands until they have reached their majority, their status as adults. Usually, on their first visit here, they are accompanied by an older bondmate who can navigate them through the dangers your world present."

This seemed a bit backward to Logan, who viewed the Perilous Realm as far more dangerous than his world. But he wasn't going to argue with her so asked Torfa, "I got Brigit's message on what you told her. Tell us about these courts that are disappearing."

The lord of the forest was happy to oblige.

"Gossip between courts has always run freely, but sometimes it's hard to separate truth from fiction for my people love to embellish stories. However, my court had a trading pact with Queen Ambrosia. We were told that her Elder, a sacred spring of healing, was sickening. We received a message of distress, but by the time we responded, her people were gone."

Brigit's face went through several different emotions during Torfa's tale. Logan found all of them disturbing and indecipherable.

She said, her eyes not leaving Torfa's, "Each court is known for one land feature that represents its queen. It's called an Elder. I knew of Queen Ambrosia's court. It was renowned for its Elder, a fountain with healing waters."

"Celia?" Logan asked quickly, but Brigit shook her head, making her tight curls bounce, "Celia is of Queen Corallina's court. As far as I know, she's safe. Her last letter didn't mention anything like this. You spoke of a Black Dog court — what do you know of it?"

Torfa told them.

"We are not as closely connected to Queen Selena's court as we dislike the hunting packs. However, once it was known we were investigating the situation of Queen Ambrosia's court, we were told of the destruction of the Black Dogs."

"What did you find when you got there? What evidence could we use to figure out what happened?"

Torfa gave Logan's questions an exasperated snort.

"There is nothing to examine. What part of gone do you not understand, human?"

Brigit grimaced at Torfa's roughness. She explained to Logan, "Due to land-law, a court binds the Elder and the queen together. In my lifetime, I've only known of one queen who died, and her Elder retreated into the Vastness. When this happens, the court is removed from the ley lines. It cannot be found again."

Brigit's face became grimmer. "I have never known of an Elder spirit dying. Only from legends, stories. But if an Elder dies, the court is also destroyed and the life of its queen is forfeit. Now you see why I was so concerned about the grove."

"The grove?" asked Torfa, on high alert, his nostrils flared wider. "What do you mean? Is something happening at your court?"

"That is for my mother to reveal, Prince Torfa. I shall not betray her through idle gossip. I've already said too much."

"Then you sentence us all to death, princess. Only if we work together can we destroy this human threat—"

Logan cut in and asked, "Human threat? You know humans are causing the death of these Elders? What evidence do you have that humans are involved?"

"As best we can, we have put together a sequence of events leading up to these disasters. Each court was visited by a human who stole a personal object of the queen's."

"The harp!" cried Brigit.

"You have had a visitor and a theft?"

"The incident happened before I was born. It cannot be connected. But yes, our court had a Bone Harp stolen."

"Was it a personal possession of Queen Elixia?"

"I guess you could say that. It's made from the bones of a murdered courtier. It plays a lament about her death."

"You are silent, bard," said Torfa, who, with the sensitivity of his kind, perceived Logan's change of emotion.

"I remember the court discussing it. I think Jib mentioned it. The púca said it was taken by a bard. One of my kind."

At Logan's statement, Torfa backed away, putting more distance between him and the human. Brigit ignored Torfa's movement of distrust. It was time Torfa learned to keep etiquette and if the proximity of a bard made him adhere to the Laws of Civility, all the better.

Brigit didn't want to tell the story about the bone harp, but since Logan spoke of it, she should.

"This is only a story I heard, so I cannot claim it as fact. One of the ladies-in-waiting, Princess Verabella, was half-fae, half-human. She was my mother's sister, so when she returned to the Perilous Realm, bringing her human lover, my mother welcomed them both."

Brigit rubbed her upper arms as if she felt a sudden shiver.

"She died. No one knew how, but there were suspicions. My mother commissioned a Cassandra to make a Bone Harp from her remains."

Torfa nodded his understanding. He told Logan, "Bone harps are rare. They are made from the bones and hair of the murdered, they will play only one tune—that of how they died."

Brigit continued her story, "It sang the despair of one who was betrayed by her lover. Before the bard could be brought to justice, he stole the harp and disappeared from the Perilous."

Hearing the story, Logan understood why Queen Elixia had a prejudice against humans.

Torfa spoke urgently, "I must speak with Queen Elixia. We could join forces, make alliances to help each other."

While Brigit didn't especially like Torfa, she saw the sense in what he said. "I will talk with her tomorrow. But for now, let's discuss the Black Dog. I asked Logan to bring him, hoping you could help us discover who he is or how he came to be in the human lands."

Without their attention, the dog had gone through the entire suite sniffing everything, licking the carpet where the spilled wine was, and jumping on the bed to wrestle the pillows.

When Torfa tried to grab him, the dog grew fearful and ran to Brigit and Logan, hiding behind their legs.

"Will he let me examine him?"

Logan sat on the floor, encouraging the dog to come into his lap. Torfa also sat down on the floor, keeping himself six feet away as Brigit had demanded earlier.

Brigit could feel Torfa expanding his magical element— Air and the weaker one of Wood. Most fae had two magical elements, but one would always be the stronger and in ascension over the other. As far as Brigit knew, only Doppelgängers were able to maintain the balance of two powers.

"He is from Selena's court. I feel the bond, but it is weakening, now that his court is gone. Soon he will be marked as a Rogue."

"Rogue?"

"A fae without allegiance to a queen," Brigit told Logan. "Rogues are seen as fair game by other fae to hunt, capture, or kill." At Logan's shocked expression, she reassured him, "Don't worry. We have him under our protection."

After they left Torfa, Brigit covered her mouth with her finger to caution Logan to be quiet. Her hand on his arm, she ushered him and the dog into a stairwell and down to the first floor. After exiting to the hall, she asked him in a whisper, "Can you use your bard sense to know if this is true? Is a human hurting us?"

"I wish I could. But I don't know enough. I would have to speak with someone who knows the truth in order to judge it."

"So you need to interview some people? Get their viewpoint?"

"It would help."

Brigit pursed her lips. She looked down at the dog.

"I think we have someone right here who knows the truth. If only he would speak of it."

"We do know he can speak."

"Dooms, sure. But those are compulsions. He must speak those. We need him to want to tell us what happened. I'm not sure how to go about that."

A few people passed them in the hall. Logan waited until

they went by before asking Brigit, "Tell me again what the dog said? The Banes."

Brigit screwed up her forehead in thought.

"The first time was at the apartment. Your mom had arrived and was worked up because I was there and you weren't. The dog ignored her. I think he was in my bedroom. She started cleaning house and that got the brownie riled. Then he showed up—"

Brigit looked down at the dog and patted his head.

"He was big, much bigger than this and had a blue aura. Like Jib goes orange, this guy goes blue. And than he predicted what would happen."

"What did he say exactly?"

"*An injury of iron will fall, spite will be both tool and cause.* Your mom stepped into a frying pan and slipped to the floor, knocking her head."

"So like you said about Black Dogs, he gave the warning directly to the person it involved and moments before the incident occurred. And what about the second one?"

"He didn't say it until Bandemer and Paul arrived. Again he was normal and suddenly his aura became blue and he grew in size. He said, *The hound of death hunts a noble prize. When the glass turns, who falls, so others rise.*"

"But nothing happened?"

"No."

"Are you sure that was what he said? Exactly how he said it?"

"Of course, why are you questioning me about it?"

"Because the first Doom has an old feel to it when you

say it. Like musty, past its expiration date. The second one seems small, not full grown. And not quite right."

"To your bard-sense?"

"Yes."

They both had their backs to the wall, hip by hip, thinking. Brigit repeated out loud the dog's last Bane, inflecting the words different, trying to get the right cadence.

"Yes, that feels right."

"It's the same words though, Logan."

"I'll have to work on it. Like one of Géza's puzzles." Logan casually slipped his hand in Brigit's. "How is your mom doing? Have you gone back to your grove? Checked on what's happening?"

"No, not yet. She's forbidden it."

"Like that's ever stopped you."

Brigit gave a snort, "Ha! Well, you know me so well, but I feel I need to be here now. At least until the end of the week. Until the symposium finishes."

She told him about Dr. Sebastian Stuart and how Bandemer had set up a meeting. "I have to move fast to get answers from him. In talking with Dr. Stuart, it seems we may need to go there to collect new specimens anyway. He wanted to see what was happening in person."

More people passed them by but Logan and Brigit were wrapped up in their own discussion. Since handholding had not received a rebuff, Logan moved his arm around Brigit's shoulders, drawing her around so they faced each other.

"I don't like this," muttered Logan. "You don't know

who that Doom was for. It could have been yours."

Brigit gave a light laugh, dismissing Logan's concerns. "I'm not high enough to fall. Besides, have you ever known me not to be able to take care of myself?"

"I'd feel better if you took someone with you. What about the brownie? Or the Black Dog? I'd suggest Granite, but he's on tour with his team."

"I'll think about it," Brigit assured him although Logan's truth sense told him she wasn't going to do that. He gave her a slight shake. "Don't lie to me. It lowers your honor."

Unlike his human friends, Brigit never got angry with being reminded that Logan could tell she was lying. She laughed again, but this time it was deeper and rather breathy. She looked down and licked her lips as she told him, "Logan, we say things to make our bondmates feel better. You need to learn to accept that."

"What do we know of Dr. Stuart?"

"He's a braggart. A human."

"A human we don't know."

"I checked into his background. He's legit."

Logan's eyes were very blue. He said in a voice that made Brigit's heart thump harder, "You don't take care of yourself."

She whispered back, "Maybe I need someone to look after me."

"Maybe someone like me?"

His mouth was just as delicious as she dreamed it would be. The third touch of their lips was interrupted by a deep woof at their feet. "My name is Devlin."

Chapter Sixteen
Dagger Drawn

rigit woke up to find her mother bending over her. Startled, she pulled herself up, bracing her back against the sofa armrest and rubbed her eyes. Brigit asked, "Is it morning already?"

Her mother didn't reply at first. Her stare made Brigit uncomfortable, and her next words put her daughter on high alert. "We never talk. I sent you that magic mirror last year. Not once did you call me."

"I've been busy," began Brigit, pulling her knees up under her blanket. Her mother sat down beside her on the sofa.

"Your sisters tell me that you've called them."

"Only Morfydd and Creirwy. Not the other four." The two sisters Brigit named were the closest to her in age and the only siblings who had also defied their mother.

"You would tell me—?" her mother began in a tone so strange that the last of Brigit's sleepiness vanished. "What?"

But Elixia must have thought better of what she was about to say, for she switched subjects, "The first conference session begins in two hours. If we want to get our hair done, choose an outfit, and select our jewelry, you need to get up."

Her mother continued to act oddly all morning. Over muffins, she asked Brigit questions about her classes and expressed interest in what she did at school. It wasn't as if her mother never asked questions about her life, but the fact she was actually wanting answers was odd.

All of this focused attention made Brigit squirm. She wished her mother would return to her usual favorite topic: herself.

"The ley lines of Tarkula's court touch the Russian steppes. Isn't that romantic?" Elixia widened her eyes, raised her eyebrows, and leaned forward as if they were co-conspirators.

"Romantic?" Brigit replied skeptically. "Sounds rather on the back end of nowhere."

The two were seated in one of the Kiburg meeting rooms on the ground floor. Dr. Sebastian Stuart was about to take the podium and the room was jam-packed. They had only gained seats because Brigit had the foresight hours ago to send down someone to reserve them.

When she had met Logan last night, he had brought her research notebooks. Brigit pulled one out from her backpack, as she thought over the only thing the dog had told them last night—his name. Well, at least it was as a start.

Her mother interrupted Brigit's thoughts by saying, "How lovely it would be to live in Castle Kiburg full time."

"Not a big enough kitchen. And no brownie."

"Have you seen the surrounding park? The trees?"

"No. I haven't had time. I've been too busy looking after you."

"After lunch, let's take a stroll. You could live here instead of that poky little apartment."

"Mother—" Brigit was prevented from saying anything more as one of the symposium organizers was stepping up to the mic, to introduce their guest speaker. This was greeted by a round of applause.

Looking around the audience, Brigit saw most were human. Many held one of Dr. Stuart's books—*The Snail's House* or *The Mountain Cave of Tomorrow*. She wondered if they got autographed copies. Clipboard lady and one of her cameramen were at the back of the room, setting up to film Dr. Stuart's speech.

Dr. Stuart's presentation was popular. The speech was witty and engaging. Instead of a stiff, off-putting, robotic talk, it felt like you were on a one-on-one with the scientist. He shared hair-raising and intimate details about his adventures, making you wish he were your best friend.

"In Norway, my fellow researcher Hans Haugen lost his life, but not his life's work."

"Didn't he tell us that story already," her mother whispered to her. Brigit hissed back at her to be quiet. Sure, Dr. Stuart was a bit of a windbag, but you couldn't argue that he was an amazing scientist with a wealth of knowledge.

At least Stuart's message was not preachy or condescending.

Her mother leaned over again, asking, "Do you believe he can help us?"

"It's worth a chance." Brigit said no more as she knew her mother wouldn't like the situation back home being discussed publicly.

Since their confrontation the day before, Elixia hadn't mentioned again anything about the state of the grove. Every time Brigit tried to steer the conversation back to the Elder, Elixia countered with a comment about who would make good boyfriend material.

"Being human," her mother confided to her, "I fear he will recommend something like a pesticide or fungicide. Humans like their chemicals. The cure could be worse than the disease."

"Better than death?" Her mother gave her an injured look, and Brigit, who was exasperated said, "Let's talk with him first and not jump to conclusions, okay?"

Trying to talk with him after the speech proved difficult. Well-wishers and fans swarmed the podium. Well, Stuart had promised to meet her at lunch. Meanwhile, there were other breakout meetings her mother wanted to attend.

Entering the banquet hall, formerly a ballroom, Brigit was happy to see that the tables had place cards. At their own table was one for Dr. Stuart, so Brigit took her seat happily, tucking her backpack under her chair.

Brigit visually checked the location of her mother's bodyguards — one was behind their chairs, another at the exit, and she knew one of her mother's ladies was checking all the food being brought to their table.

They had attended three more of the morning sessions. Overall, the talks were interesting, ranging from the simple etiquette between humans and fae to examples of successful business ventures that were already in existence.

One fae presenter was naive about humans, while another, a human, verged on being paranoid about the dangers the fae presented. She gave an internal groan as she saw the latter presenter approaching their lunch table.

"Bitter cutworms."

"Hm, dear?" her mother turned to survey her daughter. Brigit rolled her eyes, jerking her head slightly to indicate the newcomer. But it was too late as the obnoxious fae-hater was at their table.

"How delightful, Herr Parkinson," her mother said graciously. "We caught your session earlier today."

He seemed taken aback by Queen Elixia's greeting and nervously bobbed his head as he sat down. Was Parkinson surprised a fae used polite words?

"Now we can all be cozy over our luncheon. Plenty of

time to discuss your pathological antagonism towards my kind," said Elixia in that bright, high tone that Brigit usually heard right before someone got stabbed.

Summoning some patience to overcome her dislike, Brigit told her mother, "Perhaps Herr Parkinson isn't familiar enough with our kind? Or maybe a bad experience has colored his thinking, so he paints us all the same?"

During Brigit's speech, a fae approached the table and took its seat. The being had a boxy rectangular torso with arms that hung to its knees. Gills on either side of its long neck fluttered with its breathing, and round eyes gave them all an unblinking stare. A smile of greeting showed very sharp, pointed teeth.

Brigit was glad Jib wasn't about for their new companion gave off a strong fish smell. The púca would have been tempted to sink its teeth into the scaly leg.

Finally, Brigit saw Dr. Stuart arrive to complete their table. However, even Dr. Stuart's charisma could not prevent the conversation from returning to the theme of Herr Parkinson's earlier speech and his prejudice against the fae.

"The fae are too dangerous for humans to deal with, for all the power in the relationship is on their side. Case in point — at Leopold Otto, a siren preyed upon several humans, draining them to their death."

Brigit hated it when people acted like they knew things when they didn't. Why did the chancellor allow him at the conference? Parkinson was a bigoted irritant.

Brigit couldn't contain herself any longer and said, "It's hyperbole like that which fosters your kind of prejudice.

The siren didn't drain them to death! It was only a living death. Please be accurate if you are going to smear my kind."

"Your assertion that humans are powerless is ludicrous," chimed in Queen Elixia, who was enjoying the appetizers on the table. "Why, I met a human woman yesterday that thoroughly routed me. I can tell you she took me down a few pegs, and that was by human will alone. Everyone knows that to be the most powerful magic of all."

When she finished speaking, her mother cast Brigit a speculative look that the girl didn't understand. When did Elixia have time to meet any human yesterday?

"Nein!" contradicted Herr Parkinson sharply. "With magic, your kind can obscure your real intent. Make a human think something opposite of what they intended. Cast dangerous illusions. Read our minds."

"We are dangerous," agreed the sea fae. Brigit thought it unlikely the fish was as dangerous as it was pretending. She had a lot of experience with fae killers and the ones who threatened, like Fishy, were usually blowhards.

However, you never knew, though.

Brigit slid her hand under the tablecloth and down her leg to grab the handle of the knife concealed in her boot. The dryad placed the silver blade in her lap, under the napkin. She left one hand on the hilt made from hazel wood while she ate her lunch. If the creature attacked her mother, it would find that grin a lot wider.

"Of course, we have the potential to be threatening to humans. That is our biological imperative," exclaimed her mother. She reclined back to allow her bodyguard to place her entree in front of her. "Still, I consider humans far more frightening. Look at how they destroy their world."

That was throwing a gremlin into the bouncy castle! Herr Parkinson came from the school of thought that if he spoke the quickest and loudest, he won arguments. Each of his statements defending the human race was met with a tight grimacing smile from Queen Elixia.

The royal deep freeze only took about fifteen minutes before Parkinson's arguments petered to a slow stop. Like a wind-up toy that needed more cranking, he found himself out of fuel. He wiped a sweaty brow with his napkin.

Dr. Stuart, who was heartily tucking into his meal as if he hadn't seen food for over a month, finally said, "The Perilous Realm is the closest alternate dimension to earth. It is inescapable that a wide transfer of information, people, and goods will occur. We must not be foolish about these facts. Clashes are inevitable."

"There is no working with them," sputtered Herr Parkinson, who had gained a second wind. "We must shun working with the fae. We are at a severe disadvantage and handicapped, having no magic."

"Why blame my people for humankind's inability to use all the resources available to them?" said the queen in her pleasant, lofty voice. Oh, yes, someone was going to get stabbed before this luncheon was out, Brigit believed. "Humans have magic. Gods and goddesses. Old places."

In approval of Queen Elixia's statement, the sea fae opened and closed its hand in mid air. The webbing between its fingers made a clapping-slapping noise of support as fingers struck palm.

Herr Parkinson gave a menacing glare at the sea fae, holding his fork as if he would like to stab the fish. He said, "Magic doesn't exist in the human lands."

Goaded by Parkinson's words, Brigit said, "That's not true. I have a human bondmate who is a bard. He uses human magic all the time."

All the eyes swiveled to the dryad, making Brigit regret that she had spoken. However, the dryad was not the type to shy away from a contentious situation. She continued, "My roommate, Logan Dannon, is a bard."

The hand of the queen tightened on her silverware. The sea fae drew back, its mouth shaping a surprised O like a goldfish. Only the two human faces showed no expression at Brigit's statement.

"You say that like I should be impressed," said Herr Parkinson.

Brigit ignored the kick under the table from her mother.

"You would be impressed if you knew your history. Aneirin. Talisin? William Shakespeare? Bards can use their magic to perceive truth, whether it is a human or fae who speaks. They persuade people with their words. Help royalty decide justice and win wars. They should be revered. Honored for their abilities."

"A paragon," said Dr. Stuart with a bit of mockery. This surprise attack from Stuart inflamed Brigit so much she didn't feel the second kick under the table.

"Logan Dannon is," she insisted stoutly.

Herr Parkinson's next comments were said with an ugly sneer, "A parasite always loves its host. You've seduced him with your magic, fae witch. I saw the two of you last night."

In a flash, Brigit was on her feet, the hilt of her knife in her hand, the point of it pricking Parkinson's throat.

Chapter Seventeen
Knight's Tour

efore Brigit could strike, a walking stick knocked her hand upwards. In a fury, she turned to Chancellor Bandemer, with a cry of "How dare you interfere!"

"Brigit has a point," said her mother, pausing her spoon filled with orange sorbet on its way to her mouth. "She was just accused of seducing a human and is well within her rights to demand reparation for the insult."

Chancellor Bandemer lowered his cane, his face a mask of gentility, though his eyes blazed with fury. "Dueling with blades is no longer acceptable in the human lands. I expect my students to behave like civilized beings. Not start brawls."

Brigit was shaking with emotion. "Make him apologize, or I will call a Fiat against him."

"Apologize for what?" This was said by Paul, who had partnered Bandemer around the room. When they both saw the commotion at Brigit's table, the two had walked quickly over to the brewing fight.

"He accused me of using magic to sway Logan Dannon's mind. That I'm a siren or a succubus—who knows what he meant? He has a filthy mind."

"What say you, Herr Parkinson, to this accusation?" Bandemer was exquisitely polite, his tone mild. His manner seemed to display only a mild curiosity, but the hands gripping his stick were so tight that his knuckles were white.

"I say that the girl seems very agitated by my accusation she is seducing a human boy. Where there is smoke, there is fire."

Queen Elixia licked her spoon clean and placed it down with exquisite care upon her dessert plate. "Your human guest was a keynote speaker earlier today. He used derogatory words to describe the fae. Compared us to animals, actually less than animals—scum. If anyone at this table needs schooling, I dare say he should be first in the line of learning polite manners."

"I'm fully aware of his opinions on the matter of fae-human relations," said Bandemer, but the end of his sentence was as hard as the drop of a hammer. "It is why I booked him. It is hard to find a human who would talk so bluntly about the fae. For some reason," he gave Brigit a glace, "they fear speaking out against us."

Brigit, her rage still simmering, pointed a shaking finger at Parkinson. "He denies that a human can have magic equal to that of the fae. When I told him about Logan, instead of listening, he insulted me with his nasty insinuations."

"Perhaps he has never had the experience of being around a bard?" posed Paul. In his Mr. Darcy persona, he was standing off to the side as if he didn't want to involve himself in the altercation that everyone in the dining room was watching. With hands clasped behind his back, his expression appeared mild.

"Is it my daughter's duty to educate a human about their people?" inquired Queen Elixia, with that gentle air her husband knew all too well meant someone was about to receive a horse-whipping.

"Good question, your majesty," said the chancellor. "There is nothing like a first-hand experience with magic to educate a being. Darcy, locate Logan Dannon and bring him to the symposium. We shall set up some experiments to enlighten Parkinson about what human magic is capable of doing."

"No, I didn't mean—" Brigit's words were lost, for with a polite bow, Chancellor Bandemer walked away, calling out greetings to other attendees. With the luncheon and drama over, everyone rose to leave.

"I didn't mean for Logan—" Brigit continued protesting.

"Of course you didn't, dear," said her mother. Queen Elixia rose and carefully folded her napkin several times before placing it back on the table. "But you must realize that thoughtless behavior like trying to knife someone over the luncheon table does have consequences. As your father always reminds me."

Sarah Dannon was not awed by the concert hall of Leopold Otto University. Not only had she attended many concerts in palatial venues, but she made it a practice not to be impressed by anything or anyone. To be amazed meant you agreed you were inferior.

Logan found her a seat, midway to the back. As orchestra members came in and started setting up for practice, Sarah found her gaze wandering away from the ornate balconies of Rococo style to examine the people and their instruments.

People? She wouldn't describe them as such. Strange things, some from a nightmare, were testing strings and fingering keys on traditional instruments. Probably what discomfited her the most was everyone around them acted as if these aberrations were normal. Even her son chatted with a few of them before taking his seat.

It became silent when a wiry man with a cloud of white hair entered. From the violin section, the concertmaster stepped forward to talk with the conductor. Sarah was too far to hear what was said, but instruments returned to tuning, and across the span, Logan smiled at her before giving his attention to the conductor.

They were rehearsing Bach's Christmas Oratorio, or

Weihnachts Oratorium, the Cantata for the Second Day of Christmas. She'd have to ask Logan later if they were planning to do all six pieces. If so, that would be quite an accomplishment.

Sarah relaxed into the music. Logan was right—the maestro was exceptional. While she couldn't hear the conductor's words since his back was to her, she did hear the result of his instruction. Each section of the overall piece improved after he stopped them, made comments, and the members resumed playing.

Behind her, she saw a stream of light in the aisle. From the corner of her eye, she saw the silhouette of a tall man who had entered the auditorium. He came down to stand in the aisle, almost parallel to where Sarah sat. His face was in profile, but shadows obscured her from seeing any distinct features.

Suddenly the maestro called a halt with a sharp tap of his baton on the podium. He turned on his heel with a quick, stiff movement to face the newcomer, barking, "Why do you enter my domain?"

The reply was spoken gently, and a chime-like resonance to its words, "Chancellor Bandemer requests one of your students attend him now. Logan Dannon."

Sarah gasped in surprise. Logan stood up, holding both his violin and bow in separate hands. Before her son could make another movement, the conductor raised his baton to stop him.

"Is the chancellor in such a hurry that I must halt rehearsals?"

"The matter is rather delicate. And urgent," said the newcomer.

It was as if the world was held suspended on a string. The orchestra itself responded like a beast, straining against a leash, but unable to move unless the maestro released his control.

Only when the string of tension was so tight it might break, Kados Géza released it by taking one dropping step off the podium. He clapped his hands and told the orchestra, "You are lucky today. Practice is now over. If the horn section doesn't get it right by the date of the Christmas concert, Chancellor Bandemer can answer to our patrons."

A group sigh moved like a wave through the musicians. Logan put his violin away, but before he could leave the stage, the maestro stopped him. Sarah was already up, purse in hand, making her way down to the stage. She was one step behind the stranger when the group converged.

The conductor's upright posture and energy had deceived Sarah into assuming he was in his sixties; he was far older, with a lined face and liver spots on his hands. The newcomer was in his late thirties, and very handsome. She cast a worrying look at Logan's serious face.

"What is this delicate matter? Explain yourself." Géza said sharply.

The other didn't answer, but addressed Sarah instead, "We haven't been introduced."

"Sarah Dannon. I'm Logan's mother."

"Mom, this is my maestro, Kados Géza and, uh—"

"Paul Darcy, assistant to Chancellor Bandemer, of Leopold Otto."

"Oh." She didn't know what was going on, but the maestro was a stormy thunderhead right before the tornado alarms sounded.

"Mr. Darcy," Géza said the name, lacing it with sarcasm, "what brings you here to collect my student? Before you deny me again, remember, this is the third time I've requested information."

"The Chancellor desires Logan to give a demonstration at his Symposium. He will not need his violin."

A vein on the maestro's forehead started to bulge. Sarah intervened before the old man would have a heart attack or stroke, "A demonstration of what?"

Mr. Darcy answered Sarah's question, but his eyes never left Géza's "Of Logan's ability to weigh truth against lies. Isn't that what his mentor has been training him to do?"

"He's not ready. The boy still has trouble separating his preconceptions from the information he is given."

Sarah bristled at that statement. Her son knew what he knew, and some pompous conductor wasn't going to malign him in her presence. "Logan, I'm sure, can do a demonstration as long as it is fair."

Sarah fully felt there would be tricks, for Leopold Otto seemed a chancy place.

"I guarantee you, fair play will be done," Mr. Darcy assured her.

This caused the maestro to give a snort of clear disbelief. Géza measured Logan up, and said, "I've changed my opinion—the boy needs shaking up. He is too placid, too accepting of his fate. He hasn't asked once what this is about."

Under their stares, Logan blushed. "Look, it's okay, I trust Bandemer."

"That shows exactly how incredibly naive the boy is and proves my point," scoffed the instructor. "He is not ready. I shall attend this demonstration myself and learn what you intend for my protégé."

When Sarah, Logan, and Géza entered the Kiburg hotel, Paul brought them to a small meeting room and told them to wait. While Sarah and Kados Géza discussed music, Logan felt a mixture of apprehension and exhilaration. He could feel something exciting was about to happen.

Chancellor Bandemer arrived with a flourish, pausing dramatically in the doorway. He wore a coat of bright pink silk embroidered with peacocks.

As Logan introduced Bandemer to his mother, another man entered. Something in his attitude reminded Logan of his father, probably due to his size for the man was bear-like. Introduced as Dr. Sebastian Stuart, Logan realized the newcomer was the scientist Brigit was so keen about.

The next person was a round Humpty-Dumpty character of a man in his mid fifties called Herr Parkinson. Then a thin nervous woman in her thirties, who stared at Logan with greedy, bulging eyes. She was Mme. Barbier.

While the introductions were being made, a waiter

brought in three dishes with covers. They were placed on a table near where Logan was standing. He hoped it was food, for he was starving.

Tapping the floor with his stick, the chancellor silenced everyone as he began to explain the experiment he had planned.

"Logan Dannon is a human student here at Leopold-Ottos-Universität Geheimetür. Please confirm to these fine people that you are of human parentage."

Startled, Géza's hand on Sarah's arm stopped her from stepping forward. Logan told the group, "Yes, I am. Mrs. Dannon is my mother," Logan indicated her with his hand, "and my father is a banker from Texas."

"Good, good," said Bandemer, giving a wide smile to them all like a carnival barker. "Now, tell us what it means to be a bard."

So it was going to be the performing dog trick? While it irritated him how Bandemer liked to show off Logan's talents, he was now experienced in explaining himself. At least Logan had the phrases down pat.

"A bard is a talent only available to humans. I became one through an initiation." (*Better to avoid discussing the particulars of that, don't want to make mom angry.*) "The general gifts are the ability to see through fae Glamour, to recognize truth, and the art of persuasion."

At the end of Logan's speech, Chancellor Bandemer looked from one to the other of his small group.

"Ready to proceed?"

The chancellor's comments received nods. Bandemer

stepped to the first cover. With his hand resting on the handle of the dome, he told Logan, "All you have to do is tell us what you see when I lift this."

"All right, sir." It seemed simple enough, but there was obviously something unusual about the entire situation. Logan braced himself as Bandemer warned his audience, "Say nothing."

The cover lifted, and Mme. Barbier broke Bandemer's request by screaming.

Chapter Eighteen
Kibitz

andemer's guests jumped back, and Géza's grip on Sarah's arm prevented her from moving. Paul had a long-suffering expression on his face. Logan looked at the bowl's contents, frowning.

"Uh, it's a bowl of spaghetti."

"Are you sure?" asked the chancellor, raising his eyebrows.

Sensing duplicity, Logan stepped closer. Using a fork lying next to the dish, he poked the noodles. "With sauce? A red sauce? Is that what you wanted to know?"

Since the chancellor remained silent, Logan swirled noodles around a fork and took a bite. His action caused Mme. Barbier to run out of the room.

"It's a trick! He knows what you intend." This was from Herr Parkinson. He had a strident, bossy voice that hurt Logan's ears. It didn't help that his bard senses revealed that Parkinson always lied, even to himself.

"Well, it certainly is a trick, Herr Parkinson," agreed the chancellor as he replaced the dome. "But a trick for you, not the boy. As a bard, Logan Dannon sees through fae Glamour, he cannot see the illusions we cast. What you thought you saw was not what he did. Let's try the second one."

The humans in the room must have seen some enchantment. From seeing the expressions on his mother, Parkinson, and Stuart, Logan guessed it was something scary or disgusting. Meanwhile, Bandemer was amused while Paul's face was neutral. Herr Géza looked his usual self—stern and foreboding.

Bandemer removed the second cover. This time, Logan saw a bowl filled with strawberries. Instead of being repulsed or frightened, Dr. Stuart leaned forward for a closer look. He picked up a strawberry and holding it out towards him, asked Logan, "What do you see?"

"Strawberries." Logan picked one up from the bowl and ate it. It was large and juicy.

"I see," mused Dr. Stuart, carefully replacing the berry back where he had got it.

The chancellor told them, "We can compare our

viewpoints later. We still have the last to examine."

"You've coached him," insisted Herr Parkinson. His face had grown beefy red and his jowls shook.

Bandemer gave one of his laughs — it was light in weight but packed a knockout punch: equal parts scorn, contempt, and disdain. Parkinson flinched.

With a flourish, the chancellor withdrew the last cover. Sarah strangled an exclamation, by biting her lip. Logan saw a plate with a mound of whipped cream studded with cherries. The one on top was slowly sliding down the melting pile.

"Don't worry, mom, whatever you're seeing isn't real. I promise you," said Logan. He grabbed a cherry and popped it into his mouth.

Logan followed Bandemer out of the room. In the hallway was Brigit. At her worried look, he gave her a thumbs up, and she visibly relaxed.

"I still think he knew what you were doing in there. It was rigged," insisted Herr Parkinson.

Curious, Logan asked them "What did you see?"

His mom told him in a low voice, "The first was a bowl of worms, the second a stack of glowing jewels, and the last was—" she swallowed, her eyes showing remembered fear, "an egg sac. It split open and spiders, about the size of my hand, crawled out."

"Hm," said Logan. "I'm glad I didn't see that. I saw a bowl of spaghetti, strawberries, and the last dish was a mound of whipped cream with cherries."

"Except for Logan, what the humans saw were illusions," Bandemer explained with that air of a showman exhibiting a two-headed goat. Under their stares, Logan started to feel uncomfortable. "I created the illusions using fae Glamour. This is something that other fae, or a bard like Logan, doesn't see."

"Tricks," muttered Herr Parkinson. Logan saw Brigit step forward as if to disagree but Logan shook his head at her. Let the chancellor take this guy down a peg or two.

"Perhaps another demonstration will convince you?" asked Bandemer, and without waiting for a reply, said, "Let us start round two of testing Logan Dannon. We shall make this one more public, if that suits you, Herr Parkinson?"

Chancellor Bandemer took everyone back to the ballroom where lunch had been served. All the dining tables were now removed, and were replaced with rows of chairs. The audience was a mixed group of humans and fae, most were strangers to Logan.

Logan noticed a television crew setting up a camera aimed at the front of the room. A woman standing beside the cameraman scrutinized them as they passed by. Her gaze dismissed Logan and rested on the big blond guy, Dr. Stuart. She spoke something to the cameraman, and he swiveled the lens to capture their entrance.

Bandemer indicated they should take seats on the front row reserved for his group. The chancellor wouldn't let Queen Elixia, Brigit, or his mom sit next to Logan. Instead, he placed them at the far end of the row, closest to the center of the room. Logan was sandwiched between Dr. Stuart and Professor Parkinson.

Another cameraman came around to the front of the room. The big round lens panned the front row and Logan made his face appear as blank as possible. A strike of the chancellor's cane on the floor and the audience quieted.

"During our wonderful symposium, a valid question was raised. Because of fae magic, could the fae and humans ever be on an equal level? Would not humans always be at a disadvantage at the negotiations table?"

The chancellor's magically enhanced voice was the perfect pitch to reach each person in the room.

"This is a valid question and why I included an opposing opinion, like Herr Parkinson, to speak at our conference. However, humans are not powerless. They also have magic. Magic powerful enough to see through to the heart of a matter—the truth."

Bandemer indicated to Logan that he should stand.

"I have arranged a little demonstration with one of my student liaisons. Logan Dannon, a human, will be the subject of our experiment for he is a bard."

These words caused the fae in the room to start whispering. A few hurriedly left for an exit. The humans in the audience only looked puzzled.

"As a bard, Logan Dannon can see through all fae Glamour. I have just demonstrated this to Professor Parkinson." The chancellor indicated Parkinson should stand and present himself to the room. He gained a smattering of applause, but mostly boos from the audience.

"And to Dr. Sebastian Stuart, who I do not think needs my introduction." More enthusiastic applause was given as the scientist stood and bowed to the room. "Perhaps Dr. Stuart can share what he saw?"

Dr. Stuart repeated the events of what happened before entering the ballroom. His storytelling was theatrical, making the test of the three dishes seem far more dramatic than Logan felt the events were. After finishing, there was more applause as Dr. Stuart regained his seat.

Chancellor Bandemer continued, "As a bard, Logan Dannon's talents also allow him to sort lies from truth."

The chancellor beckoned Herr Parkinson to come to the front of the room. A hotel staff member walked over to Parkinson and gave him a deck of cards sealed in their original packaging.

"Herr Parkinson will be my first volunteer. Go through these, pick a card, and show it to the audience, but conceal it from Dannon."

Parkinson refused to take the small box on the platter the staff member was holding out. "It's a trick! The deck is marked. Or you'll prompt Dannon with some word or another."

Dr. Stuart stood up and took the deck himself. He examined it curiously as he said, "Sit down, Parkinson, and let a real scientist handle this."

Stuart's words got laughter and hoots. The audience wanted a good show, and he promised to give them one. Parkinson's face flushed with anger and embarrassment but he did sit back down.

Bandemer commanded Logan to turn around, placing his back to the group. He explained, "Don't break the seal on the deck yet."

The chancellor turned to the audience and explained how the game would work. "Dr. Stuart will pull a card from the deck. He will show you the card, but not Logan Dannon. When he is ready, he will describe the card to Logan. Dr. Stuart can lie or tell the truth. Once Logan has heard Dr. Stuart's identification, he will tell us if what Stuart said was true or false. Let us proceed."

The chancellor had picked a clever game, thought Logan. There was no shade of gray to these truths. The card was either the four of hearts, or not. This was something that Logan couldn't mess up.

But on the other hand, with a simple yes or no answer, he could be accused of getting it right by sheer chance.

"The Ace of Spades," said Dr. Stuart.

"False," said Logan, confidently. Stuart showed the room a card with the nine of diamonds. He replaced the card on the bottom of the deck, and pulled another.

"Three of Hearts."

"True."

They went through the 52 cards with Logan correctly verifying each statement Dr. Stuart made as a truth or a lie. Midway through the experiment, Dr. Stuart started to ride the emotional wave of the room. He'd announce cards in different voices, some squeaky, others spoken in an unnaturally deep voice, or he alternated in speaking English, French or German.

He revealed the cards like he was pulling a rabbit out of a hat, causing laughter or applause.

In the front row, Herr Parkinson looked overheated. His face a mottled color of red and white. When the deck game completed the first round, Parkinson said, "Some sort of trick. A mirror. A code word."

Stuart and his mammoth size loomed over Parkinson, "Are you calling me a trickster? A liar?"

Chancellor Bandemer, who had sat down to be out of Logan's eyesight, was calmer. He appeared bored as he examined his manicured fingernails and said, "I am willing to adapt the game in any way you wish."

Herr Parkinson insisted on checking Logan personally to determine that he did not have an earpiece. He took Logan's cell phone, and Sarah held out her hand for it.

"Blindfold him."

Once again, the game started. This time the deck made the rounds of the room. Each person, fae or human, was given a chance to stump the bard. Despite the cards traveling around three times through the audience, Logan gave correct answers no matter who spoke.

"How long do you wish to do this?" the chancellor asked Parkinson. "Why won't you admit that Logan Dannon, fully human, has an ability that you would describe as magical?"

Dissent came from a surprising quarter. Kados Géza, seated next to Logan's mother, stood up and contradicted the chancellor. "Dealing with fae, these cards could have been enchanted. Unknown to us, they could whisper the answers to the boy."

There was an outcry throughout the room: humans upset over being thought tricked, and fae angry for having their honor questioned. Still, other fae thought that if this was so, it was an impressive trick; those beings applauded Chancellor Bandemer for his cleverness.

Brigit shouted over them all, "Logan would never participate in anything so dishonorable."

Her defense gained her an opaque look from Géza. He held his hand out towards Dr. Stuart, who was now holding the deck of cards. "I have a suggestion on how this test can proceed. Hand them to me."

Dr. Stuart, hesitant to leave the limelight, but in the end he reluctantly obeyed the maestro. Whispers ran around the room, telling those who did not recognize him who Géza was.

"A Jew. He directs the university orchestra."

"Hungarian. Came into Bewachterberg during the second World War."

"I thought this cowardly country was concealed at the time?"

"Exactly. How he got here is a mystery never fully explained. He's a crafty one."

Géza appeared unfazed by the audible summations of who he was. He slowly shuffled the cards between his hands, passively surveying the audience. He waited until the murmurs died away before speaking.

"To look at a card," he pulled one from the deck, showing the face to the audience, "and to guess the truth of it is one level of truth. Be it chance? Or is it magic? But is not randomness, what we call luck, a type of magic?"

Holding the deck high for a moment, Géza placed it next on a chair. He addressed Logan, who, still blindfolded, turned his head the direction of where Géza stood.

"But there are as many faces of truth as there are cards in this deck. Let us dig deeper and mine for gold." Facing Logan, he gave his student a small smile. "Tell me the card I will select."

This command started mutterings between the fae members of the audience.

"Is a bard a Cassandra? They predict the future?"

"I didn't know Bards were prescient?"

"If so, they are even more dangerous than we feared."

Hearing the audience, Logan protested, "I can't predict the future. I don't know what card will be next."

Géza held up a hand to stop them all. He might not have the size of Dr. Stuart, but he knew how to handle a crowd.

"I am discussing truth—the larger truth. The truth that happens regardless of human action or thought. The truth of what the world is and what happens within it. Are your skills up to this, bard?"

Logan found himself growing angry at Géza's words. Why was the man putting him through this? It was just like one of the games the maestro played every week in their meetings. It made him so angry that he said without thinking, "Okay. How do we play this game of yours?"

Kados Géza laid his hand over the deck.

"Tell me what card I will pull."

"How do I know you will select any of them?"

"Good point. You're learning, boy." If he called him a boy, one more time, Logan was — "I promise you I will pick a card."

Before Géza could draw, a blinding flash of knowledge sent Logan reeling back, "That's a lie— you—"

Before Logan could finish speaking, there was a movement at the back of the room. An elegant young being, a fae crowned with a rack of antlers, stood up. Brigit recognized Torfa.

The prince of the forest shouted, "We want the truth! The fae deserve it! End this game and answer a more important question, bard. I demand Logan Dannon answer this: is a human destroying the royal courts in the Perilous Realm?"

Logan, seeing the world of truth in a different way, answered Torfa's question. "Yes."

The room broke into pandemonium.

Bane of Hounds

Chapter Nineteen
J'adoube

After speaking, Logan staggered back, his hand pulling off the blindfold. "He wasn't—" he began to say before sliding to the floor.

Brigit rushed to his side. Queen Elixia saw the expression on her daughter's face and admitted defeat. There was no helping it. Her daughter wasn't going to marry a prince of the forest, no matter how much she begged her.

She told Chancellor Bandemer standing beside her, "You seem to have a flair for the dramatic."

Bandemer gave the queen a bow, acknowledging her praise. "I surpass myself sometimes."

"But where is your conductor? Herr Géza?"

"Flitted out the door and left me to pick up the pieces. It's his way of voicing disapproval of my methods."

At the snap of Bandemer's fingers, Paul moved to where his liege stood. "Get the boy settled somewhere private. He overextended himself. He'll be hungry when he wakes. These bards always eat the pantry bare. Queen Elixia and I will calm down this rabble."

Paul didn't like leaving Bandemer on his own. Who knew what trouble the chancellor would get into without someone to restrain him. But it was a command. The Doppelgänger bowed and moved to where Logan lay on the floor. He called the med team they had on standby at the hotel.

On her knees, Sarah Dannon held her son's hand, crying, "This has her dirty fingerprints all over it."

"Who?" asked Brigit. She folded her jacket and put it under Logan's head.

The strength of her emotion made Sarah grind out, "My mother-in-law. This is the type of stunt she favors."

An Asian woman in her early thirties, wearing scrubs in dark blue with a paramedic badge on her sleeve, told the two women to move. Her name tag read Hua Cheng.

While Paul explained the events that lead up to Logan's collapse, the paramedic took Logan's pulse, checked his eyes, and attached a blood pressure cuff. She had a competent and professional attitude.

The other being of the team was fae. It wore a black trench coat that fell to the floor like a robe, heavy gloves, and a plague mask. The mask itself was a work of art—the hood was black but the projecting hooked beak was gold-plated. The eye holes were thick pieces of bottle-glass obscuring what was behind them. It all gave an anonymous, androgynous look to the creature.

It gave off a smell that Brigit recognized immediately as a combination of angelica, betony, and rue. The creature addressed its companion in a gruff voice, "Canny?"

"Seems Uncanny to me," replied Cheng. "The kid seems healthy enough, and all the readings are normal. But I'll know more once we get him somewhere private."

The two transferred Logan onto a medical stretcher. Pedal pressure raised the bed on wheels and as they headed toward a door Paul held it open for them.

The hallway was far quieter than the conference room. Sarah demanded, "Where are you taking him?"

But her question was soon answered as they stopped in front of a ground floor suite set aside for hospitality and emergencies. Cheng scanned her pass, and after the lock released, they pushed the stretcher through.

Before Paul and Brigit could enter, the Uncanny doctor blocked them. Its thick glass eyes viewed them without visible emotion. "Family only."

"I work for the chancellor," Paul explained, which only got him a "I know who you are" from the beak.

"I want to be with him," said Brigit, trying to look past the blocking shoulder.

Sarah intervened, saying in a weary air, "Let them enter. They probably know more than I do about what is going on here. If I've learned anything these past two days, it is I'm woefully uninformed about what my son has been doing."

The Uncanny doctor moved aside to let Paul and Brigit enter. Logan's mother clasped her son's limp hand and asked Cheng, "Why hasn't he woken up yet?"

"No reason he shouldn't. Everything seems fine—blood pressure, temperature, heart rate. When did he eat last? Does he have a history of fainting? Has he been sick recently? Overworked?"

"He last ate something the chancellor offered him." The glance she gave Paul was accusatory. "He said it was a cherry, but it looked like a spider."

"Sounds like something Chancellor Bandemer would do," said Cheng. "But I don't think the chancellor's poisoned anyone for what, at least ten years, right, doc?"

"Correct. And that was a tenured professor he wanted gone," the Uncanny doctor said while looking down at Logan's prone form from its bottle glass eyes. "I have never heard of him trying to kill a student. If he wants one gone, he makes them take classes with unpleasant professors. It's a less messy method."

"That makes me feel so much better," Sarah said sarcastically.

"The food was completely harmless I assure you," said Paul. "I would never countenance anything along that line."

Brigit added, "He hasn't been sick. I'd know. We live together."

Cheng raised her eyebrows at the news that a fae and human were companions, but only asked, "Any other encounters with fae beings recently? Other than yourself?"

"We have a brownie who lives with us. She fixes our food. But she's sworn fealty to Logan and would never harm him. We live with a púca—it might pull a prank on Logan, but I don't think Jib's seen Logan since it returned from the Perilous Realm a day ago."

"Nothing unusual then?" pressed Cheng, possibly because of the expression on Sarah Dannon's face.

"Well, we found a dog," admitted Brigit reluctantly. "A Black Dog puppy we took in, but I'm sure the harbinger has nothing to do with this."

"That monster sent me to the emergency room!" disputed Sarah vehemently. "It is not some innocent little dog, but a hell hound."

The paramedic said with satisfaction, "See? I was right. This case is down your dark alley, doc."

The masked doctor fished into the robe's deep pockets, looking for something. In a moment, the doctor pulled out a length of golden chain with a piece of raw crystal attached to it. The doctor dangled the pendulum over Logan's forehead. It started moving slowly, rocking back and forth, until it started spinning clockwise.

"Hm, I think you might want to cover your eyes—" but before anyone could obey the doctor's orders, a burst of blinding rainbow light briefly blinded them all. After the explosion of radiance, the light subsided to sparkles that faded away.

"Will he be all right? What is wrong with my son?" Sarah Dannon demanded again. Brigit, standing at her side, nodded in agreement. She also wanted answers.

"Overwork," the Uncanny doctor stated, pocketing the diagnostic crystal. "The being in question is experiencing a typical side effect of leveling up a Talent."

The black-robed doctor made a clucking "tsk, tsk" noise, sounding like a clock. "Why these young folk think they can become full-blown magicians at the drop of a hat is beyond my understanding. I blame television for this misconception. It's not a nose-wrinkle and a wave of a wand. Real power comes from the pain of growth."

Sarah asked scornfully, "Is that what the disco ball told you?"

"No, it's what life has taught me. The crystal just confirmed that your son's unconscious state is due to a magical overload. Now, tell me about your son."

"His blood type is A positive—"

"No, I mean—let's begin again. What does the boy like to do? What are his interests? What is his favorite food? Who are his friends? Why is he living with these fae beings—dryads, brownies, and púcas? Bringing hell-hounds home with him?"

"Technically, not a hell-hound," Brigit corrected the doctor under her breath.

Sarah's mouth gaped open for a moment before replying, "He's my son!" as if that explained everything about Logan. Meeting the doctor's blank gaze, she added hesitantly, "He runs for exercise, is that what you mean?"

"A solitary sport. When did he start that?"

"Soon after we returned from England. When he was in high school."

"No team sports?"

Feeling the question was a criticism of her son, Sarah snapped, "No."

In the awkward pause that followed, Brigit said tentatively, "He likes to read spy thrillers."

"Why?"

"Hm, I don't know. I never asked him. He just does." She shrugged helplessly.

"What else can you tell me about him?"

Sarah and Brigit alternated between sharing details about Logan: his interests, friendships, classes he was taking, a scar on his arm from a fall on his bike when he was eight, his closeness with his cousin Evelyn.

Brigit added that he shared a friendship with a fae eotan named Granite, and a human girl named Emma Walker. He had a fondness for birds, especially crows and ravens, and liked cats.

"This Emma — is she a girlfriend?"

"No," said Brigit emphatically.

"So not many human friends," observed the doctor.

"He has plenty of bondmates who will defend him." Brigit's comment was sharp with warning. The Uncanny doctor ignored the implied threat and pointed its beak at Paul.

"I see you still have not recovered full use of your MindBending ability, Doppelgänger. Stop by my office for a full check-up. Meanwhile, what do you know about this human boy?"

"He's a perceptive person," said Paul. "Loyal to his

friends. Perhaps braver than common sense warrants, but not especially foolhardy."

"According to his file, he was almost eaten by an overgrown silverfish. I call that rather foolhardy," said Cheng. The paramedic was scrolling through her phone, reviewing Logan Dannon's medical history. Her comment got an enigmatic stare from Paul.

The doctor put its hands behind its back. It paced the room, the gold-plated beak bobbing forward with each step. It looked like that bobbing water bird toy. Sarah had to repress a hysterical giggle.

"None of you have told me about Logan Dannon's magic."

"I don't feel that is relevant to—" began Sarah, but her sentence was cut off by Brigit. "He's a bard. Because he slept on Snowdon mountain in Wales when he was a teenager."

At Brigit's statement, Sarah's face became a road map of turmoil: anger, confusion, and fright.

"So he has undergone an initiation before?" said the doctor.

"I suppose so," replied Brigit uncertain. "He doesn't like talking about it, so I don't know much more than that."

The discussion of magic had angered Logan's mother. Rummaging in her purse, she grabbed her cell phone. Activating the screen, she hit a button on it as she told them, "I knew she was involved! I knew it. He's going to hear about this."

After a moment, she informed the others in the room,

"Voice mail."

A few seconds later, Sarah left a terse message, "You need to return my call as soon as possible. I don't care about you making connections or giants of finance. I'm in Geheimetür, and your son needs you. Your mother's handiwork. Call me. Now."

After she disconnected, Brigit asked, "You've mentioned her before —? Do you mean the Morrighan?"

Sarah's face flushed with fury. "She's involved. I can sense it. She's ruined our lives before with her meddling."

"Now we are getting somewhere," said the Uncanny doctor with satisfaction. "The boy is the grandson of a goddess in the human lands? That explains much."

Sarah raised the hand holding the cell phone in front of her as if it was a knife that she could use for defense. Both hand and voice trembled as she said, "She killed me once. Now, she's trying to destroy my son."

Paul spoke again, trying to reassure her, "I don't think the Morrighan is involved in this situation, Mrs. Dannon. As the doctor stated, this situation seems to be from Logan overworking his Talent in the conference room."

"Talent? It's a curse!" She collapsed into a chair, dropping the hand with her cell phone against her leg. Tears slowly ran down her face.

The Uncanny doctor crossed over to her, patting her shoulder with a gloved hand. "Good, good, best to get it all out. It helps the psychic healing."

"Bring him back, please bring him back," she begged the Uncanny, clasping his sleeve.

"When, or if, he comes back, depends on him."

Chapter Twenty
King Hunt

The cane Chancellor François Auguste Bandemer carried was a black stick, four feet high. The head was a lead ball about the size of a plum, plated with brass. It was an instrument handy for bashing in a head or two. The stick was also helpful in making an entrance or in striking a dramatic pose.

Bandemer paused, hand outstretched, his feet in a t-shape like the third position in ballet, and surveyed the room. A simple cough was not going to stop the shouting.

Far too many heads to bash with just one stick.

He gripped the cane on the shaft. Bandemer tapped the floor three times in a steady tap, pause, tap, pause, tap. Controlling the Element of Air, he removed it from the lungs of all the oxygen breathers (except for himself and Queen Elixia, whose arm was tucked around his elbow) in the room.

Those that weren't swayed by a lack of oxygen, he used a second power. The scorching by the Element of Fire caused startled yelps and screams. Finally, the room was silent.

"Now that I have your attention," said Chancellor Bandemer, "we shall politely debate the accusation that Prince Torfa raised just moments ago."

Chancellor Bandemer handed Queen Elixia to an empty seat. Once she was settled, he said (amplifying his voice with Air), "Anyone with actual factual information about any destroyed fae courts should sit here," he pointed with his cane at the empty seats, "in the front row."

In the end, only five came forward, one of those being Prince Torfa. Bandemer indicated with his hand, palm up, that the prince should speak first, asking him, "What proof of these accusations do you have?"

"Queen Summerblossom has a trading pact with Queen Ambrosia's court," said Torfa. Dressed in pencil-thin black slacks, with a forest-green silk shirt open at the throat, he managed to look deliciously at ease, despite his fierce expression.

Viewing his confident air and outfit, Elixia, wondered why couldn't her daughter be interested in him?

"Returning traders said her sacred spring of healing was sickening. The water smelled sour, and at the touch of a Unicorn's horn, it glowed purple, indicating poison. When we hastened there, we discovered her kingdom gone."

This caused a fresh round of outrage, but with the raising of Bandemer's cane, everyone hushed. No one liked gasping for breath or trying to sit on a burned bum.

Torfa turned and spoke now to the entire room, "We have heard only a rumor of Queen Selena's court. Gossip reached us about a Black Dog pack being in danger. When we journeyed there using the ley lines, we found the court gone. Their Elder, a deep cave, was dying and collapsing upon itself."

This time Bandemer didn't have to warn anyone not to speak; Torfa's statement was met by only shocked silence.

Elder spirits, or genius loci, in the Perilous Realm were well-concealed and far between. The Elder spirits were a secretive, hidden old magic that seldom made themselves visible.

They only revealed themselves when a fae convinced them to bond. And the bonding created a court, establishing a new queen. The only thing known to sever such a tie was the death of that queen.

In recent memory, the only loss of a queen was due to an accident. Afterward, her Elder, a mountain, became volcanic in despair. Her people scattered to find other courts, and her consort committed suicide.

You can feel their fear, thought Queen Elixia. She was less shocked, having lived with the reality of losing her Elder for some time. However, the thought that now creased her brow was that the disease affecting her grove was by design. She had not considered that option.

Never in recorded existence had a genius loci been

intentionally destroyed. Surely, no fae would destroy an Elder. If true, it must be a human, like Torfa claimed and the bard confirmed.

"Does anyone here have anything more to say on the matter?" Bandemer indicated the next being who had come forward. It was a short squat being with the armor plating of an armadillo and crescent shaped claws at the end of its four appendages.

"It is as the antlered one says. Queen Selena's court is no more. We excavated some of the cave's rubble, and found the Elder Spirit's life-force extinguishing."

"Scavengers," someone from the back accused it. "Grubbing for treasure more-like, dvergr."

"We were there on a rescue mission," the being snort-grunted, wrinkling its snout in disdain at the accusation. "We are bond pledged to Queen Selena. We shall kill whoever committed this atrocity, human or fae."

"What of you?" Bandemer demanded of the next in line — the fae fish being which had been at Queen Elixia's lunch table.

"Queen Summerblossom sent an emissary to gain knowledge of what could poison her water. The queen knew we had experience dealing with human pollution. We sent testing kits, but never heard the results. Or had any further contact."

The next two had similar statements. They had been appealed to or visited the courts and found them both removed from the map of ley lines.

Bandemer cleared his throat and asked, "I do not see,

Prince Torfa, why you bring humans into this matter. Why so specific an accusation? Where is the connection?"

"A rumor, a whisper on the wind reached us. I wanted the human bard's thoughts on the matter. You claim he has powers to see true. From his own mouth, he has now confirmed it!"

This roused the crowd into yelling. Fists and appendages were waved in the air. Hunting and killing humans was the most shouted call to action by the fae.

Queen Elixia noticed that the remaining humans in the audience were slinking towards exits. Even Dr. Stuart and Professor Parkinson had left, diplomatically taking a side door to escape.

"You cannot charge all humans you meet as conspiring against us," said the chancellor. He was cut short by an accusation shouted from the back of the group, "You favor humans over your own kind, Bandemer."

"I do? What about all of you? Do you want to descend back into chaos? I remember those times, even if you scrubs do not! We copied the medieval organization of courts from the human lands. We used their idea of fealty and government structure to form our courts. We made order from anarchy."

"Human lover!" cried someone else. From her seat, Elixia couldn't tell who it was.

Bandemer laughed harshly. "Do you wish to go back, scrabbling in the dirt? Haunting the lone bog? Drowning the odd human on a secluded road?"

Some of the chancellor's smooth veneer was starting to

wear away under the anger of the fae crowd. His face showed deeper lines around the nose and mouth. Queen Elixia could see the colors of his magic swirling above his head, but she couldn't figure out why among Flame and Wind there should be traces of Metal and Stone.

"You want to keep that cushy job of yours." This voice was new.

"If you think this job is easy, perhaps you would like to apply for it? In 1720, I arrived at a campus in chaos and crisis. The former chancellor, a half-blood of the royal family, murdered. The fae in Bewachterberg terrorizing the human population. A basilisk nesting in the bell tower."

"You just wanted something to do after the Sun King's death."

"Do not," Chancellor Bandemer's next words were coldly furious, even as the walls of the room flared with magical flame, "put his royal name in your diseased mouth again."

"We kill them all!" another being wailed. Before that call to action could be taken up, Bandemer singed the tail of the fae who had spoken. While it dampened that one's fury, it did not quell the growing anger now pulsing throughout the room.

"Listen!" Bandemer tapped this cane thrice again and sent out a calming spell. Under the force of it even Queen Elixia relaxed despite herself.

"Humans have evolved—kings no longer manage their government. Royalty holds only a nominal role." Bandemer's words provoked some outraged gasps. "We can't just declare a Fiat and expect a king or queen to negotiate. We must find the specific culprit or group guilty of this, first."

The fae liked this idea better. Given an enemy, the mood shifted to a goal.

"Disembowel them!"

"Cut the head off, put it on a spike!"

"Lock them up in an oubliette!"

Queen Elixia felt her heart swell with pride, and her eyes grew misty at the patriotism shown by her fellow fae. Such noble creatures.

"You would side with them over your own kind," one of the earlier speakers spoke again. The fae separated, and down the aisle came a troll. He was an Atlas type: broad shoulders, bulging with gray mounds of blocky muscles. He had a square head with a heavy brow ridge and a nose half the width of his face.

Elixia covered her eyes with one hand. Why was her husband's valet here?

Standing in front of Bandemer, face to face, the troll's body towered over the elf king. But size did not intimidate Bandemer. The chancellor's face showed no emotion at Kroll's appearance.

"Your love affair with the human race is no secret, François," the troll's voice was rough and raw. Words tumbled around the room like an avalanche. "How do we know that you wouldn't sacrifice us all if you could stay in Bewachterberg? Acting as a surrogate king to these human children at your university?"

"You malign my honor."

The troll continued as if Bandemer had not spoken.

"Elders have been lost. My queen," Kroll gave Elixia only the barest of bows as he continued "and her court are suffering from this saboteur. But you do nothing but give empty promises and prance around in your fancy clothes."

Kroll faced the audience, raising a fist bigger than Elixia's head. "Who here wants their Elder spirit dead? Who wants to live as an exile? I know I don't!"

Hissing boos, stomping of chairs or feet, and chants begged for war. Elixia could not understand why Bandemer didn't set them all on fire. Or have them die from lack of air. She would have done so in a heartbeat.

Kroll was always a painful thorn. As valet and confidante to King Ladislas, he was the only one of their court who felt he owed allegiance to the king over the queen. His stubbornness often led to tension between her and Ladislas. Elixia's dusky gray-green skin flushed with embarrassment and anger.

As usual, Kroll was where he wasn't wanted and stirring up trouble. He was probably sent here by Ladislas to snoop on her!

The mood was turning uglier by the minute. Even François Auguste Bandemer did not seem capable of turning the tide of such fierce opposition. Elixia felt uneasy, remembering the Black Dog's Doom: *The hound of death hunts a noble prize; When the glass turns, who falls, so others rise?*

"You call yourself a king, but where is your queen? Her court in the Perilous Realm?" growled the troll.

Bandemer's eyes tightened, as did his grip on his cane. "Do you need a queen to validate who I am? My allegiance to my kind?"

The chancellor's comment only changed the direction of the chanting to the repeated cry of "Where is the queen?"

Bandemer raised his cane high over his head. Using Wind, he magically stilled the crowd. "Do you demand a queen? A queen to guide us?"

In response to his rallying cry, the mood in the room panted with excitement; its rapacious hunger waiting to be appeased by the chancellor's answer.

"Here is the queen I will swear my pledge to. Queen Elixia."

In surprise, Elixia took Bandemer's offered hand. He brought her up to face the crowd. Of course, standing next to a gray monster like Kroll made her ethereal beauty shine all the more.

But more than that, as a queen, the fae were conditioned to see her rank and status as one to provide answers.

Chancellor Bandemer asked her, "Queen Elixia, did you not come to the symposium to gain aid to save your kingdom?"

"Yes," she cleared her throat, saying louder, "Yes, I did. And you graciously promised me your aid in the matter."

Kroll grumbled rocks, "And this accomplished what? Bandemer is known for his flim-flam, his empty promises. We will not fall for it!"

He shook his fist at the audience, with some copying his gesture. Others, more careful about allegiance, waited to see which would win the battle before choosing a side.

The presence of a queen had changed the mood of the

audience like a switch. Bandemer brought Queen Elixia's hand forward in a dramatic flourish, bowing over it.

"I pledge my life to save your court. To save yourself and your people." Before she could respond to the chancellor's promise, Bandemer gracefully dropped to one knee, brushing her knuckles with a kiss. "Will you accept my life, your majesty, as a pledge to save you and your court?"

Queen Elixia paused only a moment. She also enjoyed drama. With one hand, she drew the ceremonial dagger from her belt. The blade was an essential part of her regalia, for it was this instrument that marked someone during the act of pledging.

Tradition demanded a token from the candidate. She reached forward to take a lock of Bandemer's hair but his long white fingers gently stopped her.

"No, your majesty, I never give a symbolic lock. My oaths mean more to me than something that can be so easily re-grown."

Abruptly, his hand tightened over hers and opening up his other hand, he slashed the blade across his open palm. Life fluid blossomed as a line across his pale flesh.

In the ancient gesture of a life pledge, François Auguste Bandemer clasped palm to palm with the queen. Queen Elixia felt the power in that warm wetness. She now held Bandemer's Bond and with it, his life.

Chapter Twenty-One
Poison Pawn

Logan was hanging upside down from a tree. It was more than a dream, and far too close to reality.

"You've really gotten yourself in a mess this time," said his grandmother's black raven. Startled, Logan twisted to better see who spoke. His sudden movement started him swinging on the rope tied to the branch where bird perched. The other end of the rope was trussed around his ankles.

"Mara?"

"You look much bigger since we last met. How time flies." The raven cocked his head to observe the grandson of the Morrighan hanging from Yggdrasil. "I see you are still getting yourself into predicaments."

The swinging was making Logan dizzy. Seeing the world

far below him didn't help. He didn't have vertigo, but Logan also didn't choose to go skydiving.

"Where am I?"

"Is he always this stupid?" asked a white raven. She landed next to the black. She ruffled her feathers into place, before settling her wings.

"He is just a boy," Mara chided her.

"Boys grew up faster in my day," countered the white.

Logan didn't want to get into an argument while hanging upside down with only a rope to prevent him falling to a certain death. He kept his silence and thought for a moment. The last thing he could remember was a crowd of people, fae and humans, who were all staring at him. A card game. Géza!

"I saw—I saw something."

"I saw something," mimicked the white raven, who ended her mocking statement with a loud crawwwwkkk. "Almost as dense as the wood of this Ash tree."

"Don't mind Memory," said Mara. "She's cranky because you interrupted her plans for the day. Go on."

"My instructor, maestro Géza, was about to pull a card. Everything froze, his fingers on the card, while someone else asked me a question. It was like looking at a painting. Everything became flat, two dimensional but all the colors were brighter. I saw a horizon and then passed the curve of the world. I saw it all—everything—laid out in front of me. But I can't remember it now."

"I always like to hear what shamans see when their minds break from expanding too quickly," said Memory. Her croaking was a bit too gleeful for Logan.

Mara bobbed his head in agreement. "Takes you by surprise seeing the Big Picture. Blows their mind."

"Seeing what?" asked Logan. He directed the question to Mara who had once helped him as a child to bring back his mother from Between the Worlds.

"Big Picture. The Universe. Your place in the Cosmos and how insignificant you really are."

Logan was silent. The only noise was the creaking of the rope as he swayed below the branch. He looked down again at the sea and land so very far away.

"I think I know exactly how insignificant I am."

"Well, if that is all the boy has learned, I'm leaving to run my errands," said the white raven. She spread her wings as if she was about to drop from the tree into flight.

"Give him time," said Mara. "Great things can't be rushed."

"He's no Odin. I'm not wasting my time for nine days with this small fish."

"Did I say he was? But while he's a little fish, I do have an affection for him. Can't you hold off just a bit longer?"

Logan wasn't sure he should interrupt their argument, but he really didn't want to keep swinging in the wind. The blood pounding in his head was making a horrible headache.

"It was about truth. I remember now. Géza was going to pull the card, so he was telling the truth, but his truth didn't happen because Torfa asked me a question. A question I couldn't answer before, but now—"

Both birds leaned over their perch, black eyes shining

upon Logan.

"Truth isn't about what anyone thinks," said Logan, understanding suddenly. "It's about what exists outside of all that. What stands, no matter what people believe or think."

"You saw an Anchor point," croaked Mara. "A point in time that acts as an axis for all that happens before and after. It cannot be changed, but it creates all the changes thereafter."

The living rope around Logan's ankles unwound. He could feel his ankles slipping free. He frantically groped for the rope spinning away from him as he began a freefall. The birds leaped from their branch, diving to circle around Logan in a spiral.

"See, that wasn't so hard. Was it, bard?" demanded the white raven.

"Give my regards to your mother," screeched Mara.

Both birds righted their descent and the last thing Logan saw was them flying wingtip to wingtip away from him before he woke up.

From the bed, Logan said in a weak voice, "Is there anything to eat? I'm starving."

While he was eating his third sandwich he finally convinced Brigit that he was fine and she could leave. Brigit bit her lip. "I need to talk with my mother. But if you need me—?"

"No, I'm really okay."

His mom was harder to shake.

"You could stay at the Kiburg with me," she suggested, "or maybe I should go home with you?"

"You wouldn't like that. The dog is at the apartment. It's one reason why I need to get home. He probably needs out."

All this arguing back and forth only ended when the Uncanny doctor told Sarah that the crisis for the moment seemed to have passed. "However, the boy needs to learn to pace himself. You don't become a full-fledged bard overnight, or even in four years. Try four hundred."

Hua Cheng was less patient. She had packed up their equipment and was standing at the open door. "C'mon doc, the kid's fine. He'll sink or swim with his magic. That's between him and his mentor. I want to hit the dinner buffet before all the good stuff is gobbled down. Yesterday, all we got was a few limp radishes and carrot sticks."

Brigit gave Logan a quick hug under his mother's disapproving eye before leaving. To prove he was fit enough to be on his own, Logan walked his mom back to her room. He promised to call as soon as he reached the apartment.

"I'm in class until noon. Maybe afterward we can do some sight-seeing together? There's a river cruise we can take," he suggested.

Before Sarah could reply, her phone rang. His mother's face brightened as she told him, "It's your father!"

With her attention diverted, Logan gave her a wave and escaped.

When Logan reached his apartment he found Jib arguing with the brownie in the kitchen about the Black Dog. Speaking of dogs, Logan hadn't been greeted by a waging tail or a slobbering kiss. He interrupted the two, asking, "Where's Devlin?"

"Who?" asked Jib, in mock surprise, eyes wide.

"The dog, the Black Dog. And I told you his name before I left, so don't pretend you don't know it."

"Devil Dog is locked in your bedroom," hissed the cat. "You shouldn't let him roam about the apartment doing who knows what!"

Tired, Logan spoke more sharply than he intended to the cat, "He's only here for a short time. And, from what I learned today, he could have been the victim of a savage attack which destroyed his home. Have some compassion, Jib!"

There was a beat before Jib spoke again, but if Logan thought the dressing down would give the púca pause he was wrong. "Serves him right. Smelly thing. Why would anyone want him?"

"Unkind, Jib. You need to control this jealousy of yours. Brigit still loves you."

The púca turned its back and started giving itself a tongue bath that looked like it would take some time. Logan, who knew the way of cats, was not daunted by the obvious dismissive sulk.

"I learned some interesting news at the chancellor's symposium today."

"Ye did?" asked the brownie, trying to encourage a peace

between the two.

"Yes, someone is destroying fae courts in the Perilous Realm."

Jib's tongue paused for a split second in its licking before continuing the next stroke. Logan didn't miss the cat's guilty hesitation.

"What do you know about this? Don't tell me you haven't heard? A curious cat like you?"

Jib stopped the sham of bathing. It closed its eyes, hiding their fire and said with dignity, "If I spoke you'd use your Bard magic on me. I am not going to fall into a trap and betray my queen to a human."

"And by that statement," countered Logan, "it's obvious you are hiding something from Brigit and myself."

"What do ya mean about these courts being destroyed?" demanded the brownie. She was standing on a kitchen chair, her head at the height of Logan's shoulder, vigorously using a vegetable peeler on potatoes and tossing them into a pot.

"A character named Torfa asked me if humans were involved and—"

"Humans?" Jib's tone was scathing with disbelief, but the brownie covered her mouth.

"Humans," repeated Logan, "who are destroying the Elder spirits of the courts to vanquish them from the Perilous Realm."

"Wicked doings," the brownie cried out in horrified surprise. She vanished, leaving the potato and peeler to clatter onto the floor.

"Now who will fix my dinner?" yowled Jib.

After getting a deep cat scratch on its nose, Devlin ran yelping from the kitchen to retreat under the bed of the human. It was like the cave of his home den. Not that he knew that; he only felt it. Felt that the cozy darkness was comforting.

Hiding under the bed brought back feelings but no memories.

The scratch on his muzzle burned. Devlin tried to ignore it. He probably deserved it, although he didn't know exactly why. He was just trying to play, to invite the cat into a romp.

Well, he'd be more careful in the future. Even while Devlin thought that, he also knew he probably wouldn't. He had a youthful exuberance that needed an outlet and a two bedroom apartment wasn't enough to release his energy.

He heard the front door and pricked up his ears. The human named Logan was home. Voices in the kitchen included Logan, the cat who hated him, and the brownie who fed him. The voices were not happy. He whined, wanting them to be happy, wanting to be with them, but fearing he wouldn't be welcome.

Devlin shoved himself back further into his burrow.

The door to the bedroom opened. Even though he smelled Logan, the Black Dog suppressed a desire to whine or bark. He remembered a voice from before, *Stay quiet and they may pass us by.* Maybe it would work this time?

"Hey, are you scared, buddy?" Logan was on his knees and was peering under his bed. "It's safe to come out now,

Devlin. Don't worry, you're with me."

He whined, uncertain. He wanted to trust this being so much!

"I'm sorry I wasn't here earlier, but I promise I won't let Jib bother you again. The cat is just jealous." The human lay down on the floor on his back. He put his hands behind his head. "Sounds like we both had quite the day."

The Black Dog couldn't read Logan's aura like he could others. But Logan's smell was a comfort-scent, like his mother, and right now Devlin smelled that the human was tired and needed the comfort of a cuddle.

He crawled on his stomach to the edge of his new den and pushed a nose under Logan's outstretched hand. The young man cuddled his soft ears.

"Yes, you're a good dog. Indeed you are."

Not exactly a dignified conversation but Devlin still had the heart of a puppy. He gave a bark and climbed on top of Logan's prone body, causing the human to laugh as he petted him. "Oh yes, you're a good boy."

Logan looked into the dog's eyes and told him, "You've got to be brave. We may not find your family. But if we don't, Brigit and I will be your new one."

Devlin bumped Logan's hand and gave it a lick.

"I wish you could tell us more about you. More than your name."

Devlin wished he could too. He wanted to ask Logan why the human smelled so familiar to him. Whenever he opened his mouth, only a whine came out so he couldn't tell Logan he remembered him.

Bane of Hounds

Chapter Twenty-Two
Discovered Check

Queen Elixia looked over the skyline of the city of Geheimetür. Her attitude was one of melancholy introspection. She missed Ladislas and would miss him even more after she died.

"Another piece of cake, your majesty?"

One thing about dying is you didn't worry about diets. She took the dessert plate offered by Mr. Darcy (or Paul, as Brigit insisted on calling him) and returned to the table. The Doppelgänger went back to standing behind their seats, his face empty of expression. He looked like a handsome doll.

François Auguste Bandemer seemed unconcerned about making a pact that could end in his death. Instead, his attention was on peeling an orange as one of his hands was wrapped in a bandage. Elixia enjoyed the fruit's intense scent. It was one of the many pleasing things about being in the human lands. If the place didn't have humans, it would be perfect.

When they were finally able to leave the drama downstairs, Bandemer had invited Elixia to this private retreat on the roof of the Kiburg for further discussion. Paul had arrived later with staff members who set up the food and drink.

The sun was setting, and the floating fairy lights around them started to wink on, their illumination becoming stronger as the sky darkened. It was a little chilly, being autumn, but Elixia enjoyed the bite of it.

"Dr. Stuart came to us highly recommended by the rector," Bandemer told her. "Paul assures me he is what humans call a geek or a nerd. He should be of some use."

Queen Elixia made sure that when eating the chocolate cake, none of it stuck to her front teeth. She did this by licking around them with her tongue before opening her mouth to speak. "Are you sure we can trust him?"

"I'm absolutely sure we should not trust him. But if a human is at the root of these ills of our Elders, seeking a human's viewpoint could be of help."

"My daughter Brigit has always insisted that human science would hold answers to our problem. While I am not convinced, I am open to desperate measures if you think this man can help."

"Your daughter is wise. I am sure she takes after her mother." Bandemer gave a nod of deference to his companion since Queen Elixia's hand was still holding a fork and couldn't be kissed.

"My youngest doesn't take after her mother, let me assure you of that!" said Elixia tartly. "I've tried to encourage meetings with some of the most eligible princes here at your symposium. But she sneers at them all. Instead, she seems to prefer the company of this human boy."

"They do seem close. I find it intriguing. An unusual relationship since fae generally use a binding spell to ensure the affection of their pet human," said Bandemer. He finished his orange and wiped his hands clean with a scented washcloth resting in a bowl on the table.

"Perhaps he used bard-magic to bind my daughter. Have you ever thought of that?" Since this came out peevish, Queen Elixia softened it by adding, "I ask that you share your thoughts, chancellor. You are so talented in discerning the subtleties of these humans."

"Unfortunately, we did have an incident a few years back with a siren roaming the campus, binding young men, so I had Paul check. There is no spell cast between Logan and Brigit. From either side," Bandemer reassured her.

"Buy why? Why a human?" cried Elixia, frustrated and befuddled.

"They simply work well together," said Bandemer. "Logan is reserved, a thoughtful type, slow to make a decision. He lives in his head overly much. Prone to introspection. The boy is one of these humans who needs another to galvanize him into action. Your daughter provides that spark."

"He's using her? Why I'll—" but Queen Elixia's threat was stopped by Bandemer who said, "Your daughter has a quick intelligence but also a temper to match. She acts too hastily at times. So the two temper each other. I've found their partnership intriguing as it sets a good model for how fae and humans can work together."

"Working partnerships are all fine and good. I understand that. Why else would I have come here to this symposium of yours? After what we've discovered I don't think your symposium is going to be much of a success in fostering these types of alliances."

"The week is only half over," said Bandemer, unconcerned about Elixia's comment.

"I do not trust humans." Elixia, paused, taking a sip of wine before speaking again, her eyes looking off to where the city lights were glowing below them. The Kiburg sat on a hill and it gave a good view of Geheimetür. "A bondmate of mine got involved with a human. It did not end well."

"Relationships of any kind are hazardous."

Caught up in thinking about the past, Queen Elixia continued as if the chancellor had not spoken. "He was also a bard. With that sweet tongue and charismatic personality they are so well known to have. She adored him. As did we all."

She wiped a tear of remembrance from her cheek and told Bandemer, "I do not want Brigit fooled into making a decision that will destroy her life."

"Be at ease," Bandemer assured her. "I have a long experience with college students. They often fall into romantic entanglements, but after graduation, it doesn't survive the real world. Only those who are truly committed make it to the pair-bonding ceremony. The likelihood that —"

Elixia interrupted him, hopeful, "You do not think they are serious about each other?"

Bandemer sidestepped that question. Instead, he called over his shoulder to his Doppelgänger, "What do you think, Paul? You've been quiet over there hiding in the bushes. You've seen them more than I have."

Paul pulled his attention away from one of the topiaries that marked off the alfresco dining area. He said very carefully, "The two work well together, and have a strong friendship. But partnerships don't necessarily turn into deeper relationships. "

"See," Brigit's mother exclaimed, "even your Doppelgänger tiptoes around answering my question."

"I agree, your majesty. Speak plainly, Paul. I know you are not one for romance, but I am also curious about what you think of our dryad and her bard."

Paul appeared uncomfortable with the question. He cleared his throat and finally said, "They seem to like each other."

Chancellor Bandemer burst into laughter. It might have been the exhausting day, or the wine she had consumed, but Queen Elixia soon caught his mood. She giggled until she was wiping tears from her eyes.

Bandemer regained control first. "Like? We are talking about something else, *mon ami*. You've seen them. Watched them. Is there chemistry between them?"

At Paul's puzzled look, Queen Elixia told him impatiently, "Those in love stand closer together. They look only at each other when other beings are in the room. They finish each other's sentences. Smile more when the other is present—"

"Well, if those are the signs," Paul said reluctantly, "I guess my answer would be yes."

"Ah, young love," said Bandemer with a reminiscent air. To Elixia, he held up a finger, saying, "That doesn't always become a marriage and a baby carriage, as the humans joke."

Queen Elixia stopped him by waving a dismissive hand. She didn't want to discuss this any further. Dissatisfied, she set the plate down on the cafe table. Seeing her unhappiness, Bandemer decided to change the subject to the bigger problem.

"Queen Summerblossom, Torfa's ruler, had sent me the information weeks ago about Selena and Ambrosia's courts. Through Paul and my other spies, we've discovered five courts are now dissolved into the Vastness."

At his news, Queen Elixia's skin became more gray than green. "We have evacuated to prevent such a problem happening in our own court. My consort, Ladislas, removed everyone to his sister's kingdom for the time being."

Bandemer refilled both of their wine glasses. Neither mentioned the obvious fact that land-law tied Elixia's life to her court's health and that of its Elder. If the Elder died, so did the queen. In turn, Bandemer's sworn oath bound him to Elixia, putting his own life at risk. She still didn't know why he had done that.

"You didn't have to swear your life to help my court. I already had your word that you would assist me."

Bandemer didn't reply directly to Elixia's comment, saying instead, "Tell me more about what is happening at your court."

"Each moon turning we see more evidence of the disease harming our grove. We've followed all the healer's recommendations. Made potions, cast spells, and even burned the diseased trees, but nothing stopped the spread of this plague. Still, we thought the worst of the damage was contained. But three moons back, we found damage in new areas of the grove, very close to our Elder."

"Do you think a human caused this?"

Elixia sighed. "I do not like them, but I don't see how. The link seems nebulous at best. We discourage contact with the human lands. The only human who has visited my court since the killer of my bondmate was Logan. While I do not like the boy, I do not see how he could have done it. He was with us only a short time."

Paul asked, "What of this other bard you mentioned? The killer and thief? What does he look like?"

"He is not anyone here at the symposium, that I'm sure," said Queen Elixia firmly. "Though it has been long since I saw him, he had a smile you would not forget. It was long ago—I doubt he still lives."

Paul disagreed. "A human in the Perilous Realm ages at a different rate, even if they return to the human lands. Also,

I believe that bards, due to their peculiar brand of human magic, age more slowly."

For the first time, the queen became visibly frightened.

"If he is alive, I can well believe that he would destroy the Perilous Realm," said Queen Elixia. She swallowed more wine before setting the glass down on the table with a hand that trembled. "He envied the fae, while also hating us. Equal parts greedy desire for power, and contempt for those who held it."

Elixia licked her lips nervously. "His trial for the murder of my sister went against him. The bone harp told the story of how he strangled her, threw her body into the lake. There was no doubt he was guilty of the crime, for all bone harps play true."

Paul asked another question, "Was your sister a pureblood fae like yourself?"

"We shared the same mother, but she had a human father. A passing stranger. You know how these things go. A fae can't bathe naked in a sacred stream without a human thinking he's desperately in love with her. Those affairs are short lived. I wish my sister's relationship had been."

"Caught and convicted. How did he escape your retribution?" asked Bandemer, in a neutral voice.

"Only through the duplicity of another female did he escape. A harpy. Despised by many, she fell for the first sweet words she heard. She believed herself in love, and removed him from his prison. And gave him the cursed instrument so I cannot even lay my sister's body at peace."

"A love triangle?"

Queen Elixia replied with contempt, "The man loves no one but himself. He left his accomplice behind to be executed."

"So what was his justification for committing such an act?" inquired Paul.

"He thought —." Queen Elixia waved her hand at them, turning her head away to gaze over the lights of Geheimetür, as she said, "It was ridiculous! He thought he would replace his bond partner with me. That I would put aside Ladislas and welcome him as my consort. The man was delusional."

"Perhaps he interpreted your flirting as the favor of a queen? Only to discover later, he was but a plaything?"

Elixia neither confirmed nor denied Paul's summation of events.

"You think there is a connection between this old story and current events, Paul?" Bandemer asked.

"Queen Summerblossom believes that every vanished court had an item stolen by a human. Each possession had a link to the human lands and was a personal object of the queen. Your harp is from the bones of a half-human woman. There is nothing more personal than a relative."

Bandemer snapped his fingers, "Contagious magic. Your relative shares your blood. What can be done to the harp, can be done to you. If he had the power or could access someone that does, it could explain the attack upon your grove."

"You think it is due to me that my court is dying? That he has sent this foul disease to the Elder through the bones of my dead sister!" cried Elixia.

"Grudges between humans and the fae are expected. But this goes far beyond just an affront to dignity or purse. This entire situation stinks of a vendetta. Something all very personal."

Chapter Twenty-Three
Zwischenzug

J t was early in the morning when Queen Elixia was escorted off the roof by Chancellor Bandemer. After they left, Brigit emerged from the topiary on the Kiburg rooftop.

Paul, who was putting dishes on a tray, told her, "Those who hide in the shrubbery to eavesdrop seldom hear flattery."

"I guess I owe you a Debt since you didn't reveal my presence to my mother or Bandemer."

"I'll exchange the Debt for a word of advice. You need to stop acting like a child."

Nothing incited a behavior like a statement condemning it. However, Brigit managed to control herself, saying tightly,

"If I wasn't treated like an infant, I wouldn't have to snoop for information. When I saw you sneak away after Logan woke up, I knew you were up to something."

"Do not assume that the chancellor did not know you were listening."

"What if he did know? I'm investigating matters that could destroy my home. I shall do as I please."

Brigit was about to leave, when Paul stopped her by repeating the Bane of the Black Dog, "The hound of death hunts a noble prize; When the glass turns, who falls, so others rise? You cannot stop a Bane no matter how hard you try. It will find a target."

"So I should be reconciled to this?" snapped Brigit, sweeping a hand around her. "To my mother's dying and the loss of our court? What wise counsel, Paul. Perhaps you should look after the chancellor. From what I just heard, he's tied himself to our fate."

"Don't worry about Bandemer," Paul assured her. "He never gambles unless the dice are loaded."

"Hm, how comforting."

"A further word of advice—"

"More advice? I'd sooner eat compost."

"The Black Dog. It's the key. Discover the meaning of its riddle, and you have the solution. Prophecies are always a puzzle and they turn around on themselves. The dragon eats its tail."

Brigit struggled with the desire to tell Paul to jump off the Kiburg's roof. She managed to choke out, "How informative," before leaving.

Brigit trotted down the stairs of the Kiburg, deep in thought. Emerging into the lobby, she bumped into one of the potential suitors her mother kept urging her to talk to — Serio.

"Sorry, I was in a rush," she apologized for accidentally bumping into his arm. Her emotional storm had blinded her to what was in front of her.

"*Sem problemas,*" he replied in Portuguese.

At least her mom had good taste, for he was a good-looking guy. Serio could have starred as the hero in one of those daytime soaps that Jib liked to watch. But Brigit had no time for glossy black hair styled in perfect waves or deep brown eyes. Or a swoon-worthy smile of bright white teeth.

However, Brigit did have time to ask questions and investigate a subject vital to her.

"If you could spare a moment, Prince Serio?"

"For beauty such as yourself, I have more than a moment."

Comments like these were exactly why Brigit was finished with court life. All this posturing and flattery made her want to gag. Why couldn't these guys be more like Logan? Talk to a girl like she was their equal and not something needing false praise laid on with a trowel.

"Perhaps we could talk in one of the meeting rooms?" suggested Brigit.

Serio readily agreed, and after searching the ground floor, they found one room unlocked and deserted. Sitting down across from each other, Brigit asked, "Dr. Stuart was in your neck of the forest last summer, wasn't he?"

"*Si*, the doctor was. He reviewed the results of an initiative that he and his team implemented some time back. It was a great success."

"Can you tell me more about it?" asked Brigit. "I've read his other research projects but the only paper I saw on this one didn't go in depth."

"He plans on publishing a paper next year as a five-year study. Your mother tells me you are studying botany. Is that why you are interested?"

"My mother, the queen," Brigit reminded Serio of Elixia's rank, "and our court are thinking of having Dr. Stuart work on a special project in the Perilous Realm. I'm conducting a background check."

"Ah. He is a very competent scientist even without all the glamour attached to his public persona."

"You've had dealings with him?"

"A few. I am not a scientist myself," Serio said humbly. "My position is more of an adviser. We are interested in protecting the ecosystem where my court crosses into the human lands."

"Can you tell me more about the project? And Stuart?"

"Dr. Stuart likes to be on stage, holding the mic, the one in control. You may have noticed his ego already. It is hard to miss."

Serio smiled; Brigit grimaced.

"Yeah, I saw a bit of that. Wanted to control the crowd when my bondmate, Logan, was giving the card demonstration."

"Exactly. If you let him have the limelight, I have found Dr. Stuart an intelligent human to work with. You may do the work but let him take the credit and all will go smoothly."

"Hm. Okay." Brigit didn't like the sound of that but if it was necessary in order to save her court she could do that.

"The work he did for us was quite valuable. In the human lands, a vine became troublesome. It was initially imported by humans from another country to use as erosion control, where the forest was decimated. It spread rapidly, and became invasive, destroying native habitat. The problem was removing it without using herbicides that would harm the surrounding native plants."

"That's interesting. My mother is worried about using human chemicals in our fae court. How did Dr. Stuart accomplish this without using poison?"

Serio pulled up his phone and flipped through some screens. "You can read about it here—" He was about to hand Brigit his phone, but she waved his offer away.

"Sorry, my fae magic likes to drain cell phone batteries at a touch. Best if you just explain it to me."

"He used a specialized bacteria, and gene-spliced it. It was released into the plant. The more the plants grew, the more it replicated its own destruction."

"Sounds like a risk. Why didn't the bacteria not move onto other plants in the region?"

"Genetic coding tied it to the plant we wanted removed."

"Hm. Can you email a link to those articles to my

bondmate, Logan?"

"Sure."

Brigit dictated the email to Serio. She wanted Logan to print out the papers and bring it to her.

"Thanks, Serio. I appreciate it."

"Does this makes a Debt between us?"

These guys —! Brigit gave an exasperated sigh.

"A small Debt. Unless your information proves invaluable or something."

It wasn't until the afternoon when Logan had a chance to drop by the Kiburg and meet Brigit. He handed her the packet of print offs of the research she had emailed to him.

"Thanks, Logan," she told him, taking the bulky envelope. "It's some research Dr. Stuart did in the rainforest. I wanted to take time to read it before I meet up with him."

"The scientist that might help with the grove?"

"Hope so."

This close, Logan couldn't help himself. He asked, "When will you be coming home?"

Brigit gave him a lopsided grin. "As soon as I can. If you think being here with my mother is fun, ugh, think again. I'm being smothered."

"Tell me about it," Logan muttered in agreement.

"I have a lot to talk with you about," she confided. "Things are going badly at home with the grove. Everyone in the court was moved to my aunt's kingdom. My mother and Jib hid that from me. Who knows what else they haven't told me."

"Could you go home? Visit the grove yourself?"

"I thought about it but mother has forbidden it. And they watch me like a hawk. Even now, her bodyguard over there is staring daggers at me."

Logan turned to look where she indicated. The guard, wearing a black t-shirt, jeans, and combat boots, turned away. Probably trying to disguise his interest in Brigit.

"Amateur," sniffed Brigit. She turned back to Logan. "Anyway, thanks for the this. Dr. Stuart has copies of my research and we've been discussing the next step to take."

During their conversation, the two closed the space between them, talking in lower voices. Looking at Brigit, the sweep of her black eyelashes concealing her downcast eyes, and the curve of her cheek, it was hard to resist touching her.

Logan cleared his throat and said, "I wanted to talk with you about the Black Dog. The Bane it gave when you were with your mom. I think we could approach it a different way —"

"Well, do I spy two little love birds?" Torfa's appearance and comment made them both jump away from each other. Brigit clasped the envelope packet to her chest, and Logan stuck his hands into his jean pockets.

"Ha ha, Torfa," said Brigit, sarcastically. "Hilarious. I know a beer hall in Geheimetür that has an open mic for comedy on Saturday nights. I'll give you a flyer about it. You'll bring the house down."

Brigit's sarcasm didn't seem to inflict any damage on

Torfa's ego. He leaned a shoulder casually against the wall, careful that his rack of antlers didn't bump the paneling. The woodland prince gave Logan a curious once-over stare. "I'm beginning to think I know why your mother is seeking a match for you."

"My mother was matchmaking for me when I started to crawl. She's a queen. Always moving her subjects across a game board only she sees. I'm just one of those pieces. But unlike my sisters, I refuse to play."

"And such a delicious game token, though. You certainly gained Serio's interest. He couldn't stop talking about you over breakfast."

Logan's bard sense showed him that Torfa's words were true. That this fae, Serio, really did like Brigit.

"Serio had some useful information for me," said Brigit. "He forwarded it to Logan for me."

Before Torfa could saying anything else, Brigit took Logan's hand and moved them further away from the fae prince. To fae, who kept each other at a safe distance to prevent attacks, the meaning was clear: she trusted Logan.

"Logan is my bondmate, Torfa. You and Serio are not. Never forget that." She gave Logan's hand a squeeze, and kissed him on the cheek. Her perfume of wildflowers teasing his nose. "I've got to run before mother's guard comes over and starts punching your face to a pulp, Torfa."

Brigit ran off, casting Logan a smile and wave.

Torfa snapped open the Japanese fan he was holding. "She seems to pay you favor, human, unlike her mother."

"I don't want to date her mother."

For once, Logan was thankful for his mother's appearance. She was walking across the lobby and waved at him to hurry, or they would miss their bus.

Bane of Hounds

Chapter Twenty-Four
Protected Pass Pawn

L ogan loved his mother, but sometimes it was hard to like her. For hours, he heard about her thoughts on how strange the fae beings she encountered at the Kiburg were.

"That young man almost looked human. If you could forget seeing the antlers and pointed ears. Is he one of your new friends here?"

"Only someone I know. Not a friend."

Taking a bus to meet up with the boat tour on the river, Sarah commented about the quaintness of Geheimetür, and how backward the town was.

"How bizarre that they don't allow regular cars

downtown. Using a car would be more convenient than these buses."

"They don't want the pollution."

"But horse-drawn carriages for deliveries down the main street? How ridiculous."

"We have a town like this at home. Mackinac Island."

"That's for tourism."

Whenever Logan challenged her world-view, she always had a ready answer for him. What was more exhausting was the never-ending questions about who his friends were, what classes he was taking, and how they pertained to his degree.

"A headache, dear?" asked Sarah as they exited down the ramp from the boat tour.

"Somewhat."

"I don't think you've been feeling well since that Incident." She never referred to his collapse after the card-truth game as anything but the Incident with a capital I.

Logan knew she was right, which was irksome in itself. Still, he didn't plan on telling her about the lightheaded episodes of vertigo he sometimes experienced. Or the strange dreams. If he did, she'd start in again about him transferring from LOTTOS to a stateside university.

"Working on a paper due next week. Late hours."

Sarah said brightly, "Your father is coming down for the last day. He wanted to meet up with you before we have to head home again."

Oh, Logan bet he did! Logan was sure that his father recently had many a late phone call from his mother filling his ears about their son. He'd hear something from his dad about him staying (or not) at Leopold Otto.

"I think I'll head home early tonight if that is all right with you, mom?"

"Sure, dear. You don't want low grades on your transcript."

Transcript as in transferring. Dad would be here soon. He was usually sensible and would listen. He talked sense. Mostly.

They hugged goodbye, and Logan left as quickly as he could. The apartment was lonely without Brigit, but he had the dog to look after. Besides, if he put on a home improvement show, the brownie would join him.

Feeling better the next day, Logan set up to meet Emma Walker at a bakery located on the corner opposite the main entrance to the campus. Logan became friends with Em last year when she hacked the library database to get Granite some test answers. Emma's actions had resulted in an adventure that exposed a monster destroying the books at the Abbey library.

Per usual, Logan found Emma already hunched over her laptop, scanning the screen when he entered.

"Hey, Em."

"Just a sec." While Emma finished up what she was doing, Logan went to the counter to pay for a Brez'n, or a soft pretzel, before sitting down at the table.

Emma's long bangs flopped over one eye. She still had

her hair shaved on the sides but her crest was purple. She pushed her glasses up her nose and peering closer at the screen, murmured, "Huh. Gotcha."

Since the reason Logan met Emma was over her hacking into the library, he didn't want to know what her exclamation of victory meant. He pretended to ignore it, by looking idly out the window. From here you could see the clock tower.

"Done." She closed the laptop lid and gave Logan her full attention.

For a moment, he thought about introducing her to his mother. Emma Walker was one of his few human friends at Leopold Otto. But the colorful hair, black leather jacket, and ear piercings would probably irk Sarah.

"I need a favor."

"If I can." She pulled out the flash drive from her laptop. In her hand, it changed to Obake, the dwarf flying squirrel. The tsukumogami spirit from Japan was Emma's constant companion. In squirrel-form it was an adorable little monster.

"How's it hanging, Logan?" said Obake.

"Just ignore that," cautioned Emma. "It's trying to learn slang so it doesn't sound so robotic. Now it sounds fifty years out of date."

"Uh. Okay," said Logan, but he did tell the tsukumogami, "I'm doing fine, Obake."

"Why do I have the feeling you are distracted?" chittered the dwarf flying squirrel. It examined Logan with black eyes the size of peas as Logan felt the prickle of its magic examining him. "Embarrassed? Is it about the favor you want to ask? Why can't Brigit help? Does the favor concern Brigit? Do you want us to do something illegal? Will it be exciting?"

Its quick-fire questioning made Logan laugh as he told Em, "I see training Obake to restrain its curiosity isn't working out so well."

Emma reached up and held the flying squirrel up to her face, eye-to-eye. "As you can see, it is still a busybody."

The tsukumogami often angered or embarrassed people by revealing secrets. Logan didn't hold it against the squirrel, for he knew Obake couldn't fight its nature. Being an ancient Japanese key, later inhabited by a spirit, it was under a compulsion to unlock things, just as Logan recognized truth from lie without trying to do so.

Last year, Logan discovered that his bard talent provided some shielding of his thoughts. This latent bard talent was probably the only thing that saved him from the tsukumogami telling everyone about Logan kissing Brigit.

"To answer your question, Brigit and I recently found a lost dog. A puppy, really. But both of us are tied up. She's with her mom at the Kiburg attending a university symposium," Logan explained. "A week-long function at the castle that's supposed to bring the fae and humans together."

Emma asked after what she felt was the most important, "Brigit's mom is here? Oh, boy."

"Yeah, and so is mine. She's also staying at the Kiburg."

At Em's alarmed expression, Logan grimaced. "Yes, it is

that bad. But they leave in a few days."

"You've got a dog at your place? I can't imagine Jib playing nice with a dog," said Em skeptically.

"No joke. Jib is pouting. The brownie feeds the dog; I take him out with me during my morning run. But I need someone to come by in the afternoon and take him out for a potty trip. I'm not getting back until late in the evening most days."

"Sure, I can do that. Probably can't go over until after lunch. Will that work?"

"I can't be choosy." Logan leaned closer, with a confidential air, as he told Em and Obake how they found the dog. "Brigit figures he's too traumatized to tell us what happened. Who hurt him. We do know his name: Devlin."

"Maybe Obake could discover that for you?"

"Maybe we can try that together at a later date. Right now I'm still winning his trust. I don't want him thinking he's under attack. He gets enough of that from Jib."

"But what about Logan's secret?" demanded Obake, as it scampered up Em's arm to ride on her shoulder. "I want to know what it is! Let's discuss that."

"Maybe you should just tell Obake before he drives us both crazy with begging to know it? Don't worry, Logan. Unlike Obake, I can keep a secret."

"Uh."

"C'mon Logan, you know Obake won't stop demanding to know. It's like living with a crazy hamster. Just spill it. I promise I won't laugh. Did you wear mismatch socks or something?"

"No, I, uh—"

"Not at all like you to be tongue-tied. By chance, is this about Brigit?"

Logan flushed. "Yes."

"Fight? Is that the real reason she's at the Kiburg and not at home?" When Logan didn't answer, Emma smirked. "So its finally happened, huh? You two are an item. Are you going to make it official?"

"Not official. Yet. I mean, it was only a kiss. Nothing more."

Logan's blush deepened. He wasn't used to speaking about his love life to anyone, let alone a short girl with glasses who he considered a little sister.

"Sure, mate, keep telling yourself that."

"We haven't talked it over yet. I don't know where I stand."

"You don't? Why not? I think it's rather obvious."

Logan toyed with his food, looking down at the remains of his pretzel.

"Maybe it is to you, but until Brigit tells me—"

"Ha! Try maybe to everyone. By the way, I need to know the date of the kiss. Granite and I had a bet on it." At Logan's outraged expression, Emma laughed. "Look, you two were living and working together. Hanging out twenty-four-seven. What did you think everyone was going to believe?"

"You can have friends of the opposite sex, you know."

"Sure you can, Logan. You and I are friends. Granite and I are friends. But we don't make eyes at each other, or go out of our way to touch each other. You two finish each other's sentences for crying out loud."

Em gave an exasperated shrug that caused Obake to grip her jacket with both paws so it wouldn't fall. "Granite thought you'd already sealed the deal, but he was thinking like himself. Do you know I had to set up a spreadsheet for him to keep track of his girlfriends? Took me hours of data entry."

Logan asked doubtfully, "So you think it happened just because we hang out together? Familiarity and all that?"

Emma raised her eyebrows at Logan's statement. "I have my thoughts, but what are yours? Because all that really matters is what you and Brigit think."

"I wish I could talk with her. Get things out in the open. Brigit can't use a phone or a computer. It's not like I can text, call, or send an email. Every time I see her, Brigit is with her mother, the chancellor, or Paul."

Emma picked up Obake from her shoulder and started playing with the flying squirrel as she talked. She rotated her hands, one-by-one, under each other, so Obake could jump from palm to palm.

"You could send her some flowers. That's clear-cut and states your intentions. Dating is your intention, right?"

"Yes. That's an idea, but Brigit doesn't like cut plants. Though she does love potted plants. She brought the one in the hallway of my apartment inside to live with us."

"Generally, I'm the last to give love advice, but I'd recommend doing something. Nowadays, if you don't respond within seconds, people think no one cares about them. Blame technology. Everybody does."

"Speaking of technology," Logan said, glad to change the subject, "How's the work at the library going? Is it helping out with the budget?"

Having parents barely able to support her at Leopold Otto was why Emma had hacked the library in the first place. Now she was working to restore the database and improve the library's security.

"Oh, that tight-wad Bandemer set up a shady scholarship program. I'm the only recipient. But it only pays my tuition fees. Paul and Burkhalter were pretty angry about Bandemer's penny pinching, but I told them to drop it. I'll find other ways to pay for meals and my apartment."

"Nothing — you know—?"

"Illegal?" asked Emma, smirking again. "No, nothing dodgy. Just some small freelance jobs, all legit, that Paul finds for me. Like your website for being student liaisons. He squeezed some money out of the LOTTOS budget to compensate me for that."

"I know I've said it before, but the website is a life-line. We were going crazy with fae creatures showing up, who knows when. And human students weren't any better."

"I'm glad it's working for you. Paul found the money because I put something in the back end of the system to send him IP records of anyone harassing you two."

"Oh," said Logan, unpleasantly surprised. "So that's the real reason why the late-night knocks stopped. I thought it was because we came up with a good system to help everyone."

"Paul only interferes with the real whackos."

"That sound's ominous."

"It's no big deal," Emma said, even while Logan's bard sense pinged it as a half truth. "He lets them know what behavior is expected from a student at Leopold Otto. Sorts them out. I'd be thankful, not worried about it. Some of these fae think they can do what they want to humans and ignore the law."

"I guess," Logan said hesitantly. "But don't tell Brigit. She wouldn't like Paul's interference, even if it was well intentioned."

"Our dryad does have it in for the poor guy. Can't think why. Paul advocates for her all the time to Bandemer. I think he feels fatherly toward her."

Fatherly? What a strange idea.

"Maybe that's the problem?" mused Logan. "She distrusts authority figures. Being a Doppelgänger, his power puts her at a disadvantage. She can't feel equal to him and I know it unsettles her."

It was hard to be with friends and not gossip. Logan didn't want Brigit to accuse him of going behind her back. At the same time, he didn't want anyone to see Brigit in a poor light.

"Yeah, I've noticed that," said Em. "Even Granite acts weird when Paul is mentioned. It's why I don't discuss what Paul's fae sept is with anyone."

By sept, Emma meant the various clans that the fae identified themselves as. Jib was a púca, part of the Trickster sept; the brownie was from The Kindly Ones, which helped humans; and Brigit and Granite were Naturals, a sept close to human in appearance, that was closely tied to nature.

"By the way, have you seen that new face that Bandemer gave Paul?" asked Emma.

"Actually, no. As a bard, I see Paul as he really is."

"So does Obake. I wish I could see him as a wyvern. Celia said he was gorgeous. But, me? I see whatever illusion he slaps on his face. Every time he comes by the library, Burkhalter does a double-take. You can tell she senses something odd about him. Like she's trying to figure him out."

"How is Frau Burkhalter doing? I've only seen her at a distance this semester. I noticed she was out of her arm sling."

"She can't type for very long or lift anything. Still going every week to physical therapy for the damage that monster did, but Burkhalter doesn't let it slow her down. After killing that book-eating monster, she's become a hero to her staff."

"That's good to hear." Logan looked out the window, thinking of Burkhalter being swallowed by the thing from Outside that had devoured books, removed Paul's magic for disguise, and had come to the attention of the griffins. "By the way, have you heard from Celia?"

"A few emails. Sounds like her mother and sisters are keeping the naiad pretty busy at their spa." Emma squinted suspiciously at Logan. "Is there a reason for the question? I thought last year you rather liked her. You're making me feel as paranoid as Brigit."

The problem with being a bard is that Logan could give

her a lie, and taste like he was about to vomit. Or he could say a half-truth, which would only be moderately nasty on his tongue. The easiest route was to stay silent, which incurred no penalty.

However, he could tell when Emma lied to him. It was an imbalance of power, and as a friend, he tried not to give her lies of any sort.

"I did have a bit of a crush on Celia at the time. Nothing more. But I do consider her a friend, and Brigit learned at the symposium about a threat to the Perilous Realm courts. I want to make sure Celia and her family are safe."

"What type of threat?"

"Humans take personal things from the queens and use it against them."

Logan didn't add the information about the Elders dying. He didn't want to deceive Emma, but the Elders seemed to be a holy thing for the fae. Brigit had cautioned him about discussing it.

"Hm. Celia hasn't mentioned anything like that," Em said. "They do a lot of business with humans, though— healing services, massage, cosmetic Glamour. But from what she's said, that side of things is run by her sister group. Her mother, the queen, is out of the picture mostly. Retired was my impression."

"I'll send her an email later today about it. Better safe than sorry."

Hearing the bells of the university clock, Emma started packing away her laptop and its cord. She put the tsukumogami on her shoulder where it grabbed her ear lobe and changed into an earring that was an ancient Japanese key.

Slinging the bag's strap over her head, she told Logan, "Hate to cut and run, but I've got to get back to the salt mines at the library."

"No problem. I'll tell the brownie you're coming. She'll let you in."

At the door, Emma paused and said thoughtfully, "Look Logan, it seems to me that Brigit likes you. But she's fae and that path could be dangerous. Especially since she's a princess. You don't want to make a mistake—"

Logan's mother would have recognized the expression on her son's face. Logan was not going to be budged from what he had set his heart upon.

"Don't worry about me. I know what I'm doing."

Logan ignored the sour taste of the half-truth.

Bane of Hounds

Chapter Twenty-Five
Discovered Attack

Logan must have fallen asleep on the sofa again, for one of those terrifying dreams came to haunt him. He was a child again, holding his mother's hand. She pulled him along, admonishing him, "We mustn't be late!"

Trotting beside her, Logan felt his arm tugged again. In response, he looked up to see a hazy blur of a face. Was this his mother? Suddenly doubtful, his step slowed, making him trip. The voice floating around him urged him forward, "We can't be late."

"Late for what?" he lisped. In the dream Logan was young, maybe about seven?

"The fun fair."

As dreams do, the situation changed without explanation. Now, he was on the spinning cup ride, his hands too short to grasp the safety rail. Instead, he desperately tried to wrap his arms around his mother as the cup pitched them around the bowl.

She was laughing hysterically, and Logan clung tighter. His little body was slung against the side of the cup as it turned, jerked, and spun again. Turn, jerk, spin. Lights flashed in front of his eyes, blurring his vision. Logan felt sick to his stomach.

The only thing holding him in place was his lifeline, his mother. Still, it wasn't enough, for his hands were too small and he couldn't grip her hard enough. He slid along the slick plastic of the seat, slamming his head and shoulder against the inside of the amusement ride.

"Having fun, dearest?"

He was falling, in that dizzying way unique to the Perilous Realm. He reached out, trying to grip anything that would stop his descent. His hands slapped against a slick wall as he continued to drop.

Logan opened his eyes to find he was in a hall of mirrors. The maze of reflected images was himself. They weren't twisted like a true hall of mirrors but were standard reflected images of Logan. But none were the Logan of today. Instead, it was him at different ages, younger and older. Some had faces filled with arrogance, and others appeared sad.

Drawn to one, Logan reached out to touch it. His fingers meet the other's. Instead of feeling the smooth surface he expected from the glass, Logan felt the warmth of skin. His fingertips merged with the mirror's.

Instinctively Logan pulled back, causing the image in the mirror to lurch forward. Their faces now nose to nose, and Logan felt images start to flip through his mind, showing a timeline that had never happened—one where his mother, despite medication and counseling, never recovered. One where he never went to Snowdon. One where he went to a university in his home state.

It was all a truth that could have been. Could have happened. But never did.

Overcome, he pulled back harder. The image in the glass gave him a solemn look before fading away. The glass darkened to black and showed no reflection.

Dream Logan rubbed his eyes, trying to make sense of it all.

Hesitantly, he reached out to another mirror. The same thing repeated. His fingers entwined with the image and Logan felt another rush of knowledge. Another timeline where his grandmother never came to visit that summer long ago, and where his cousin Evelyn died in a car accident.

Not true. This wasn't true.

Walking through the maze, touching each image, Logan discovered another story to tell, another divergent path his life could have taken. It was like working a jigsaw puzzle—with each piece, you saw the complete picture of the sky with clouds take shape.

Eventually, Logan stood alone, surrounded by nothing but black mirrors.

Suddenly, the mirrors vanished, changing into trees. But not just any trees, these were the ones Logan remembered seeing at Brigit's court. Logan recognized their strange shiny white tree trunks. Over his head, silver leaves moved in the breeze, making a chiming language few could understand.

The trees, sparkling like frost crystals, parted to make a path. Logan started down it, his shoes crunching on the brittle grass under his feet. Looking down, he saw it wasn't grass, but dead leaves his shoes were smashing.

Suddenly, Logan understood what the leaves were weeping.

"Save us. Save them. Save her."

Her mother asleep, Brigit was on the couch still reading the report on Dr. Stuart's research when she heard a scratch at the door. The bodyguard on duty was getting up to answer it, but Brigit waved him back and did it herself.

"Hey, what are you doing here?" Brigit whispered.

"Couldn't sleep. Can we talk?" Logan asked.

"I'd love to get out of here. Let me grab my coat."

Like kids sneaking out, Brigit and Logan went down the stairs and out the back door of the Kiburg, near the pool. Outdoors, the cold crispness on her face made Brigit give an involuntary startled gasp. Logan handed her his gloves, and she drew them on.

She told him, "I really do need to buy my own pair."

"At least you have a good coat now," said Logan observing her jacket.

"It's pretty cool looking isn't it? Magic makes it look like leather, but it's really just wool. My mom bought it for me."

Brigit lead them, and they walked side by side, down a slope.

"I'll be glad when this week is over."

Brigit understood what Logan wasn't saying. That he wanted things back to a normal routine, without parents. She heartily agreed and asked, "How's your mom doing?"

"She's fine, physically seems to be okay. But she's a high-maintenance mom, and needs a lot of attention. She means well, I know. And I love her—"

"But she's always giving advice. Always in your business. Everything you say is weighed and judged. Says she trusts you, while at the same time thinks you are making a mistake with your life?"

Brigit's list got a reluctant chuckle from Logan.

"That's about right. I think I've seen every tourist hot-spot in all of Geheimetür by now."

"You'll have to show me a few. I doubt I've seen any, unless they're trees. When does your mom go home?"

"The day after tomorrow. But first, my dad is coming down from Berlin. He wants to talk to me."

"Oh. Hm. Dads. She's determined to get you to leave Leopold Otto, isn't she?"

"I won't leave. Don't worry."

Their boots crunched over the dried grass as they entered the parklike grounds of the Kiburg's gardens. They met a sidewalk that would take them deeper into the maze of hedges that was a feature of the formal gardens.

Brigit decided to change the subject. "Have you seen the maestro since he played cards with you?"

"No. I don't have another meeting with him until next week. I went by his office, but he hasn't been there during his office hours."

"Sounds like he's avoiding you."

"That's what I thought."

One thing about Logan, he wasn't the type of guy who would push himself onto a girl. Not like Torfa. On the other hand, a girl sometimes liked having a bit of pushiness. If he wasn't going to take the initiative, Brigit would. She linked her arm with his and pulled herself closer against him. Logan slowed his long stride to match hers.

"Why do you think he took over that card test? What was he trying to do?"

Logan didn't reply for about five strides. He said slowly, "I've mentioned it before, but I don't think the maestro wants to improve my violin playing. Our sessions never cover technique or advice on what I could do. It's all about these stories and interpreting them."

"Hmm, I remember you telling me that." Wearing a thick coat and gloves made the chill outside worth tolerating. Especially if that meant Brigit got private time with him.

"I think he's teaching me lessons about truth. There's the simple truth about whether someone is lying or not. It's why Bandemer wanted a simple test that the audience could understand. But a person who thinks they are telling the truth can still be lying."

"Because they say something they believed was true?"

"Right. However, Géza wanted me to predict the truth of an event that hadn't happened yet—or might not happen at all."

"Drawing or not drawing the card. Got it."

"I've never done anything like that before. I didn't think it was possible."

"Precognition—future vision—I thought that was only a power given to Cassandras."

"Cassandras?"

"It's a fae sept, and one of the few that both fae and humans can have. It's the ability to know the future. Like the Greek priestess cursed by Apollo to tell prophecies. Like the banshee."

"So the Black Dog is a Cassandra?"

"No. Devlin is a Harbinger."

"This is confusing!"

Brigit's laugh caused powder puffs in the frosty air.

"Harbingers only give news of a certain type: Dooms. Their power is limited to their need to provide one specific pronouncement, unasked, and without control. It's why the Black Dog can speak his Bane while he is still struggling to speak about what happened to him. But Cassandras can see the future on demand, although not always clearly. Ask them a question about anything, and they can give an answer."

"Okay. I see. I think I get it."

The two stopped in front of a fountain. Since winter was approaching it didn't contain water. The cupids riding the dolphins were draped with evergreen garlands and twinkle lights.

"The more you're around us," said Brigit confidently, "the more you'll get the hang of it."

"Will I be hanging around with you?"

Brigit turned to face Logan. His arms wrapped around her waist and their jacket fronts brushed against each other.

"I want you to."

"But what about Serio? And all those other fae guys? And your mom definitely does not like me. Or your dad for that matter."

"I make my own decisions. Don't you?"

In the dark, under a waning moon, Logan's blue eyes appeared darker, almost without color. He bent down to her, his forehead resting against hers as he said, "May I have this kiss, your highness?"

Brigit's response was to rise on her toes and put her warm lips against his. These kisses were as good as the first ones, especially when they didn't have a dog to interrupt them.

They only broke apart when Brigit rocked back on her heels, unable to stay on tiptoe. Smiling, she told him, "The difference between you and Serio is you don't have to ask my permission. We're bondmates."

Logan picked her up and Brigit wrapped her legs around his waist. She snuggled in as they began to kiss again.

"Do you know how cold it is out here?" demanded Jib, as the cat jumped up to the fountain's rim.

"Go chase some mice, Jib," Brigit told the púca.

Frost on the pumpkin! That cat needed to have a bell and collar on it! This was one of the problems of being a princess. Everyone thought they owned a piece of you. Dating was her business. Not a nosy púca's.

"Are you going to run off and tattle to mother now?" she demanded.

"I am your chaperone," Jib reminded her.

"For the human lands, not for my relationships! I'm a big girl if you hadn't noticed."

With the appearance of the True Beast, Logan's arms started to loosen, and Brigit jumped back down to the ground. At least Logan kept his arm around her shoulders, while she held hers around his waist.

"You two can smoosh your faces together later," meowed Jib. "We have a bigger problem here."

"That I wanted to forget for a while," sniped Brigit. "Thanks for reminding me."

Logan squeezed Brigit and gave her another kiss, a quick warm one, on her temple.

"We have time," he reassured her. "All I needed to know about us, you told me." In a conciliatory gesture, Logan asked Jib, "Do you mean the problem about Brigit's court? About the trees?"

The cat mimicked Logan sarcastically, "Brigit's court? The trees? Of course I do! We need a plan to help Queen Elixia not die!"

"What do you think I've been working on!?" demanded Brigit. If she had a rock in her hand, she would have thrown it at Jib. Perhaps sensing her desire for violence, Logan tightened his grip on her.

"We all want the same thing, Jib. Brigit is working with Dr. Stuart to come up with a way to save the trees."

Logan's comment made Brigit shake her head as she broke from Logan's arms. She put her fists on her hips and said vehemently, "Stuart is not going to save us. If anything, he's the man behind it all. I've been reading a paper of his—he bio-engineered a microorganism that concentrates iron within its cells, in order to kill plants. Iron that kills some fae. A perfect weapon."

Logan tasted the ring of truth of what Brigit said on his tongue.

Jib grew to panther-size and said, "Let's kill him."

Chapter Twenty-Six
Pawn Storm

It took a couple of hours to convince Jib that they couldn't kill Dr. Stuart outright.

"Well, not until we have more proof. Then we'll see," said Brigit.

"But he should dieeeeee!" Jib only stopped yowling when when Brigit told the púca, "If he's guilty he'll be punished, never fear."

"Good," sniffed Jib, its tail angrily lashing back and forth.

"How do you plan on getting proof?" asked Logan, not addressing the possible method of punishment. Sometimes when it came to the fae it was best not to know things. "Tomorrow is the last day of the symposium. We need to catch him before he leaves."

"Is the film crew still here?" asked Brigit.

Jib, who had amused itself by following them around to see the behind-the-scenes action of filming, told her that yes, they were still there. "They have one last set up tomorrow morning. Some interview with the local newspaper that the chancellor wanted them to film."

"Perfect!" Brigit outlined her idea to them, asking Logan. "Do you think Emma will help?"

"I'd think she love to do it. I get the feeling she's getting bored with a life of law and order."

"This guy's arrogance will be his downfall."

After making a call to Emma to see if she would agree to their plan, Brigit gave Logan a quick kiss. "It's so late. I've got to go."

"I know."

But neither of them went. They shared several more hugs and kisses before they separated. Logan to return to his apartment to discuss with Emma the finer points of their plan. Brigit and Jib to return to the Kiburg.

The doorman held the door and Jib, waving its tail in the air, trotted off down to the elevator.

Following him, Brigit passed the hospitality room where Logan had recently recovered. The door was open, and she saw the profile of the Uncanny doctor's beak. She hesitated. The elevator doors opened for Jib, and Brigit told the púca, "Go head. I'll be up in a moment."

She tapped on the open door to get the Uncanny Doctor's attention.

"What can I help you with?"

"Well, uh. I have a problem I'd like to discuss with you," said Brigit. The Uncanny's gloved hand beckoned for her to enter. Brigit closed the door behind her. She didn't plan on anyone overhearing her.

"My human friend, Logan, you helped him earlier."

"Yes. But I cannot discuss his case with you. Human law forbids me divulging medical information without permission."

"Oh, not that, it's just, hm," Brigit looked around the room, embarrassed and stalling. The place was tidy, with snacks and drinks stacked on one side, medical equipment on the opposite side.

"Well," began Brigit, not sure how much time she had to talk before the human paramedic would return, "Logan visited my home in the Perilous Realm and got really sick afterward. I'd like him to come back again, but I don't want him to get ill from the visit. Is there any way I could prevent that from happening? Medically?"

The doctor was still as a statue. Brigit wondered what was under the mask, robe, and gloves. Probably better not to know.

"Tell me about this illness."

Brigit described it to the Uncanny. "Like when humans get the flu. He was shaky, ran a fever, and was weak. It took almost two weeks for him to recover, and even then, he was still tired a lot."

"That is a typical reaction—"

"But I don't get it!" protested Brigit. "Humans travel to

the Perilous all the time. Some live there. Why would Logan get sick?"

The Uncanny folded its hands in front and returned to stillness.

"When crossing dimensions, it takes time for the body to adjust. For a human, it is best they experience the Perilous in short visits. It allows the body to become accustomed to our world. Did you not experience any disorientation when you arrived at Geheimetür? Or had you visited the human lands before that?"

"No, you're right," Brigit frowned, remembering. "It was the first time I had come to the human lands. I actually fell out of my tree, and someone looked after me for a week or two before I felt like my usual self. But I didn't get as ill as Logan did. I only felt under-the-weather, didn't want to eat, and slept a lot."

"Yes. You experienced the adjustment, the metabolic change that happens when one crosses over to a realm that is not one's own. It wasn't as intense for you as it was for your friend, Logan. We are all individuals, after all."

"Why do we get sick at all? And how can I stop him from getting sick again?" Brigit asked, her frustration showing.

"Immunity comes from experience. You have resided in the human lands now for how long?"

"A little over two years, on the human calendar."

"Have you seen changes with what you can do here?"

"No, not really—wait, I think there have been some changes. When winter comes in the human lands, I start to slow down and feel sluggish. About a month back, without thinking, I picked up Logan's cellphone. The battery didn't die. I just thought I hadn't touched it long enough."

"I would suggest you test yourself occasionally. See what has changed for you. Brownies can work in their homes or barns due to a long association with humans. Knockers and kobolds handle the ore found in human mines without issue, because of their familiarity with the human lands."

"So, the longer I am here, the more I'll adapt to being able to handle human machines like cellphones and computers?"

"Perhaps," said the Uncanny, hedging like all doctors on a diagnosis. "Remember, though, each being's experience is its own."

Brigit, though, had already gone back to thinking over her own problem and barely heard the Uncanny's prognosis.

"So Logan needs to keep dipping his toe in the cold water, in order to acclimate himself to the Perilous? Instead of diving into the deep end all at once?"

"An apt analogy." The beaked nose nodded. After a pause, the creature said, "I was surprised by your relationship with Logan Dannon."

"Surprised?" Brigit's quick temper was ignited. "Because he's a human and I'm a fae? We can't be bondpartners because of that?"

"Fae and humans being associates isn't anything new. A partnership being on equal footing is. You have not beguiled Dannon to be your friend."

"At least you can see that, unlike that idiot, Peterson."

The Uncanny doctor's stillness was soothing, although at times unsettling; it was easy to forget it was a living being. Brigit started talking with less reticence than she usually would with others.

"It makes me mad to have others compare me to a being like Sibyl. I'm not a siren using some magical power to seduce a human. It makes Logan look pathetic. Implying that he doesn't have any ability to resist me or can't make his own decisions. Like he's my mindless puppet!"

"The opinions of others about your bond partner appear to anger you?"

"Of course it does! It's a personal affront to my honor."

"You cannot change the worlds and what they think of you."

"Huh. Jib has already tried that psychology stuff on me."

Brigit made a move to leave, but stopped when the Uncanny said, "I thought, when you entered, your purpose was to discuss the Elder lying over your heart."

The dryad's hand instinctively flew to where the silver leaf from her home lay under her skin.

"What do you know of it?" she asked suspiciously.

The Uncanny Doctor glided closer, and Brigit noticed that its movement was not the gait seen in a two-legged being. It did not touch her, but its glove hovered above her chest.

"I see its aura. Which is exceptional."

"I can't see yours. Your aura, that is."

"I have muted it, so it will not interfere with treating my patients," explained the Uncanny. "You continue to surprise me, Brighid Holly. I have never seen an Elder outside of the Perilous Realm."

"It's not an Elder," Brigit countered. Her fingers curved protectively over where the leaf rested. "It's just a leaf from my home grove in the Perilous. Our trees gifted it to Logan, and he gave it to me."

"Your Elder radiates joy and sadness."

Brigit resisted the Uncanny doctor's judgment, and said stubbornly, "It can't be an Elder. If it had that much power, then why can't I understand what it says to me in my dreams?"

"Only a queen can communicate with an Elder. Speak with your mother, and see what she says about it."

There was no way Brigit was going to tell her mother about the leaf. The Uncanny doctor could forget that!

Emma Walker tapped lightly on the apartment door. When the door started to slowly open, she came through. No on was visible but she figured it was the brownie. Em had never met her for she was shy, but she took care of things at Brigit and Logan's apartment.

Emma tossed her backpack on the sofa and sat down. Without Brigit and Logan, the apartment seemed to have an odd quiet to it which was a bit unsettling. Like someone watching you that you can't see. Since working in a haunted library, Em was far more sensitive to atmosphere.

Rummaging in a pocket of her bag she brought out a pouch filled with dog treats. Logan hadn't time to introduce her to the Black Dog but Em figured a few peanut butter snacks would sort out their relationship.

"Hey, Devlin," she called, rustling the bag in her hand. "Logan sent me over to take care of you. My name's Emma."

She didn't hear anything in response to her call. It wasn't a big apartment. The door to Brigit's room was closed and when Em approached it, she felt a need to leave. Okay, probably not inside there.

The dog wasn't in the kitchen or trapped in the hall closet. Nor was he hiding behind the group of house plants set up like a forest in the living room. Nor was he behind the television cabinet.

"He's in Logan's bedroom," said Obake. In its flying squirrel form it was perched on the top of Emma's head so to have the best view.

"Devlin. C'mon out pup," Em said as she entered Logan's bedroom. Ripped up pillows, their inner foam shredded and cast all over the bed and floor, causing Emma to groan, "Uh-oh."

The lump on the bed moved as the dog dug deeper under the covers. A long black plume of a tail remaining outside the bedspread started to wave a welcome.

"Someone got bored," observed Obake.

"I see." Emma thought over the problem and told the dog, "Don't worry, Devlin. I'll clean it up and we can go out for a walk. Maybe chase a ball around? Okay?"

Em carefully slipped the top blanket off the bed. Laying it on the floor she started tossing all the broken foam bits onto it. Her plan was to use the blanket as a carry-all to take the destroyed pillows down to the main trash area.

The clear outline of the dog was more visible under the sheets left on the bed. He was about the size of a pillow himself. As Emma talked to him, the tail would sometimes wag. Eventually a black nose poked out from the edge of the sheets.

Obake spread its side flaps and glided down from its perch on Emma's head to the bed. The dwarf flying squirrel clawed up the headboard. It perched on the top and watched the dog out of its bright black eyes.

Emma had most of the mess in her blanket sack.

"I'll be right back, Obake. I'm going to dump this. Then we'll use the vacuum cleaner."

Emma left carrying the bundle slung over her back like Santa's bag. As soon as Obake's sensitive ears heard the front door shut, it spoke to the dog, "You can come out now, Devlin. The human is gone. Let's have a chat, just us two."

The nose became a head with soft brown eyes and two large floppy ears. Devlin wriggled out from the covers and sat up, waving his tail. He gave a deep bark, as if inviting Obake to play with him.

"Hm, what a smorgasbord of secrets you are," mused Obake, its eyes glistening with greed. "Oh yes, I see. Fascinating. Tell me more."

Emma was delayed in returning because of Logan's phone call. When she returned she called out, "We have a mission from Logan and Brigit. Wait until you hear, Obake. You'll love it!"

Sitting in the living room was the dog. Obake sitting on his head.

"I have so much to tell you, Em," said Obake. "Devlin was brought to Geheimetür by Logan. Well, another Logan."

Chapter Twenty-Seven
Fianchetto

Emma Walker approached the woman in charge of filming Dr. Stuart's documentary and flashed the press pass she had created on her computer.

"Oh, so you're finally here. I thought your paper was sending over a guy?" asked the woman whose name tag read Dani Johnson. Her dismissive look took in Emma and her dyed purple hair, blue jeans, and boots.

"He's barfing in a toilet this morning," lied Em. "Covered the opening of a new beer hall and tasted too many samples."

"Reporters," Dani muttered. She gave an intimidating stare at Emma. "Okay, so give me a list of the questions you're going to ask Dr. Stuart."

Emma's smile grew into a grin. "That would be a big no. I'm a news reporter, not a public relations hack for your homeboy. Anyway, isn't this a film documentary? The truth and nothing but the truth?"

"Fine," growled Dani. "I'll edit out all your mistakes later in post-production."

Emma gave only a faint half-smile in reply. With a muttered growl, Dani turned away to speak with her two cameramen. She rattled off a series of instructions.

It was early morning, and they were standing near a decorative pavilion set in the center of a maze formed by evergreen hedges in the Kiburg gardens. There was a chair where Dr. Stuart sat, getting his hair and make-up fixed. Beside him, there was another for Emma who would be interviewing him, allegedly for a local newspaper.

After Logan's call last night, Emma hacked the newspaper's website. On their staff page she put up a photo of herself with a fake bio. In about ten more minutes that page would vanish. Her media pass was easy to make from equipment she already had at home.

While she worked on the fake ID badge, Obake had filled her in on all the details of Dr. Stuart's research. The tsukumogami loved information and quickly compiled a list of questions, based upon its data mining, that they could ask the scientist.

It was a bit of a push to get everything done. Emma

hadn't a moment to tell Logan what the Black Dog revealed to Obake. It was something she wanted to discuss in person with him, not over the phone. Em figured it could wait.

Obake was in her ear posing as a Bluetooth earpiece. It would feed her all the questions and information she would need to interview Dr. Stuart. From keys to flash drives, to memory cards and phones, anything dealing with revealing information, Obake loved to disguise itself.

Waiting for the light test on her face and clothes, Emma wondered what tree, bush, or leaf Brigit was hiding within. The hedge maze made a half-circle around the shelter. Brigit was bound to be watching and waiting to make her move.

The lighting people were all arguing. If they had set up inside, they could have controlled the light better, but the cameraman couldn't find access to an empty conference room. Emma smiled to herself, knowing that Logan had made sure all the doors of empty rooms were locked before the documentary crew swept through.

"First time in front of the camera?" asked Dani as she came to where Emma sat. At her nod, the director told her, "Okay. Well, just do the best you can. I'll edit something passable out of what we get."

"Okay," said Emma, pretending to care. She figured none of this would ever see the light of day, considering her intention.

The man is full of secrets, said Obake in her ear.

"Full of something," Emma murmured under her breath.

It took a certain level of hard-headed self assurance to

be a female who did well in gaming, and Emma did very well in that world. She had seen plenty of posers online and at tournaments. Keeners didn't impress her.

With a firefighter dad and a schoolteacher mom, Emma had seen many blustering liars: parents who wanted her mom to change a grade, and kids who cheated on tests trying to deny it. Those who fawned over her dad one day with a "thank you for your service" when he wore his uniform to a dinner out with family, but refused to vote him a living wage.

Emma was as cynical as only a twenty-something could be.

She didn't think much of Dr. Stuart, but that would be true even without being told about Brigit's suspicions. She wasn't into authority figures, especially ones who called her "girl."

But while Dr. Stuart didn't intimidate her, that didn't mean he wasn't trying. He was a big guy—he loomed, coming into her personal space more than necessary. His knees were about an inch away from touching hers, and occasionally, he would bump Emma as if by accident in the middle of a question.

He cut Emma off, jumping over the end of her words to make sure his agenda was recorded. To throw Emma off her game, Dr. Stuart would use scientific words in a patronizing tone expecting her to look ignorant. That didn't work, for Obake quickly unlocked any word Emma didn't recognize and whispered the definition into her ear.

After a warm-up of about fifteen minutes of soft

questions, Emma shifted her cross-examination, "What new working relationships with the fae have you formed here at the symposium?"

Dr. Stuart, now feeling reassured of Emma's harmlessness, leaned back, crossing his legs (foot jarring Emma's ankle) and said, "One particular connection is with the fae Queen Elixia. Her majesty has an interesting problem with her kingdom in the Perilous Realm. It seems her trees are dying."

"Because of your scientific background I can see why that would be of interest to you—"

"A court in the Perilous Realm is a self-sustaining ecosystem," Dr. Stuart lectured on, oblivious to Emma's comment, "and thus its environment serves as a perfect place to conduct scientific inquiries."

"Like the Galapagos Islands or Antarctica?"

"Similar, but the kingdoms in the Perilous Realm are even more isolated from outside contact. Even travel between courts is controlled. And Queen Elixia's kingdom is known for being insular. Rarely do its inhabitants visit the human lands. Their seclusion makes them vulnerable."

"To what? Can you explain, please?"

Stuart waved his hand vaguely about, "Take the queen's daughter, Princess Brigit. She attends Leopold Otto, breaking tradition and encouraging new ideas in the fae simply by her presence here. I've heard her attendance has increased fae enrollment at Leopold Otto."

Let's wipe that grin off his face, chittered Obake in Emma's ear.

"Are you talking about new ideas and how they change people? That sounds like a good thing, opening up the fae to new experiences. Isn't that what the symposium is all about?"

"On the surface, it might seem like a good idea, but from my experience, when environments overlap, uncontrolled transmission happens. Whether it is ideas or disease, both can be equally as dangerous."

"Oh, like indigenous people exposed to diseases they haven't experienced before?"

"Yes. While fae creatures do visit our world, their native flora and fauna remain in the Perilous. It's an environmental bubble that can be easily infected or damaged."

A bush behind Dr. Stuart's head shook slightly. Emma ignored it and continued her interview, "What you're saying is the Perilous Realm makes a perfect petri dish. A terrarium. Which can be observed—"

"It would make an ideal place to conduct research in real-time. An experiment we cannot do here because of the likelihood it would escape and cause harm elsewhere would be a perfect test to do in the Perilous Realm."

Probably because of the film crew, a small group of fae and humans had gathered to watch the filming. One of them was a guy with antlers who looked like he was a member of a K-pop band. Fae or maybe someone cosplaying.

Dr. Stuart continued, "An enclosed, pristine environment with little, if any, contact with our world would provide a perfect place to study disease. An immaculate setting where we could introduce whatever we want."

"Have you ever tried anything like that? Or are you purely speculating?"

He looked as coy as an older, large man could. Or maybe sly. When Dr. Stuart didn't give a verbal reply to her question, Emma pressed further by challenging him, "I don't believe that it wouldn't leak over to our world. The fae cross over all the time. Wouldn't a biological agent introduced into the Perilous come here too?"

Dr. Stuart gave one of those big guffaws that invites others to share in his hilarity. Emma didn't. The fae in the audience didn't seem amused either.

"It's doubtful it would impact us at all. Zoonosis."

An infectious disease that passes from non-human to human, whispered Obake.

"While it's rare that disease crosses from animals to humans, some do. And when they do it can be devastating," said Emma thinking at the same time, *gotcha.* "Something coming from the Perilous Realm, connected with magic, could be lethal to us."

"I think it more likely that something from our world entering the Perilous would present the greater danger," said Dr. Stuart with condescension. "Their world is too specialized. Too self-contained. The fae rely upon magic to fix their problems. It is one of their many flaws."

"But what of the risk to the fae who live in the Perilous? What would happen to them while you are conducting these theoretical experiments?"

Like many who had grown used to the cameras following

them, Dr. Stuart was too comfortable being filmed. Perhaps it was because it was the last day of the symposium that emboldened him. Or maybe it was Obake, unraveling his secrets the longer the interview progressed. Whatever reason, his mask was crumbling away with each word he spoke.

"The mortality rate would depend on the experiment. However, you need to remember that the fae are little better than animals. Some may appear human-like but they are not."

"So they will be your lab rats?"

At this point, Emma saw Dani's eyes widen, but she didn't stop the cameras.

She wants something dramatic to film, said Obake. *Let's give it to her.*

The tsukumogami had been using its talent for unlocking secrets to loosen Dr. Stuart's tongue. Obake applied more magical pressure, and Dr. Stuart's self-condemning words tumbled out at a faster rate.

"Like rats they turn upon each other under the right conditions. The fae are a warlike people, constantly having vendettas and duels against their own kind. Any deaths due to my trials would be negligible compared to what they've done to themselves."

Only the distant sound of bird song broke the silence. Unaware of the consternation he was arousing, Dr. Stuart mused, "It would be best, though, to have access to their dead."

"Like, for autopsies?"

"Yes. Of course. We use human bodies for the same purpose."

"Those are donated to science," Emma pointed out. "If the fae don't believe or care about science why would they —"

"We would pay them," said Dr. Stuart smugly.

"Like a bounty?"

"An excellent idea. We could even foment dissension, cause them to turn on their own. Take the leftovers of their battles and thus increase the materials we need for an accurate assessment of these creatures."

It felt like everyone was leaning towards where Emma and Dr. Stuart sat.

For Emma, it felt like time was slowing down. She blinked. Her mind felt foggy as if she had just woken up. She coughed and tried to sit up straighter.

Something is happening at the Kiburg, said Obake in her ear.

Dr. Stuart was looking past her right shoulder, his gaze on the castle hotel. Slowly a smile spread over his face. He said, "Yet despite all their magic, the fae are easily tricked. It is their belief in their superior position, relying upon their powers, that eventually betrays them."

Emma squinted, trying to bring Dr. Stuart back into focus. Behind him, a dark arm was reaching out of the bushes. It clapped the scientist on his shoulder.

Before anyone could react, Dr. Stuart disappeared.

Bane of Hounds

Chapter Twenty-Eight
Forced Move

Queen Elixia had not planned on attending the last day of the symposium. She was tired, with a weariness that could not be repaired by rest. She was also fretful and had woken with a headache behind her eyes. She waved away her hovering attendants and asked the púca, "Where is my daughter?"

"She left this morning to go see that scientist fellow. He's going to be interviewed on television," said Jib. The cat was sitting loaf style on a sofa cushion, its eyes half closed in inward contemplation.

"That girl is never where one needs her," fretted Elixia, pulling on her coat jacket. She adjusted her belt holding her

knife and facing the mirror, twisted to check the back of her
skirt. "What do you think?"

Jib opened its eyes wider and took in the queen's outfit.
"You look like a powerful queen who means business."

"Good."

The queen headed to the suite's door, but before her
guard could open it, she stopped. She didn't look at Jib as
she said, "Swear upon your pledge to me that you will
remain at Brigit's side. That you will serve as her guardian
no matter what happens to me."

"I would do that regardless of my pledge, your majesty."

Jib referred to the Oath of Fealty between courtier and
queen when a lock of hair, or in the cat's case, a shedding
of a claw tip, was given in a formal ceremony. This harmless
method replaced the ancient one of swearing fealty, which
had involved blood-letting or maiming.

"You might be a Trickster, Jib, but you have a loyal
heart." Her words, said in a flat, dry tone, were worrisome
and unnatural.

Her lack of emotion made Jib uneasy. She should be
enjoying the drama of her soon-to-be entrance. The púca
felt sympathetic until she said, "And stop being silly about
that Black Dog. It is beneath your notice."

"As you wish, my queen."

Queen Elixia found her daughter loitering in the Kiburg
hotel lobby. Brigit was dressed in a pale pink long sleeved t-
shirt, and the jacket her mother had given her. It was the
only gift of the many Queen Elixia had bought her that

Brigit had seemed delighted with.

"You look very nice," said her mother, who reached over and twitched the collar of her daughter's jacket so it would stand up to frame her heart-shaped face. "What are you up to today?"

Her daughter gave a look familiar to Elixia; Brigit wasn't going to tell her the truth.

"I'm meeting with Dr. Stuart after his interview this morning. Bandemer sent over a local reporter to ask us questions. A tidy conclusion, to show the symposium was a success." Elixia arched her eyebrows at her daughter's answer.

Brigit protested, "That is what I'm doing. Honest. What are your plans? You smell extra nice. Something to woo the crowd, huh?"

"Only the humans, dear. These Glamour scents don't work on our own kind, though I wish they did. Life would be far easier if a fae courtier thought itself half in love with me, before I had to demand something from it."

Logan Dannon and the Black Dog arrived. At least the boy did not say anything to her, other than an appropriate greeting of, "Merry meet, your Majesty."

Elixia would rather discuss the dog. "Any other prophecies of Doom?"

"No, but the Black Dog did give us a name—Devlin. I think he's starting to heal from his trauma. Mother, I told Logan what the Black Dog said, and he thinks—"

Elixia didn't want to know what a bard thought. She cut off Brigit and asked, "What are your long term plans for this dog?"

"We haven't discovered his court, yet, and from what we've heard from Torfa, his court may have been destroyed. We both," Brigit indicated Logan, and a silent message passed between them, "have taken him as a bondpartner."

"A harbinger? Really, dear, how original. Well, I guess someone must." Elixia gave an aggrieved sigh. "If you bring him home, make sure he has a bath first."

"Mother!" Brigit exclaimed, annoyed. "He's very clean and a good dog. Don't be so elitist."

"We are a cat family," spoke up Jib, sitting on its haunches at Elixia's feet. The dog whined at Jib's words, earning him an orange stare from the púca.

"Hm, well, your father always wanted a dog. So you can discuss it with him when he arrives."

"Father is coming?" Brigit asked, delighted. "Good. It's about time. He should have been here earlier."

"He had our court to settle at Queen Titania's," Queen Elixia reminded her daughter. Last night, Elixia had sent one of her ladies-in-waiting with a message to Ladislas to come to her, but she wasn't going to admit to Brigit how much she missed him. Elixia was trying to be brave, and her need for Ladislas seemed a weakness. Besides her daughter would just say I-told-you-so.

"Moving the court will be a wasted trip. We will all return soon," Brigit stated hopefully. Her mother gave a sad shake of her head at her daughter's words.

Before they could argue, Queen Elixia saw the chancellor and his shadow, Paul Darcy, walking down the opposite hall.

Attendees of the symposium were starting to congregate outside the conference rooms.

"Have fun with your dog, child, but when your father arrives, we have much to discuss."

Elixia swept away, chin raised, with Jib trotting beside her high heels. The cat gave one look back at Brigit, Logan, and the dog, giving a quick aggravated flick to its tail.

When Elixia passed Bandemer, she exchanged a regal nod, but he was busy talking with others. Several of the princes stepped aside to let Queen Elixia precede them into the banquet hall. It was here where wrap-up speeches would be given to mark the end of the week-long symposium.

The queen took her time, hovering at the entrance as if she was in a receiving line. She collected cards and good wishes. She exchanged more greetings, especially with the three other queens who had attended.

Elixia even spoke to a few humans she was contemplating for future commercial joint ventures. The CEO of a florist company that dealt in exotic flowers for the rich; and a clothes designer who was intrigued by how Brigit's faux leather jacket had been made without harsh chemicals. Her perfume worked its subtle magic, and she signed their symposium schedules with the flourish of a rock star.

Despite trying to maintain a cheerful attitude, her headache was increasing. Elixia felt as if she was floating, out of her body. No one was aware of the dire threat to her home court, so all this cheerfulness felt more like the steps to a macabre dance.

Still standing near the door, a face Elixia knew peered into the room. Feeling that having a nice verbal duel would make her feel better, Queen Elixia stepped over and greeted Sarah Dannon.

Logan's mother came straight to the point, "I was to meet my son in the lobby. You don't know where Logan is? He doesn't answer his phone."

Elixia's eyebrows rose at the woman's question. Did she think a queen troubled herself about a human's whereabouts? Elixia's surprise must have communicated itself to Sarah for she said with some pique, "I just thought you might know. Since he seems to be with your daughter so much."

Stung, Elixia in her best careless, superior queen voice, said, "Brigit is with Dr. Sebastian Stuart being interviewed by a reporter. They are discussing science. Important things you wouldn't understand."

"Would you?" asked Sarah Dannon who was never shy in saying exactly what she wanted.

Elixia ignored Sarah's parry and in an offhand manner said, "I thought I saw your son in the shadows, hovering about with his dog."

Sarah blinked but otherwise didn't show her repugnance and fear for her son's new pet. Feeling she scored, Elixia said, "You are not here for the symposium, then?"

"When I planned this trip to visit my son, I didn't know there was an event happening here. Otherwise, I would have stayed somewhere else."

"Because my kind is staying here?"

At this moment, Chancellor Bandemer, crossed to where they were standing.

"Ah, I see the mothers of my two student liaisons have met."

It could have been the chancellor's mustard yellow coat and the purple stockings tied with hot-pink garter ribbons that caused Sarah's confused expression. The riot of color in the chancellor's dress was his vice. It was almost as out of control as Elixia's love for chocolate.

"Do I know you?" asked Sara frostily. Paul, ever standing in the shadow of the chancellor, did the introductions.

"Chancellor François Auguste Bandemer of Leopold-Ottos-Universität Geheimetür, Bewachterberg, may I introduce Mrs. Sarah Dannon, of Austin, Texas, in the United States of America."

In antiquated fashion, the chancellor kissed her hand, declaring, "*Enchanté*. Your son is doing good work with my office as a student liaison."

Between Fae and French charm, Sarah stood no chance. She always softened when someone praised her son. "Yes, he mentioned that, but I don't know exactly what that position means."

"Neither does he," purred the cat at their feet. Jib's jab was ignored by all.

"Like a debate club." Bandemer's reputation for navigating tricky situations was well earned. He waved his hand, fluttering lace cuffs, in a vague motion. "Your son convinces others to come to a mutual understanding.

Mediation between fae and humans. It will be invaluable on his resume."

"That phrase is often used when there is a great outlay in time that bears little in terms of tangible return," said Sarah. If something went against the best interests of her only son, she could resist the most powerful Glamour.

Paul may have been hiding a laugh behind his hand. To cover it, he gave a cough and told them, "We need to take our seats, chancellor. It looks like they are about to start."

"Why don't you join us, Mrs. Dannon, on the front row?" suggested the chancellor. "Afterward, we can talk further about your son and his work here at Leopold Otto. I would enjoy hearing more about his life before he came to us."

During this discussion, Queen Elixia found herself growing more distracted. It started as a nagging worry. Like she had forgotten or mislaid something. She had been feeling it all morning, and it was why her first thought this morning was about her missing daughter.

Since entering the room, her feeling of an unsettled preoccupation increased. She started looking around, trying to find whatever was bothering her. It had a hint of magic.

Sarah Dannon and the chancellor moved away, still talking about Logan. Jib was meowing and rubbing itself around the queen's legs. She paid the púca no mind.

"Is something wrong?" asked Paul.

"I don't—" began Elixa, frowning, "something is here."

Before she could say more, Queen Elixia saw the harp. It was set up at the edge of the dais located at the front of the room. In a corner, past where Chancellor Bandemer and

Sarah Dannon were now sitting.

This was her harp — her bone harp — stolen so many years ago. The harp made from the bones and hair of her murdered courtier, her sister. The promise of its song beguiled her.

She couldn't stop herself; Queen Elixia started towards it. Paul threw out an arm to prevent her advance but Elixia easily sidestepped his block with a dancing step. The púca's warning meows were turning into a wail. Jib tried to trip her. She stepped over the cat.

Standing in front of the harp, Queen Elixia licked her dry lips. Her heart was beating faster. She reached out and touched the strings, and as she did so, a bead of blood formed on her fingers.

The spell to kill her unlocked.

Bane of Hounds

Chapter Twenty-Nine
Double Attack

rigit's touch on Dr. Stuart's shoulder brought him into the Perilous Realm. She ripped him from the human lands and threw him down on the forest floor of her home. Her hands shook with fury.

Stuart recovered quickly and staggered to his feet. Crossing the boundary of the worlds affected humans in various ways, from something as mild as vertigo and nausea to vomiting and fainting. The fact Stuart wasn't more disoriented told Brigit that he was familiar with the Perilous.

Brigit didn't have time to dwell on it for the wrongness of the woods shocked her. Feeling their pain, she closed her eyes, her hand over her breast, where the leaf pulsed, throbbed achingly.

While the tie between the queen and the Elder spirit was the strongest, Elixia's family also experienced a deep connection to the magical power. Brigit and her sisters served as handmaidens to their mother, the Pythia, or High Priestess, of the grove.

Lost in a trance, the trees warned Brigit of Stuart's movement. Her eyes snapped open. She glared at the scientist. "I read your paper about the work you did in South America. That's how you did it here, isn't it?"

"Oh, yes," said Dr. Stuart, as if the two were back in the Kiburg having an ordinary conversation. "Magnetotactic bacteria are fascinating, don't you think so? I encountered them first during a deep cave exploration."

"They have magnetic iron inside their cells."

"To navigate," agreed Dr. Stuart. He looked around with a curious, examining air at the trees around them. The stark silver of the tree trunks glittered like new ice illuminated by the bright morning sun. "I started this experiment on your trees years ago at the request of my patron. Making the gene-spliced MTBs was a fascinating project. They've been in your trees growing and replicating, building up the concentration of magnetite, which you fae creatures are so susceptible to."

"Iron," said Brigit. She felt sick to her stomach. The iron that was so dangerous to her own kind that humans used it to ward against them. Only fae who worked in the human lands, like brownies or knockers, could tolerate prolonged exposure to the metal.

"Since your grove is actually one organism, connected by an extensive root system, I thought the trees would spread the bacteria throughout. I'm glad to hear my hypothesis proved to be correct."

Brigit slid her knife out of her boot and felt the smoothness of the handle against her palm. That big grin that Stuart flashed for the cameras faded as he viewed the blade in her hand.

"Why did you do it?"

"For science, of course. What institution would fund a bio-engineered disease in my world? It could possibly get out of hand. Who would pay for that type of research? But here?" He gestured around him, taking in the dense circle of trees. "The Perilous is the perfect spot to indulge my desire for pure experimentation. And of course, there was the money I was given to make it happen."

"Money? Who paid you?" Brigit demanded sharply.

"Queen Elixia knows him. He was once her brother-in-law."

Brigit barely restrained herself from throwing the knife into Dr. Stuart's heart. "Tell me how to heal them."

Stuart shrugged, hands out. "I can't. No one can. By the time you see the result of the bacteria, it's too late to do anything about it."

"Do you hear that, Logan? He's admitted to poisoning our trees in an attempt to kill my family."

Behind a group of trees, Logan had been hiding with the Black Dog. Brigit had brought them earlier, setting them into place to spring their trap. Hearing Dr. Stuart's words sickened him. It also disturbed Devlin for the fae beast was now the size of a lion. Blue sparks flickered over its fur.

He and the dog stepped out from their concealment.

"I know, Brigit. He's telling the truth. It makes me sick." The Black Dog was staring with a fixated gaze at Dr. Stuart while it gave a low growl. "He doesn't believe you can reverse the damage."

"I'm glad you see it my way," said Dr. Stuart. Between Brigit's knife and the isolation of being in the Perilous Realm, the scientist was tense. "Let us leave now."

"Why the rush?" asked Logan.

"Because Queen Elixia is about to die," snapped Dr. Stuart. "When she does, this Perilous Realm court will fold in upon itself like a collapsing star. We don't want to be here."

"Yes, she's dying because of you!" screamed Brigit, letting her anger break free.

"No," said Logan, holding out his hand as if to hold Brigit back, "he means a more imminent danger. What do you mean?"

A wind picked up, and the leaves and the branches above them started to sway, the leaves crackling against each other like brittle glass. The ground began to shake.

"I was given an enchanted gift to set up in the Kiburg. Right before we left, I felt Queen Elixia wake the spell."

"What are you talking about?" demanded Brigit.

"It was a bone harp. My patron provided it. He told me to set it up in the morning conference room, where she was invited to attend the morning session. The harp has a spell on it to kill Queen Elixia."

"He's telling the truth," Logan repeated to Brigit. She was so angry she almost slapped Logan for providing the information. "I don't care about truths! We need to save my mother and the grove!"

The leaf inside Brigit was tired of being ignored. It had tried to speak to the dryad, but she wasn't the Elder's partner. Now, returned to its place in the Perilous Realm, it spoke directly to the Elder. It wanted to share all that it gained from the human lands.

The Elder agreed: *Return to us—it is time.*

Before Brigit could throw her knife at Dr. Stuart, the Elder leaf took control of her. The grove was connected, root to root. It would bring her to join with the Elder so the healing could be done.

The potent magic of the Elder transformed the body of the dryad. It stretched her, so she became a tall, willowy tree trunk, her skin dappled and her face formed the swirls and knots of rough bark.

When the change hit her, Brigit flung out her arms over her head in surprise. These became branches. Her fingers became a canopy of leaves. The shoes on her feet cracked and fell away as Brigit's legs burrowed into the ground which embraced them.

It all happened so quickly and was so unexpected that Brigit had made no sound during the transformation. As the roots underground connected with the Elder, Brigit felt her consciousness swept away like an acorn tossed on the turbulent current of a flooding river.

It was not like a typical dryad-tree joining. In those instances, Brigit and the tree retained their separate identities. Now, Brigit tried to hold fast, to anchor herself among the vast wave of rushing awareness that overwhelmed her. All she could do was hope to keep her own concept of self. Instinctively, Brigit folded her essence into a tight kernel.

She felt the leaf, that had been with her since her summer in France, fragment. Its veins, midrib, and stem dissolved, as its essence returned to the Elder. And with its dissolution came the understanding of how the Elder planned to save itself through Brigit's sacrifice.

As Brigit transformed into a towering tree, the earth rose under their feet. Dr. Stuart, Logan, and the Black Dog stumbled back with the dog recovering the quickest. It flew at Dr. Stuart, launching a frenzy of threatening barks and growls. Its snapping teeth kept the man cornered.

Logan regained his balance by instinctively putting out a hand against one of the trees. Instead of the chill and hardness he expected to feel, the bark was warm under his palm, with a fleshy spongy surface. He jerked his hand back.

Brigit's tree was as large as a young Redwood. Although he'd seen Brigit merge into many wood forms, he'd never seen this sort of transformation. Logan would have to trust Brigit to know what she was doing.

Dr. Stuart grabbed Logan by the arm, shouting in his

face, "We have to leave! Now. Or die."

Logan shook him off, replying, "How do you expect us to do that? You've just angered the one person that could lead us out of the Perilous Realm."

"The dog! Use the dog."

The Black Dog's snarling lip showed plenty of teeth, all aimed at Dr. Stuart.

When Brigit had brought Logan to the Perilous Realm hours back, they hoped the dog would be able to give them new information about himself. But while it was evident from its wagging tail and excited barks, the Black Dog was happy to be back to the Perilous, there was no evidence he remembered anything more.

"That creature," Dr. Stuart said, pointing a shaking finger at the Black Dog, "it can get us out of here—"

"It wasn't him that brought me here. He wouldn't know the way back. It was Brigit. You destroyed his home court. Devlin can't remember anything because of the trauma you caused him."

"I didn't destroy his court," argued Dr. Stuart, strangely offended at the accusation.

"Only Brigit's court?" asked Logan, suddenly understanding that Dr. Stuart was only a tool, a weapon that someone else must have used to gain their end. It was odd to see such a big man look frightened, but Logan couldn't find any pity for him.

Logan demanded answers from Dr. Stuart, despite the howling wind rushing through the trees and the smashing glass noises of leaves falling.

"Tell me who paid you. How do we find him?"

"You can't. He contacted me. I never knew his name. Only that he was once wedded to Queen Elixia's sister and has an abiding hatred of the fae. He's a bard like you."

"So, you didn't have anything to do with the other courts being destroyed?"

"No!" Stuart shouted back. He held his arms over his head to protect himself, but the sharp-edged leaves slashed his forearms, and a few shards gashed his face. The foliage fell like sheets of ice from a roof.

None of them touched Logan or the Black Dog.

"How did he contact you about harming Queen Elixia at the symposium?"

"A note was sent to my room. I was told there would be a package for me at the hotel's loading dock. It told me what to do. Where to set it up so she could find it. The spell was already on it."

"If I took you back to the Kiburg, could you stop the spell?"

"Yes, yes, take me back!"

"You're lying."

While Logan resisted the impulse to strike Dr. Stuart, the Black Dog did not. The lion-sized beast lunged forward, knocking Dr. Stuart to the ground. Its weight kept him from rising. Dr. Stuart held his arms over his face for protection.

Logan tried to remember what Brigit had told him about her court and the trees. But before he could think things through, there were a series of popping noises, like gunfire or champagne corks.

Logan ducked, looking about wildly about trying to figure out the sound.

It was the trees—parts of the outer bark were bursting off—chunks breaking away to fall to the ground. The pop-popping sound grew, causing Logan to cover his ears. The Black Dog starting barking again, and Dr. Stuart screamed in fear and rage.

Bane of Hounds

Chapter Thirty
Spite Check

Entranced, Elixia's hand stroked the frame of the harp made from the bones of her sister. Her hands started to shake, thinking of the last time she had seen Verabella alive.

A bone harp was made from the body of a murdered being. The bones were shaped by magic to make the frame, and sinews or hair became unbreakable strings. The levers to change the pitch were created from the vertebrae of Verabella's spine.

And when it played, it told the story of her murder.

Unable to stop herself, Elixia's hands played across the strings of the bone harp. Instead of music in the traditional sense, its notes sang the story of her sister's tragic death at the hands of her love.

Tread lightly, she is near
Under the snow—

The design of whorls and loops that spelled her sister's fae name lit up as if written by fire as the lament continued.

All her bright golden hair
Tarnished with rust—

But something else was attached to the harp: a death spell keyed to Elixia activated when she touched the strings. When the music ended, so would her life.

Elixia tried again to pull her hands away from the strings, biting her lip against the pain. Blood dripped from her fingertips. But she could not stop their movement as they plucked the strings.

Around Elixia, the hotel room was spinning as if she had drunk too much mead. She thought first of Ladislas, and secondly about her daughter, her youngest.

The queen had thought she would die when the Elder passed. But now, if she were to die first, the Elder would retreat and her kingdom vanish.

Elixia wept as she played.

Paul cursed himself for not being more alert. He should have checked the room earlier this morning, but Bandemer's frantic search for a missing garter had thrown off the schedule.

Paul cursed under his breath. It was a long string of

oaths in Russian, Latin, Norwegian, and French.

By the time the Doppelgänger realized the danger and tried to stop Queen Elixia, it was too late. The spell had caught her like a moth on a spider's web. Nothing would be able to stop her from reaching her destination.

Like a key turning the tumblers inside a lock, Paul saw the spell click into place upon Elixia's touch on the bone harp.

As a Doppelgänger, his magical elements controlled Time and Memory. It was with Memory that he was able to present a different face to anyone he met. Magic that received a crippling blow last year when he encountered a thing from Outside. Even now, his Talent for Memory would take time to fully recover.

But Time? That was still his to control. He could bend it.

If he had reacted fast enough, Paul would have been able to rewind to the moment when Queen Elixia entered the room, but even that was now too far past. It was dangerous to go backward. It would cause the growth of multiple time-paths. It was enough to cause a Doppelgänger to lose his mind.

No, it was easier and safer to shape a moment that was happening in Paul's current time. Simpler also to bend time in a constrained location. The conference room would serve.

Snarling with anger and concentration, Paul pulled at the weave of time which surrounded him that only he could see.

All in the room paused in mid-gesture, half-laugh, as the

seconds were split not once, but twice, now thrice. Their movements became suspended like cold honey dripping from a spoon. Gestures were frozen. Mouths opened to shape a word that wasn't uttered. A tear welling at the corner of Queen Elixia's eye stayed quivering in place, unable to fall.

Paul bent the micro-event of this moment upon itself, folding it so tightly no action could move forward. It was a temporary solution because, for each moment he held it, Paul risked losing his sanity.

But the Doppelgänger needed time to think of a better solution to save the queen's life. He'd stopped Elixia's playing for the moment, but unlike the flickering candles back in his cave under the library, he could not loop her forever.

Each person in the room had a timeline straining to move forward, desiring to fulfill a destiny. Even now, Paul could feel Bandemer's timeline thrashing against Paul's leash trying to free itself.

No, he could not hold them all in his hand. But when the regular pace of time returned, which it must, so would the death spell continue.

Or Paul could spend all of his power. Wind time into a pretzel. Put it into a never-ending Möbius strip. Fix this moment like a spinning top and laugh as it made its pretty pattern that would dazzle the eyes and senses forever.

This devil's whisper to destroy them all was why Paul seldom used this talent. It took discipline to resist indulging the temptation to show mastery over what ruled the life of many.

No, I won't do that, Paul reassured himself.

Really? Do it.

Not for the first time, Paul told the voice in his head to shut up.

The Doppelgänger needed a way to save Queen Elixia and to re-start time. Before he became insane from holding the time strands of 30-odd people in his mind.

Paul was the only one able to move. He walked to where Queen Elixia was frozen in her chair, the harp leaning against one shoulder, her fingers hovering over the strings.

Like all fae, Paul saw the world differently than humans. The auras of individuals showed bright pulses of colors defining their being and magic to his sensitive eyes. However, his Doppelgänger magic saw more.

He saw the construction of spells.

The song of the harp, its lament, wasn't a spell in itself. The harp was a tool formed by magic, from the body of the dead. Its purpose was to tell a tale, and only that story. The bone harp existed separately from the death spell coded to start at Queen Elixia's touch.

Because of its link to Queen Elixia, it had been an ideal tool for a spell using contagious magic. Contagious magic could be worked by humans or fae. It took a personal item and linked its owner to the spell worked upon it.

Employing an instrument made from her dead sister to weave a death spell for the queen sent a very personal and savage message. However, the death spell was not as potent as the cláirseach's magical need to put a voice to its song. This could work in Paul's favor.

Bending time often dealt with the isolation of one event, one strand, where something could be held, twisted, or changed. Too many younger Doppelgängers rushed in and started their work without thinking things through. That led to disastrous results, making rip tides in time that could destroy lives.

Paul had learned the hard way to wait and be patient.

He bent closer, examining Elixia's position. The queen's right forefinger was touching a string. Her other fingers were paused right before taking another stroke along the strings of the bone harp.

With the precision of a surgeon, Paul moved time forward by milliseconds. Elixia's right forefinger lifted, thinning the sticky web of the death spell. While her left ring finger lowered, coming to a paper width from touching another string, it thickened the spell web.

While the harp was resting against her shoulder, that contact was not what kept the cláirseach and queen connected in their dance of death. It was Elixia's playing. Yes, the strings were the problem.

Paul slowed Elixia's movement again. He let the queen's hands approach the harp and draw back again after fingering the strings. Yes, here was where the web of magic thinned the most!

The Doppelgänger stopped time again and saw where the two events could be separated. He sliced the anchors that held the harp in time with Elixia. Like carding strands of wool, he collected the sticky web of the death spell. Winding up the spell like a woman does her ball of yarn, he took the layers of the sorcery and twisted it back upon the harp.

Like the candles in his cave retreat, he set the harp to play on a continuous loop. Now, the lament would never end, and the death Geas, trapped by the harp's litany, would never complete.

To make sure no one else touched it, Paul cast the harp into an unused time eddy—a dead end of worn possibilities that would never come true. No one but himself would ever be able to reach it.

There was a reason why Paul rarely used such dangerous magic. It had the potential to kill him.

Paul's hold on the people in the room slipped away, causing time to re-start. He staggered, fell first to his knees, before landing flat-faced on the floor. The room exploded into noise and confusion, none of which Paul heard.

Bane of Hounds

Chapter Thirty-One
Endgame

Queen Elixia arrived in the Perilous Realm with fingers dripping blood and a panther-sized black cat at her feet.

"What are you doing!?" She had to scream because of the noise, and even then, Logan barely heard her. He pointed at the tree which had replaced Brigit, "Brigit, that's Brigit!"

Elixia was breathing hard, a line of blood crusted one nostril. She kicked off her high heels and ran to Brigit, embracing the tree. She pressed her cheek to it, listening. Logan made his way to her side but didn't touch the tree or Brigit's mother.

"Dr. Stuart told us your life was in danger."

"It was," spat Jib, whose coat was coated with licking flames. "Someone left a death spell tied to a harp. The Doppelgänger broke her free. When we woke, the queen knew we were needed here."

At Jib's mention of her, Elixia's eyes opened. They were a wild kaleidoscope of colors, spinning and reforming prisms. Her voice was hoarse, "Brigit is with the Elder, but I can't reach either of them. What happened, Logan? And why is that human here?"

Logan didn't need to look back to where she pointed.

"Dr. Stuart has admitted to poisoning the grove."

"Jib, kill him."

"Gladly," hissed the cat.

Logan had only his body to put between the scientist and the púca. While he considered Jib his friend, he knew that wouldn't stop the cat from going through him to get to Dr. Stuart. He said in a rush, "He may have information we need. Someone paid him to poison the trees. An old enemy of yours, your majesty."

Elixia's snarled as she told Jib, "Take him to Queen Titania's court and if the king hasn't left yet, inform Ladislas of what we know at this time. Imprison Stuart in a cloven tree until we can deal with him. "

Logan said, "Don't kill Stuart. We need him to take the burden of the Black Dog's Bane."

"Whatever are you talking about, human?" Elixia snapped impatiently. She still had one hand on Brigit's tree as she cast a black glare at Dr. Stuart standing behind Logan.

"*The hound of death hunts a noble prize; When the glass turns, who falls, so others rise?*" Logan quoted the Black Dog's Bane.

"That prophecy was meant for me—or Chancellor Bandemer. Maybe the Doppelgänger."

"Was it?" asked Logan, cocking his head and raising a questioning eyebrow.

"Explain and be quick about it! I just had a near-death experience, and we have more important things to do."

"You all took it to mean it was directed at one of you in the room. That it was a statement. But I asked Brigit to repeat it. It was a question and not a statement. The Black Dog was asking you, not telling you, of the Doom."

Elixia started laughing hysterically. When she got herself under control, she told Jib, "Take the Black Dog with you. Let him play with this human, chasing it all the way to Ladislas. But don't break Stuart's neck until I can be there to enjoy his execution."

Before Logan could protest further, Jib blinked out, as did the Black Dog and Dr. Stuart. Logan opened his mouth, but Queen Elixia held up a forefinger covered with her blood.

"Do—not—question—me!"

Logan gave a quick bow. He was in the Perilous Realm in Queen Elixia's court. He would try diplomacy later, for Dr. Stuart's death would do no favors to Elixia or the fae in the human lands.

Elixia pursed her lips and dropped her hand from the tree. Her fingers left a bloody trail on its bark. She told Logan, "Come with me."

As they walked, their feet cracked the leaves and bark lying on the ground. Logan wore shoes, but Elixia's naked soles were cut by the sharp edges she trod upon. She left smears of her blood behind as they traveled through the fae forest.

How far they went, Logan didn't know. The trees without their bark were now dark. Like they had been burned by fire. Without landmarks Logan could identify, the scenery was gloomy and monotonous.

The land had calmed upon Queen Elixia's appearance. Now it was quiet as a cemetery at midnight. From ahead of him, Queen Elixia said, "Tell me what Dr. Stuart did."

Logan cleared his dry throat and began, "After Brigit read some research of his that wasn't published yet, she suspected that he had used the same method to infect the grove."

"What research?"

"He used a microorganism that naturally had iron to kill off an invasive plant in South America. Because of the fae being susceptible to iron, Brigit thought he used it as weapon here."

"Yes, I see," mused Elixia. "Our grove is actually one being—the Elder. All of its trees are connected. Anything placed in one area of the forest would eventually travel throughout, to infect them all."

Since she was walking in front of him, Logan couldn't see her face, but he saw the queen's shoulders move with a heavy sigh. "Iron remains a problem for our kind. Only fae who live in the human lands develop a tolerance for it."

The queen stopped and, with one raised hand, pointed ahead of her. "The Elder."

If Brigit's tree had been the size of a young redwood, this one was ancient. It was no longer silver, but black, like the smaller trees. But under the charred appearance was the glow of orange, like fresh lava under old.

Elixia looked up, and Logan followed suit. The height of the tree was such that its crown could not be seen. It disappeared into a sky that was gray and stormy. Logan felt a drop of rainfall on his cheek.

The queen placed both palms on the scorched bark. She was silent for a few long moments before explaining to Logan, "The Elder is working a Great Magic. I have not felt this intensity since we created the court so long ago."

She closed her eyes and put her forehead to the tree.

"It is trying to heal itself from the poison." After a moment, she pushed herself away and faced Logan. "Tell me what happened to my daughter."

"Dr. Stuart confessed that he had hurt the trees on orders from the human who was once married to your sister. Then she turned into a tree."

"Dryads don't become trees. That's a Greek urban legend. They step into trees."

"I can only tell you what I saw. Brigit transformed into that tree! Is she in trouble? In danger?"

Queen Elixia didn't answer Logan's panicked questions. She asked him for more details on what happened. "Did Brigit bring something back from the human lands with her? The Elder keeps telling me something about a leaf. I don't understand what it is referring to."

"Oh, yes, a leaf." Logan wiped the rain out of his eyes, threading his fingers back through his hair. "When I visited the court, after the riddle game, I picked up a leaf that fell from the grove. I gave it to Brigit."

"What did she do with it?" Elixia's expression made Logan hesitate. Had he done something wrong?

"I — well—" Logan stumbled at first but decided to tell the queen all he knew even if it made Brigit angry with him later. He had a sinking feeling that something was wrong about Brigit being a tree.

"Brigit carried it around with her. Last summer, it attached itself to her under her skin. She couldn't get it to let go. It sent her dreams she never understood. I don't know anything more than that."

Elixia gasped, her hand reaching out to grab Logan by the wrist. It was a strong and fierce grip that dragged him closer to her. He might have been afraid, but his thoughts were all about Brigit.

The queen choked out hoarsely, "Brigit brought back the leaf — and it is the cure. I don't understand how, but the grove is using it to heal itself."

Raindrops landed on Elixia's face, their watery trails mixing with her tears. "The leaf used Brigit. Traveled the human lands. Exposing itself to your world. Now, the Elder has taken its child back, but I cannot find my own child within her. It can be easy to become lost within the Elder's greatness."

Queen Elixia brought Logan closer to the Elder tree and

ordered him, "Touch it."

Gingerly, Logan did as she bid. The magic was hot under his hand but did not burn him.

"Brigit is not responding to me, but she never listens to me," her mother told Logan. Logan could see the retraction of her pupil and the fine age lines at the corner of her eyes.

"But she likes you. You will bring her home to me."

Before Logan could ask how, Elixia moved quickly. She yanked him forward with the grip on his wrist, and Logan fell into the Elder.

"Find my lost child."

Logan opened his eyes and found he was at the Weberhaus, a popular Biergarten in downtown Geheimetür. It must have been a Friday or Saturday night as the place was packed. It was here that he had met Brigit almost two years ago.

He scanned the crowd, trying to see if he could locate Brigit. Logan knew he had to find her. But all he saw were the backs of heads. Seeing one with dark curls, Logan started making his way in that direction.

"Excuse me, excuse me," he said, worming his way past shoulders and elbows.

Someone bumped his arm, and Logan saw that it was a fae being. It wasn't a bog sprite, but some leafy creature. Its triangular head had two large bug eyes like a Praying Mantis.

"Do you know a fae dryad named Brigit? Have you seen her?"

At Logan's question, everyone in the beerhall turned and stared. They crowded around, blocking any way for him to escape. Now that he could see their faces, he could see they were all leafy creatures. Although they had no mouths, Logan heard a chant: "Who is Brigit? Who is Brigit?"

The fae creatures pushed and shoved him. They were moving him to the end of the room, and up on a stage. It was here Granite had done his stand-up comedy routine so long ago.

Bright lights blinded Logan. He reached up a hand to shade his eyes as a microphone was shoved into his other hand. The chanting question grew louder: "Who is Brigit? Who is Brigit?"

Logan coughed into the mic, and the screeching peal showed it was live.

"Oh, sorry about that," he instinctively apologized. "Brigit? If you can hear me, can you come to the stage?"

The chanting stopped, and the restaurant became quiet. Due to the light, the crowd was now anonymous black blobs. Logan spoke into the microphone.

"If any of you know Brigit, I'd like you to help me. If you don't know her, she's a fae dryad. A short girl with black hair and brown eyes. If someone has seen her, can you tell her that Logan Dannon is looking for her?"

Logan's appeal gained only a heckle from the audience. "Why do you care?"

"I care because—" Suddenly, Logan remembered where he was: inside an Elder tree in the Perilous Realm. The memory of another mission to retrieve a lost loved one.

And he knew it would take more than a physical description to bring Brigit Cullen to his side. He began again, speaking Truth, "Brigit Cullen is the bright star in my life. A friend that values loyalty above her own life. Who cuts a fine line with fairness. She's smart, but also clever. She loves trees and anything made from them. And once she saved an entire library of books from annihilation because of that love."

Maybe it was the same heckler, but another shout made Logan squint trying to find who spoke, "Sounds like a million other girls. What makes her so special?"

Logan thought of Brigit, the way she'd cock her head and give him a knowing smile when Logan tried to weigh both sides of a problem. Her passion for justice. Her contempt for fae who didn't adhere to the Laws of Civility. The excitement she had over trivial experiences, like discovering candy canes for the first time.

How she'd read stories out loud to that potted plant she had rescued from the hallway. Or when she insisted that he take that coco mat home with him to Texas over the summer because it would be lonely if left behind.

The feel of her cooler hand in his warm one. How her nose would scrunch up when she was displeased. The way she said his name when teasing him.

"She's the woman I love."

The crowd broke out in wild applause. Logan blinked against the spotlight that did a wild rotation of colored spots before landing on the fae girl stepping onto the stage.

"Logan," Brigit said.

"Glad to see you," Logan replied. "You had me worried for a bit."

"I was worried for a bit."

Brigit wrapped her arms around him and placed her chin on his chest to look up, her eyes the darkest brown. Brigit was so slight, so small that it was easy to lift her with his embrace. She wrapped her arms around Logan's neck, and he held onto her waist, suspending her off the ground.

"Are you done saving the world?" he asked her.

"Only saved a corner of it. And only because the leaf brought back the antigen, the immunity from surviving the human lands. The Elder replicated it. Inoculated the grove against the iron."

"Sounds complicated." Logan was not interested in discussing science. Instead, he kissed Brigit's face, scattering kisses on her forehead, nose, and cheeks. She snuggled closer, their breathing matching each other.

"I'll tell you about it later."

"Hm-mm."

Logan's progress had finally brought him to Brigit's lips. His mouth was tender on hers, causing Brigit to tighten her hold. Surfacing, she asked him, "Can you take me home? I've seemed to lost my way."

"Your mom is waiting for you. She's awfully worried."

Brigit put one finger over his lips.

"Home with you."

The Weberhaus faded away, and the two found themselves under a sky filled with stars. They stood on the Kiburg's roof, and the night breeze was chilly. Neither noticed.

"Do you really love me?" Brigit asked.

"I'm a bard. I always speak the truth."

"Ha! No, you don't." Brigit dug her elbow in Logan's ribs and he let go of her as she slid to the ground. "You fib all the time, Logan Dannon. What about that time when you skipped class because you slept in and told your study group you were sick?"

"This isn't a lie."

Holding his hands on either side of her face, he bent down and gave her a deep kiss.

Bane of Hounds

Chapter Thirty-Two
Post Mortem

hile using his power to hold time in place had drained Paul physically, lying in a hospital bed to recover was boring. With a knock at the door and the entrance of Queen Elixia, Paul started to rethink if boring was really all that bad a thing.

Today, Queen Elixia was cosplaying Lady Caroline Lamb, Lord Byron's lover. Her Regency dress was cut indecently low, and her dampened undergarment was designed to cling to her form. Since her husband, King Ladislas, accompanied her, Paul studiously avoided meeting her gaze, opting to direct his stare past the king's shoulder.

"Dear," Elixia addressed her husband, "this is the brave Doppelgänger who shaved a century off of his life to save me."

More like a loss of fifty years. However, Paul had no plan on being humble about his accomplishments to their majesties. He knew why they were here. To negotiate the Debt they owed him.

The conversation started like two dogs circling each other, sizing each other up.

With his life partner dressed like someone from a sexy version of a Jane Austen novel, Ladislas was wearing a coat and breeches so tight that they may have been a second skin. Being of an imposing build, Ladislas may have thought he could intimidate the figure lying in bed.

"He looks very pale, my love. Perhaps a fruit basket?"

"That would be a nice gesture," said Paul, stressing the last word. He weakly pulled himself up. When Queen Elixia rushed forward to readjust his pillows, it put her bosom very close to his face. Paul hastily closed his eyes.

Paul didn't know if Ladislas would decide that killing him in a duel would be an easier path than paying their Debt.

The end of the bed moved down from the pressure of someone sitting, and Paul cautiously opened his eyes. Good, Elixia was farther away.

"It is unfortunate that my beloved," said the king, "came under danger while accepting your hospitality."

Good, Ladislas might not kill him after all. He was opening negotiations, trying to barter.

"Some could argue that she brought the danger with her

since it was an old enemy of your court who set the bone harp as a snare." Paul might be weak, but he wasn't dead. The Doppelgänger would give as good as he got.

"I do believe the invitation guaranteed some safety if you attended—"

The king's comment was interrupted by Paul, who was starting to feel irritated, "There was fine print on the back in invisible ink. I'm assuming you didn't read the disclaimer about death, dismemberment, or being resurrected from the dead?"

The silence that followed Paul's comment showed that neither of them had read it. That wasn't surprising. Paul doubted anyone attending had. The fae were not known for their caution.

As Elixia twisted a ringlet around a finger, she addressed her comments to the air, "The queen is the most important player on the chessboard. What shall we give a fae who returned her?"

Something passed between the king and queen that Paul couldn't decipher. It involved Queen Elixia wriggling her eyebrows, and King Ladislas giving a moue of disagreement with his eyes and mouth. But it seemed Elixia won the argument as Ladislas gave a heavy shrug of his shoulders and told Paul bluntly, "What do you want for compensation? Half of our kingdom? The hand of our daughter in marriage?"

"I am not interested in lifebonding with Brigit," said Paul, exasperated.

"There are two others you can choose from. One is off

playing at being an Amazon warrior. The other is working as a brain surgeon. I will warn you though, of those three, Brigit is probably the most manageable."

At the king's words describing his youngest daughter, Paul almost choked. "Uh, no, thank you, your majesty. However, Brigit is part of how you can pay off your Debt to me."

"I had planned on a more advantageous marriage—" began the queen, only for the king to contradict her, "A Doppelgänger! What a catch! Imagine having one at our court, my dear."

Paul cleared his throat.

"I don't mean to disappoint you both, but payment for my Debt is something other than marriage to your daughter or land in the Perilous Realm."

The royal eyes staring at him were disconcerting in their intensity. Paul steeled himself and continued with the plan he had worked out while staring at the ceiling last night.

"My Debt will only be canceled if I let your youngest daughter, Brighid Holly, known to me as Brigit Cullen, pick her own bond partner, when or if she wants one, here or in the future, without any influence, command, threat, or enticement, by you or your representatives."

Before Queen Elixia could voice her protest, King Ladislas grabbed Paul's hand in a hearty grip. "Expletus!"

Paul anticipated an argument from his liege when Bandemer learned his Doppelgänger had canceled such a great Debt with such a simple request. He was surprised when the chancellor, upon learning the news, only said mildly, "You will get no quarrel from me, Paul. Relax. Let the heart monitor go back to normal."

Chancellor Bandemer had appeared at the side of Paul's hospital bed with flowers, chocolates, and a fruit basket. He proceeded to open the box of sweets and eat them one by one while discussing recent events with his spymaster.

"That's a cunning Debt returned. Now Brigit Cullen will owe you. She will be more useful for our needs than Queen Elixia. As much as I adore Brigit's mother, she is a handful."

"That is not why I did it," Paul protested weakly.

"Are you in love with her? I thought you rather fancied my pet librarian, Frau Burkhalter?"

"I fancy no one," growled Paul in aggravation. Sometimes he enjoyed these word games with Bandemer, but he felt out-of-sorts today. Why couldn't he be left alone to be bored? "I have no plans on telling Brigit that I have done this. As a gentleman, I request that you don't either."

"Hm. You do realize that the Code of Chivalry died some centuries back? And even when it was in place, few knights adhered to it?"

Looking out the window, to see ravens fly by, Paul asked, "Have you never been in love?"

"Plenty of times," said Bandemer stoutly. "I enjoy the process and heartily recommend it. Good for the liver. But I do not let love dictate policy. That would be sloppy. Don't tell me you are in love with that young dryad?"

"No, of course not. But I feel Brigit should make her own decisions. It is not pleasant to dance to another's tune."

"Are you referring to your position with me?"

Paul changed the subject to something that was bothering him. "I thought you would be angry since I could have used my Debt to release you from Queen Elixia."

"Not at all, *mon ami!* That is already resolved to my satisfaction."

"It is?" asked Paul. Perhaps it was the headache, but he couldn't figure out why Bandemer would be happy owing a blood Debt to a Perilous Realm queen.

"I don't gamble unless I know I can win," said Bandemer smugly. "I had already discussed the danger to Queen Elixia's court with the banshee before she left for her new position in the United States."

"That Cassandra? What did she say?"

"Oh, she acknowledged the danger, but also told me Queen Elixia and her court would be saved before the symposium ended. With no risk or inconvenience to me."

"So it was all an act?" Knowing Bandemer, Paul should have known. "But that doesn't take care of your larger Debt to discover the villain who is trying to destroy the Perilous Realm."

Even in his weakened state, Paul could feel the drawing of Bandemer's power, its intensity electric, as his liege replied. "If the Perilous Realm does not vanquish its enemy, what does my life matter? Or yours, Paul? We either fight together and win, or lose and die."

As Paul considered the seriousness of what Bandemer told him, the chancellor fingered another chocolate. He asked, "You don't like these jelly-filled ones do you? I didn't think so," and before Paul could reply, ate the last one from the box.

Paul woke to find Jib sitting on his chest, purring.

"I figured a little cat-magic wouldn't be amiss," the púca told the Doppelgänger. Paul reached up, and when Jib didn't move, he started stroking the cat's fur.

Jib told him, "I heard how you canceled Queen Elixia's Debt. What a romantic you are."

Paul groaned in embarrassment. "I guess everyone knows."

"Only those closest to their majesties will be aware of your grand gesture. However, our dryad princess needs to know that she is free to make her own choice. Don't worry, I will tell her and spare your delicate sensibilities."

Paul kept petting Jib. It was comforting to feel the little rumbling purr under his hand.

"Where is Brigit? And Logan?"

"In the Perilous Realm. Dr. Stuart must be sentenced for his villainy."

"That is going to cause a problem with the humans. I've seen the television news. They are calling for the scientist to be returned."

The cat's purring grew lower, and Jib had a look of contented satisfaction on its face.

"He'll be returned. In perfect condition. Somewhat."

"What have you done?"

"Who knew you were such a worrywart, Paul? Logan argued the human's case. Brigit agreed with him. She is learning how to balance her Debts. Logan is good for her," mused the cat.

"How so?" At Paul's questions, the cat narrowed its eyes.

"You don't know much about bond partners, do you? Watching you bumble your relationship with Anna Burkhalter, I should have know you were naive about love. Logan helps Brigit by being at her side, supporting her," explained Jib as if it was talking to a child.

The cat started to knead Paul's blankets, adding, "I think you need to extend your circle, Paul. Good thing I consider myself now your bond partner. I will manage your social calendar for you."

"You? My bondpartner? I don't—"

"Don't protest. I know you want me to be in your inner circle. You're so obvious! Keeping a cat bed at your desk? Petting me? Next, you'll be buying me my favorite treats. I prefer salmon-flavored ones, by the way."

Paul sighed. Life had grown complicated since he first posed as Logan Dannon, so the human boy wouldn't appear to miss class.

Jib continued with its opinions, "Their majesties may have forgiven the Debt for saving Elixia's life, but that doesn't cancel what I may feel about what you did for my princess."

There was a light tap-tap at the door of Paul's private room. The Uncanny doctor entered. "How is our star patient feeling?"

"Weak, tired, and bored," said Paul.

"I am not here to discuss your physical welfare but your

336

magic: your control of time and illusion. Have you tried to use either?"

Jib jumped from Paul to the windowsill causing the Doppelgänger to expel a grunt. The cat pointed a paw at the Doppelgänger and asked the doctor, "What do you see?"

"A handsome, dark-haired man in his mid thirties."

"That's the face Bandemer gave him," purred Jib. "What I see is a patient from the cafeteria who shared his breakfast milk with me. Someone younger, in his human teen years. Since we see two different images, it seems Paul's Doppelgänger abilities to shield his true visage have reset."

Paul immediately felt better hearing this news.

"What about your control over time?" The Uncanny doctor pointed the beak of the mask to the room's window. "Can you reverse a snowflake's descent?"

Paul tried. He grabbed the flurry outside of his window and rewound the snow's travel by a fifteen seconds. The swirl of snowflakes moved backward before blowing away to form a new pattern.

"A little. It's hard, but yes, I can do it."

"Good, good."

The door pushed open again, and a young man came in holding a tray. Smelling lunch, Jib jumped back onto Paul's bed. Balancing on Paul's leg, Jib walked over his prone body. The púca opened its orange eyes opened wide.

"Bond partners share things. Especially chicken."

Bane of Hounds

Chapter Thirty-Three
Food for Thought

$\mathcal{A}$rthur Dannon appeared to be a man in his mid fifties, with dark hair, mild eyes, and a bulky build that might be fat. A rational human being on the surface. But Chancellor Bandemer knew that he was also the son of the Morrighan, the Celtic goddess of war and sovereignty, and eyed him warily.

When Rector Maximilian Schubert received Mr. Dannnon's request for an interview, he had forwarded the request to Bandemer's office.

"This seems to be one of your messes to deal with," a harried Schubert had told Bandemer over the phone. He wasn't far off the mark. As rector, Schubert dealt with the everyday administration of Leopold-Ottos-Universität Geheimetür, while Bandemer handled the fae and the more colorful aspects of fundraising and schmoozing.

After introductions were made, Arthur Dannon said, "My wife has told me that our son Logan had an incident at a university-sponsored event that required medical care."

"He's fine. A minor thing," Bandemer assured him.

The two were seated in the chancellor's office. Instead of taking his usual position behind his desk, Bandemer was in one of the more comfortable club chairs, a coffee table between him and where Arthur Dannon sat opposite.

"It might have been a minor thing to you," said Logan's father, "but it was at your instigation that my son was at an off-campus event, which had nothing to do with his school studies."

"Are you so sure that it didn't involve his studies? His extracurricular studies?"

The man was hard to read for his face revealed nothing, neither did the tone of his voice.

"I assume you mean this position you have given him as a student liaison? My wife told me about this. Why don't you explain why you have put my son in danger?"

"I think your son can put himself in danger without my assistance, Mr. Dannon. Within a month of arriving here, he started dating a siren."

Arthur Dannon gave one slow blink and a growly dismissive laugh. "Young men go to college for experiences. We both know what the world means to them. Dating."

"So it doesn't concern you that he was involved with a siren, and now consorts with a fae dryad? Who he is currently living with?"

"My wife told me about the girl. It does not shock me for I have a far wider acquaintance, shall I say, with the world than she does. I was raised in a hippie commune. Unless you are telling me he is living out of a car, doing drugs, with three to four girls in his bed at the same time, I don't really care."

Viewing the man in the Oxford shirt with stripes and the business suit, Bandemer blinked as he tried reconciling the past with the present.

"No, no, I can't honestly report that he is doing those things," Bandemer said.

"I wish my son to be released from these duties. And I want to know how you will protect him from the fall-out of being your catspaw."

"No, he seems to be your mother's tool, the Morrighan's pawn."

There was a long silence. A muscle jumped in Mr. Dannon's jaw, showing he had clenched his teeth. The growl had deepened as he told the chancellor, "I will deal with my mother and her plans."

"I am not a father, but I do know something about power. Your son will be someone's puppet if he doesn't learn how to protect himself. I thought that was why your family sent him here? For Logan to grow his bard power?"

Bandemer could see that Dannon was digesting his words, thinking over what the chancellor had said. Crossing his legs, and folding his hands over one knee, the chancellor told Arthur, "Now, let me explain to you my plans for Logan Dannon's education."

Emma Walker met up with Logan Dannon and Brigit Cullen at the Weberhaus two days after the Dr. Stuart interview. She was eager to hear what happened after Dr. Stuart disappeared, and she also had her own news to share.

Logan and Brigit arrived after Em did, so she and Obake had plenty of time to observe them making their way over to the table she had grabbed for them.

Obake was hanging in her ear, back to its favorite disguise as an earring. It whispered to her, *They look quite friendly.*

Don't embarrass me, Obake, Em warned the tsukumogami.

I'll be as quiet as a dwarf flying squirrel, promised Obake. Knowing the worth of its promises, Em figured she should have left it at home.

"Hey, Em!" Brigit said, giving her a friendly greeting. While their relationship had started in a tumultuous way, Emma was now part of Brigit's bond circle since she had helped with the library matter. Brigit unzipped the backpack she had placed on the chair, and Jib poked its head out.

"Hi Jib," said Emma, as the cat climbed out to find a place on the table.

"I see you brought your delicious squirrel thing with you."

Em touched the earring in response to Jib's comment,

but Obake chose not to change. The tsukumogami probably thought it safer not to tempt the cat with its rodent form.

Logan had gone off to flag down a waitress, but the Black Dog, which had come in with them, stayed behind. He gave a woof of greeting and spread out under their table, his fur brushing Emma's legs.

Logan arrived with some beers and set them down, taking the seat next to Brigit. Em almost laughed at the casual way Logan draped his arm around the back of the dryad's chair. Things have gone public, and he's staking out his territory.

"You have to catch me up on what happened," Em said, leaning forward.

"Can we get some food first?" Jib gave a pitiful meow.

"I've ordered. You can wait." Logan told Jib.

Brigit told Emma about taking Dr. Stuart to the Perilous Realm, the leaf that went back to the Elder, and how the trees were cured.

"Amazing! But that doesn't explain why your eyes have changed color."

Brigit lowered her lashes and bit her lip, "Well, I guess merging with the Elder had some side effects."

"I think they are pretty," said Logan, who hurriedly added, "not that your brown eyes weren't pretty. But green and brown. Well, they are striking."

"I might have to start wearing sunglasses."

"Not around me."

Emma rolled her eyes at both of them. "Tell me what's happened to Dr. Stuart?"

"We were both there for his trial at Queen Titania's court. My aunt officiated the case since my mother was the plaintiff. Logan was able to help with the questioning because he pointed out when Dr. Stuart lied. It's now confirmed that Stuart was paid to infect our trees."

The Brotzeit arrived. The platter had black bread and Obatzter, a soft white cheese mixed with chives and onions for spreading. It included pickles, radishes, and sausage.

"You'll burn your tongue, Jib. Wait until it cools," cautioned Brigit, as she cut up some sausage and put it on a small dish just for the púca.

Jib dramatically flopped to its side, knocking silverware to the floor with its back feet. A spoon hit Devlin on the head, causing the dog to whine. Brigit left to go get clean forks.

"It really couldn't be as easy as Brigit is describing," said Em.

"It wasn't," said Logan, grimly. "I'll tell you the gory bits later."

"And I've got something I have to tell you about your dog. Something Obake discovered about him." Seeing Brigit returning, Em mouthed to Logan, "Later."

"You did a marvelous job interviewing Dr. Stuart. What happened after we snatched him?" Brigit asked, curious. She started spreading cheese on her bread, taking a mouthful.

"Oh, all hell broke loose. I acted like I didn't know anything about it. While they were searching the bushes, we slipped away, but not before I had Obake copy all the footage before deleting it. I didn't want my face broadcast all over the news, but I figured we could share some of

Stuart's incriminating statements online."

"And the reporter who was supposed to come for the interview?"

"He got called to a plum assignment about the grand opening of a distillery. Too bad that the bus he took coming back had a flat tire and delayed him getting to the Kiburg."

"Imagine that," Brigit said, giving a wink to Em.

Em asked, "What about you, Brigit? You came to LOTTOS to find a cure for your trees. What now? Are you going to stay here?"

From Logan's face, Em saw that he hadn't considered this turn of events.

"Oh, I'm staying here. I don't want to go back home. After the Elder marked me, mother wanted to make me some sort of senior priestess serving the grove full time. I can't imagine anything more boring!"

Logan relaxed his death-grip on the back of Brigit's chair at the dryad's comment. Brigit continued talking about her plans as if she hadn't noticed the tension, "I still want to complete my degree, but now that the pressure is off, I can take some other classes that have personal interest to me."

"Tell her about the Kiburg," said Logan.

"Is this about that floating dog?" asked Em. "I saw it hanging in mid air when I was coming up to the hotel. By the time I finished the interview, it had vanished."

"Paul was holding the dog with a spell," said Brigit, sidetracked. "But when he saved my mother, the Doppelgänger had to release his hold on it. I heard from Serio that Prince Fidalo ran yelping with his tail between his legs all the way home to Queen Tinlaxi's court."

"Served him right," said Jib. Pleased with the dog's humiliation and the sausage, it was taking time to clean its whiskers.

"Brigit is moving out of the apartment," blurted out Logan, who didn't care about arrogant pug-dogs getting their comeuppance. "Her mother insists that she take a room at the Kiburg if Brigit wants to stay at LOTTOS."

At Em's surprised look, Brigit gave an aggravated sigh. "Logan's mom made a big deal about me rooming with her son. She threatened to kick me out since Logan's parents control the lease. My mother wasn't going to wait for them to do that. Pride, you know. She immediately transferred her Kiburg suite to me."

"Oh. That's rotten. No brownie for you. And where will Jib live?"

The cat said loftily, "Jib will live where there is sausage. And no dogs."

Brigit gave the púca a quelling look. "The brownie will stay with Logan. He's going to see if Granite would be interested in taking over my room."

"And the Black Dog?"

"He'll stay with me," asserted Logan. "There's going to be a huge investigation by the Perilous Realm courts into what happened. To find out who planned this attack. I'm hoping that they find some of Devlin's kin, but regardless he's always got a home with me."

"And Devlin's Bane? What about the Doom?"

"That's complicated. I think the original Bane was meant

for my mother," Brigit stopped Logan from interrupting by shaking her head, "It was, Logan. You know it was. But my mother survived, and all Banes must be satisfied. Logan twisted it somehow, and it became Dr. Stuart's fate instead. He was a man of high standing who fell, so he fitted the brief."

"And missing class for the week?" asked Em.

Brigit shrugged. "My grades will take a dent from it, but it was worth it."

More food arrived, Flammkuchen, a thin-crust pizza. All of them dived in again as their beers were refilled.

"Can we stop talking about the dog?" complained Jib.

Brigit smiled at the cat, asking, "What do you want to talk about?"

"Where are you taking me over the winter break? I want to start planning our vacation."

Bane of Hounds

Epilogue

At Dr. Sebastian Stuart's sentencing, Logan had argued that the human scientist couldn't be killed or vanish for long without causing comment.

Dr. Stuart was a well-known personality. He would be missed. People would demand answers.

However, the queens of the Perilous Realm insisted justice be served. After the destruction and pain Stuart had caused, willingly cooperating with another human to destroy fae courts, he had two options: be imprisoned forever, or put to death.

It took some time and diplomacy, but eventually a compromise between all the parties concerned was reached.

It involved a dragon taking Dr. Sebastian Stuart through the Perilous Realm back to the human lands. The dragon gave gravity to the situation. By his presence as executioner, the serpent elevated the entire situation to the high drama the fae loved.

The dragon stepped from the Perilous to a nexus of the ley lines located in the human lands. He wrapped his serpentine body around the scientist, keeping the man contained within the circle of his coils.

His claws were longer than Dr. Stuart's body. His round eyes, with their horizontal pupils, were mesmerizing. The scientist looked away, keeping his gaze on the fog that surrounded them.

"Queen Titania has requested that I release you here."

"Where is here?" demanded Stuart.

"Snowdon, Wales," the dragon informed him.

Dr. Stuart thought it over. He had been on bigger mountains. Yes, it was winter. Hypothermia was a risk, but he was a survivor. He could do this. His mind was already thinking about finding a cave. Or he'd make a burrow where he could conserve his body heat.

"Are you done with me? Can I go now?" Stuart had only briefly lost his confidence when the scientist thought he'd die in Queen Elixia's court. He had quickly regained his equilibrium when he realized that the fae wasn't going to kill him. Logan could have told him that decision by Queen Titania wasn't made out of kindness.

The dragon preferred warmer climes himself, and was also feeling the temperature. But it had been a long time since he had played with human prey in his natural form. He wanted to enjoy teasing the human a bit longer.

"Do you not wonder why here? What is special about

this place?"

Clearly Stuart, who was starting to shiver, did not. The dragon, though, blinked his crystal-blue eyes. He spoke like thunder and prophecy, "Snowdon, where King Arthur killed the giant eotan, Rhitta. The place Merlin, as a boy, was initiated into the Mysteries. The bosom whereon Aneirin and Taliesin slept, coming down the mountain in the morning as poet-bards."

"Pshaw," Dr. Stuart scoffed. While he wore a sweater, it was not comfort enough against the wind that battered at him. He needed to find shelter and soon. "Let me go, as Queen Titania commanded you."

"Oh, I am letting you go," said the dragon. He uncoiled, lifting his tail and breaking the circle. "You will either come down this mountain a poet-bard or insane. I doubt you will withstand the induction into the Mysteries. It takes a certain flexible mind, which I doubt you have."

Dr. Stuart didn't hear the dragon's words. He was already moving off into the mist, looking for a place where he thought he could hole up until daylight. He was mumbling to himself, and the sound echoed back, the supernatural forces of Snowdon already starting to follow their fresh prey.

François Auguste Bandemer thought it a good ending. He stretched his wings, flicking his long tail. Would he fly back to Bewachterberg, or just slip through the Perilous Realm to Geheimetür? Hm. Fly, he decided.

He would enjoy it, and Bandemer was all about life's pleasures.

Bane of Hounds

Requiescat
by Oscar Wilde (1854-1900)

Tread lightly, she is near
Under the snow,
Speak gently, she can hear
The daisies grow.

All her bright golden hair
Tarnished with rust,
She that was young and fair
Fallen to dust.

Lily-like, white as snow,
She hardly knew
She was a woman, so
Sweetly she grew.

Coffin-board, heavy stone,
Lie on her breast,
I vex my heart alone,
She is at rest.

Peace, Peace, she cannot hear
Lyre or sonnet,
All my life's buried here,
Heap earth upon it.

Bane of Hounds

Acknowledgments

A book becomes greater with so many helpers. I've had the support of some wonderful readers who have provided advice and support: Andie K. who lent me German assistance; Laurie H., Giselle S, Astrid M., Jessica F., Amirah, and Yishai. Thanks to my editor, Kate H. for catching typos and verb abuse.

I love reading your comments and reviews. Your review doesn't need to be long — even a line or two makes a difference in helping others discover new books. Your feedback is the best encouragement we authors can receive to continue writing.

Thank you for reading Bane of Hounds. I'd love to give you a free story via my website (ByrdNash.com). Here you can discover more about me and my magical worlds.

Bane of Hounds

Bane of Hounds

Glossary

HUMAN LANDS

Leopold-Ottos-Universität Geheimetür, Bewachterberg: Affectionately called LOTTOS, was founded by the royal family in 1521.

Geheimetür: German for "Secret Door." A university town located in Bewachterberg.

Bewachterberg: German for "Hidden/Guarded Mountain." A country located south of Germany and Switzerland.

Treaty of Sigismund: A treaty between the King of Bewachterberg and the fae which resulted in the country being hidden for 99 years and a day.

Bard: A human who has gained powers of persuasion, understanding truth, and seeing through deception (fae Glamour) of supernatural means. Two famous Welsh bards in the early Medieval period were *Aneirin* and *Talisin*.

Science

- **Magnetotactic bacteria** (MTB): Bacteria that grow particles of magnetic iron inside themselves, which they use to orient and navigate along the earth's magnetic field.

- **Ecotone:** A transition area between two biological environments, where two different biological communities meet and integrate.

- **Extremophile**
  An organism that prefers to live in environments that are usually hostile to life, such as volcanic springs, alkaline lakes, hydrothermal vents, or extreme heat or cold.

Lady Caroline Lamb (1785-1828): An Anglo-Irish aristocrat and novelist.

Tsukumogami: A magically created creature in the human lands, region Japan. In Japanese folklore, a tool that had been used a long time (the length of time often given as 99 years) would often become alive and a self-aware spirit. Emma's companion is a shapeshifting spirit so would be an Obake and Bakemono, a subset of Yōkai.

Geas: A magically-enforced command or prohibition.

Canadian

Keeners: term for posers.

Gaelic/Irish

ó Conchobhair: O'Conner

Cláirseach: This traditional Celtic harp was once associated with the ruling classes.Its image is on Irish and British coins, and on the coat of arms of the Republic of Ireland.

Scottish

The baw's on the slates, and the game was over.
The ball is on the roof, and the street game is over: go home!
skelpit lug: blow to the ears.

French

Mon ami: my friend (said only to close friends).
petit chien: small dog
bête noire: black cat

Food

Vol-au-vent: A canapé made of puff pastry
Flammkuchen: a thin-crust pizza.
Brotzeit: a German savory snack tray which could include bread and butter, hard and sliced cheese, pretzels, pickles, radishes, onions, hard boiled eggs platter had black bread
Obatzter: a soft white cheese mixed with chives and onions for spreading.

FAE CULTURE

Perilous Realm

The faerie world is composed of many kingdoms, just as the Human Lands has many countries. Each kingdom is ruled by a queen who is equal in status (theoretically) to all the other queens. However, in reality courts differ in status due to size, magical ability, and political strength.

Courts

- *Court Elixia:* Brigit's mother and court.
- *Court Corallina:* Celia Rivers's court.
- *Court Ambrosia:* Elder is a sacred spring of healing. Destroyed.
- *Court Selena:* a Black Dog court. Elder was a deep cave. Destroyed.
- *Court Summerblossom:* Torfa's court. Had an alliance with Court Ambrosia.
- *Court Tinlaxi:* where the pug dog is prince.

Fae: (plural or singular, the word fae remains the same) — beings that call the Perilous Realm their home.

Beings: The preferred term to describe another fae.

Bondmates: Instead of using the term "friends."

Banes or Dooms: Dangerous prophecies of the future, usually given by Harbingers or Cassandras.

Wyrd or Wyrding: A magical statement that is an important declaration of truth or truth that will soon come to pass. While the banshee has spoken in a Wyrding voice, so has Logan. This is a crossover talent, attached to Cassandras.

Contagious Magic: A magic that uses something closely tied to a person in a spell in order to work magic upon the owner. Not to be confused with Sympathetic Magic which might use a doll that looks like the victim in order to inflict harm upon that person.

Affiliations: Fae magical abilities are from seven affiliations: Wood, Metal, Stone, Water, Wind, Flame, and Time/Memory. It is possible for a fae to have more than one affiliation, but there is always one that is dominant.

Glamour: A magical working that conceals, deceives or creates an illusion. The fae can choose to view the Glamour or what is true underneath it. Shape-shifting is not a form of Glamour.

Questing Journey: A physical journey in the Vastness or Between the Worlds to find an Elder.

Elder (genius loci): A magical wellspring that exists in the

Vastness until it bonds with a fae queen and forms a court.

Pythia: The queen serves as High Priestess in secret ceremonies that honor the Elder.

Vastness/Between the Worlds: A term for the space between the known worlds of the human lands and the Perilous Realm.

Ley Lines: Magical pathways connecting places of power both in the human lands and the Perilous Realm. They are used by the fae for traveling to other courts since the kingdoms are standalone bubbles of existence.

Anchor: An important point in time or a person that a vast destiny is attached to. A crossover term as it happens both in the Perilous and human lands.

Pledge of Fealty: Contemporary pledges of loyalty from a fae to a queen is done with the taking of a lock of hair or nail with a ceremonial blade used by the queen upon the one who pledges. A life pledge is far more serious and ties your life to your word. In ancient times, these pledges sometimes resulted in more serious bloodletting (the removal of a finger, hand, foot, or arm).

Rogues: A fae without allegiance to a queen or the protection of a court. Rogues are seen as fair game by other fae to hunt, capture, or kill.

Laws of Civility: All kingdoms acknowledge a code of behavior called the Laws of Civility.

Debts of Honor: Something owed, acknowledged between both parties.

Fiat of Harm/Injury: An official and binding declaration against another being.

Expletus: The formal word used by a debt-holder to acknowledge the debt is at an end.

FAE CLANS

Septs

Clans of the fae are grouped by type. It can influence allegiances as those of the same clan feel familiar to each other.

Naturals

Keep to a human form, and are closely connected to natural materials found in the human world. Think trees, streams, rocks, and mountains.

- **Nymph** (Elixia): a fae being associated with trees, usually affiliated with wood. They are tied to one tree as a home.

- **Dryad** (Brigit): a fae being associated with trees, usually affiliated with wood. They can move from tree to tree for homes.
- **Eotan** (Granite): beings with supernatural strength. Contains giants, trolls, dwarves. Usually affiliated with stone or metal.
  - Dvergr: a dwarf in old Norse Mythology. Their degree of human-like appearance varies greatly.

The Kindly Ones

A branch of fae who like to help humans. Because they have a long history with the Human Lands, they are immune to iron.

- **Brownies:** Fae spirits inhabiting homes and barns who are helpful. Logan's housekeeper is a brownie. If used cruelly they become nasty boggarts who some humans have mistaken as poltergeists.
- **Tommyknockers:** (Knocker, Knacker, Bwca, Bucca) lives in mines and tunnels.

True Beasts

A fae that presents physically as an animal and cannot change into a human form.

- **Fenrir:** A monstrous wolf from Norse Mythology.
- **Púca:** Jib is a púca who is also a True Beast. However, some can change into human form like the Kelpie (see *Never Date a Siren*).

Tricksters

A self-described Sept that crosses over others (such as Jib who is a Trickster and a True Beast). Many are True Beasts (horses, cats, dogs), or Shapeshifters. Magical affiliations vary greatly.

Dragons

- **Wyvern:** A bipedal (two legged) dragon with wings and a tale that ends in a diamond or arrow shaped tip. It is a favorite heraldic beast.

Time/Memory Affiliated Groups

- **Harbingers:** Fae creatures who are compelled to give specific Dooms and Banes. They do not control what they say or when they say it. It is usually about one future event.
- **Cassandra:** A being who has prophetic powers, who can be fae or human. Cassandras, like the banshee, have general prognostic abilities. They can answer any question at any time as long as it doesn't concern themselves.
- **Doppelgänger:** (German usage is capitalized, same form in plural as singular). They hold the highest form of fae power, Mindbending.

CHESS CHAPTER TITLES

Backward Pawn: An isolated pawn with no other pawns to protect it from attack.

Knight's Gambit: The Knight is moved to an empty pawn square, where the player gains an advantage.

Queen's Wayward Attack: An attack by the Queen, often leading to checkmate in four moves.

Knight's Tour: Attempt to move the knight 64 times, landing on each square only once.

Kibitz: A comment made during the game by a spectator.

J'adoube: French for "I adjust." Where a piece is touched by a player, but not moved.

King Hunt: A prolonged attack on the King, which removes him from a defensive position.

Poison Pawn: A pawn easy to capture which gives the player who loses it a chance to launch a strong attack.

Discovered Check: When a pawn is moved to reveal another piece which places the enemy King in check.

Zwischenzug: German for "intermediate move." A move that seems to be forced upon the player, but actually improves their position.

Protected Pass Pawn: A pawn that has the protection of another friendly pawn.

Discovered Attack: When a pawn is moved, it reveals a surprise attack upon the enemy King.

Pawn Storm: The advance of two or more pawns in an attack on an enemy King.

Fianchetto: Italian for "on the flank." With the movement of a pawn, the Bishop's position is advanced.

Forced Move: A move for which there is only one logical response.

Double Attack: Two friendly pieces launch a combination attack upon the enemy.

Spite Check: Faced with inevitable checkmate, the soon-to-be loser puts the other player in a checkmate that is easily defeated.

Endgame: The final phase of a chess game.

Post Mortem: (Slang) Analysis of the game after it is done.

Lightning Source UK Ltd.
Milton Keynes UK
UKHW021001021020
370915UK00012B/781